THE JACKALS

A NOVEL

ADAM SHAW

MOONSHINE BOOKS

Published by Moonshine Books, Louisville

ISBN-13: 9780578971223

Cover design by Matthew Hanover

Printed in the United States of America

This one's for you, Ruben.

SUGGESTED LISTENING MUSIC

ONE

I never planned on Mark finding out I'd slept with Beth.

In the moment, when the sleeping with happened, I didn't think about that part. It was 2:00 a.m., Beth and I had both had a few too many beers, and we were lying on our backs on her living room floor. I also didn't think about it when I kissed her. And when she kissed me back, climbed on top of me, and ran her hands up my body until they gripped either side of my face, any chance of consideration jumped out the window. By the time it ended and there was no sign of Mark coming home, I almost forgot it even happened.

It did, though. And Mark found out.

The thing is, we didn't mean for it to happen. It was a mistake. We loved Mark. She'd been dating him for two years at that point, and I'd been his friend since the seventh grade. Mark and I got through high school by sticking together. We stayed over at each other's houses, consoled each other through breakups, and started one of Lafayette's most popular bands. We were, for all intents and purposes, best friends. And Beth, she came into his life and didn't miss a beat, falling into line with all of us like it was always meant to be.

The night the sleeping with happened, Mark was supposed to be home. We were going to hang out, but he stayed over at work, which had become an almost daily occurrence. It had gotten to the point where we expected him to bail more often than not, which stung, so on that night, Beth and I drank. And kissed. And slept together.

I was staying at Mark's the weekend he found out. It was a shitty place, but it beat staying at my parents'. He and Beth rented a little house, and, as a result, I had a free place in the basement when I wanted to crash. It wasn't ideal. The walls were wood-paneled, and Mark and Beth rarely opened the blinds, making it look like a crossover between an '80s sitcom and a Sam Raimi horror flick.

We'd been doing the *You, Me, & Dupree* act for a year now, so we pretty much had it down: I'd crash in the basement, sometimes with my brother, Brian. Kenny, another friend of ours, would come and go as he pleased, staying until 4:00 a.m. one night and coming back at 2:00 p.m. the next day. At that point in our lives, the five of us were like family. Beth would make the occasional snack or go on a beer run when we were too drunk to, and, for the most part, she took care of us. She wasn't taking care of us the night Mark found out, though, because she and I had slept together two weeks prior, and this was the first time we'd seen one another since.

I don't know why I expected things to be normal. Beth had given me no indication that they would be. I called her when Mark invited me to crash, but she never picked up, not the first time, not the third, and she ignored every message I sent. In hindsight, I probably should have noted that this meant to stay away, but clues aren't easy to pick up on when you're twenty-two. So I came over, took my place in the basement, and had some beers while we watched a few movies.

Brian and Kenny weren't there that night. I remember

thinking that maybe they knew, that Beth had told them to stay away, but I'm not sure that was the case.

A few minutes before Mark found out, he and I were sunken into his couch and watching the end of *Revenge of the Sith*. Without looking away, he leaned over and asked a question I knew he knew the answer to. "What's the best lightsaber fight?"

I leaned forward, hoping for some acknowledgment from Beth—she'd taken my side in this argument before—but she sat tight in an old plaid recliner, knees huddled against her chest, face buried in a Lauren Conrad book. I hate that I remember this, but I'd never noticed before that moment that Lauren Conrad had books, or that people read them.

Either way, she didn't look up.

"*Episode III*," I said, falling back into my seat. "Hands down."

Mark laughed. "Bullshit."

"It's the only one that made me cry."

"Also bullshit," Mark said, cracking open a soda. "You cried when you watched *Jedi* for the first time."

"I was fourteen, and I hadn't seen *Episode III* yet."

Beth looked up from her book and shot me a glance. She'd put on glasses, which I'd never seen her wear before. I wondered if she even needed them, or if she'd just put them on to distract herself from the fact that I was there.

When Beth spoke, I almost threw up.

"Let's settle this," she said.

Mark raised an eyebrow, and I looked away and across the room at a poster for his dad's frozen custard joint, King's. The two bears on it were holding hands, each with a cone of their own while they stared out across the room and the people whose lives were about to change. I've thought about those bears from time to time since then, sometimes when it's hot, sometimes when I'm missing Mark, mostly when I'm jealous of their bear friendship that, at least as far as I can tell, is pretty much perfect.

"This *Star Wars* shit," she said. "You're comparing apples to oranges."

I opened my mouth and started to ask her a question, but she dodged it by turning toward Mark. Her blonde hair fell from behind her ears in a way that kept me from reading her.

"What do you mean?" Mark asked.

"Let's start with the new trilogy," she said. The way her eyes widened for him made me want to sink through the couch and disappear. "The lightsaber fights are one hundred percent different than what they were in the original trilogy. These days, they can play with speed, chain actors up for flips, and set backdrops that are just better than what they were able to do in the seventies and eighties. The thing is, these fit you guys too. You," she said, pointing at Mark, "don't need the bells and whistles to appreciate a movie. You enjoy the aesthetics and limitations, especially when it comes to something like *Star Wars*. Jack, though," she said, hiking a thumb at me, "he likes the explosiveness. He lives for shit getting wrecked or seeing someone do five backflips before slicing someone else in half."

I tried to object, but Beth held up a finger, still looking at Mark. "It's just a matter of taste. That's the thing—they're too different to compare."

I rolled a wad of couch fuzz between my thumb and fore-finger. "But what—"

"I have an idea." She reached across the side table and grabbed a couple old receipts from her purse, which she stuffed in Mark's hand.

"Give him one," she said, nodding my way. She shuffled in her purse for a second and tossed us each a pen, reaffirming my long-standing belief that Beth was prepared for any situa-tion. "We'll take a look at four categories: skill, emotion, overall impact on the *Star Wars* universe, and aesthetics."

"What about soundtrack?" Mark asked.

"Doesn't count. *Phantom Menace* wins every time."

I smirked. "Good point."

She gave me a nervous, lips-sealed smile that looked so forced I thought Mark would ask her what's wrong. "You're going to rate each category on a scale of one to ten," she said. "Whichever has the best average score is the best lightsaber fight."

Mark stared at his receipt as if it were a riddle. "We get to make a defense for ours before we vote, right?"

"No," Beth said. "You've been doing that for years."

"How will we calculate the winner?" he added.

She closed her book and set it on the side table. "I'll run the numbers."

Mark shook his arms out as if preparing to throw a pitch. "Let's do this."

Beth smiled at Mark, an authentic thing that showed her bright white teeth, then tapped the head of her watch. "Five minutes."

"Five?" Mark balked.

"Four minutes and fifty-six seconds," she said.

He scoffed like a teenager who'd been told to get to bed at nine, but he turned immediately to his paper. I wanted to work on mine, but being here with both of them, I couldn't think about anything. Not *Star Wars*, not my beer, not the bears on the poster. All I could focus on was Beth in her chair, knees hugged to her chest as she stared at the credits rolling into the top of the TV.

Mark turned his in first, folding it in half and slapping it into Beth's hand. He stared at me after this, making my palms sweat as if he knew what Beth and I had done and was waiting to pounce or kick my ass. Beth stared too, her blue eyes narrow slits.

"How much time?" I asked.

"Thirty seconds," she answered, not even looking at her watch.

I didn't care about *Star Wars* in those thirty seconds. I knew it was a gimmick, that it wouldn't solve anything, and that we'd still be arguing the same things for years to come. The only thing I cared about was getting out of here with Beth and figuring out what was going on, so I scribbled some numbers for each category and wrote a note:

We need to talk.

After I handed Beth the piece of paper, she unfolded it and started comparing it to Mark's. She said nothing as she did this, leaving us to ourselves as she tried to calculate the results of almost a decade of debate.

"There's no fucking way you win," Mark said.

I forced a smile and stared at the now-blank TV.

We sat in silence while Beth looked at the receipts, listening to the crumple of paper as she thumbed her way back and forth between them. The room, full of junk and books and everything else the two of them had collected over the years, felt like a closet. I scratched the back of my neck as I looked from Mark's collection of Steven King books to Beth's basset hound figurines. My mind wandered to stupid things, like if a horror book with basset hounds would even work. Or if it existed. Were there bassets in *Pet Sematary*? I looked at Mark, wondering if he'd know.

Before I could ask him, the crinkling stopped.

"I can't do this," Beth said.

Mark arched an eyebrow. I realized then that my lips were dry, that a lump had made its way up into my throat, and that I was about to throw up.

"What's up?" Mark said.

Beth sighed. It was a heavy thing, and she sank into her

chair, curly blonde hair spreading out behind her head. I used to tell her that her hair looked like a mane. I'd joke that she looked like a lioness, even though lionesses don't have manes. In hindsight, that was a stupid gimmick.

"We need to talk," Beth said.

Mark pushed himself up in his seat. "About the winner?"

I raised a hand, as if to stop her, which I've since realized made me look like a child.

"About Jack and me," Beth said. "We slept together."

Mark's face froze, looking like his jaw had locked and someone had tattooed wide arches of eyebrows onto his forehead. I wanted to say something—I wish I would have—but I couldn't figure out how, like the words ran up my throat and tripped over one another before they came out.

After what felt like an hour, he spoke. "You mean you, like, shared a bed or something?"

Beth breathed in through her nose, a long thing that I thought might buy us time. I expected her lip to quiver, her eyes to squeeze out a tear, something, but she stared past him, past me, like she'd somehow numbed herself to the whole situation. "No. We had sex."

Mark turned toward me. "Really?"

"We can sort this out," I said. I didn't mean to, but I'd started scooting away.

Mark coughed up a laugh and shook his head. For a second, I thought he actually thought it was funny. "We can?"

"Look, I'm sorry. I should've—"

"Did you or did you not have sex with my girlfriend?"

"Just listen," I said. "We—"

"Did you do it?"

"I can—"

"Jesus Christ," Beth said. "Just fucking say it."

For the first time all night, she looked me in the eye. She

was biting her lower lip now, and her blue eyes had glossed over in tears.

"We had sex."

I've lost count of how many times I've thought about the five minutes that followed. Mark's face—eyes narrow, mouth wide like he wanted to bite my head off—screaming my name. Beth yelling at him to stop, as if she hadn't anticipated Mark being pissed. Mark grabbing his half-empty soda and throwing it at me, cutting my forehead and covering me in the smell of Dr. Pepper's twenty-something flavors. Every time I replay it, I look for a way out, like a dungeon master planning out a D&D quest or a movie critic outlining his thoughts, and every time, I come to the same conclusion: I fucked up.

The moment that lingers longest, though, is Mark, pinned to one side of the couch by Beth, staring at me with large, heavy brown eyes. His black hair stuck to his forehead in thick clumps, his cheeks red, huge things filled to the brim with the hate he was ready to spew.

"Fuck you," he said.

"I'm sorry," I told him. "I'm so, so sorry."

Before I could say anything else, Beth asked me to leave. I sat on their back porch for a few minutes afterward, thinking of ways to apologize while I listened to them yell at each other. I thought about buying a gift, asking them to talk, or even getting them a card, but nothing seemed right. When they quieted down—when the screaming stopped—I stopped as well, deciding I'd make it up to them one day, when they'd forgotten about it or moved on. I told myself we'd laugh about it after their wedding, that time I was an idiot and slept with Mark's girlfriend, and Beth and I would forget about any feelings we had or could have had. Everything would be good again. All we needed, I told myself, was time.

TWO

That was seven years ago, and I haven't talked to Mark since. And, as of last night, Mark's dead.

A lot's changed in those seven years. For starters, I dropped out of college and ran away from my small, Midwestern hometown of Lafayette, Indiana, to the friendly confines of Louisville, Kentucky. It was all I could do after the falling out with Mark, really. Word traveled from one person to another like head lice or fleas, and before I could do anything about it, everyone who mattered knew what I had done, and they hated me for it. See, Mark was Lafayette's golden son. His family owned the local frozen custard joint, King's, and he was the one you could count on for anything. Flat tire? Mark would help you. Lawn mower broken? Mark would bring his over, and he'd probably even cut your grass.

Me, though? I was the guy who fucked him over, so I left to start over and grow up.

The morning after I learn about Mark's death, I wake up alone and an hour late to work. I reach for my phone, hoping for a message from Brian, my brother, telling me it isn't real. There's no text, though—just alerts from Apple News and the

Weather Channel—so I sink my face into my pillow and try to wish it all away.

Brian called in the middle of the night to break the news. He said, "Mark's dead" as if he'd said it a million times before, like he was ordering a sandwich or explaining a funny YouTube video he'd found. At first, I didn't believe it. You don't lose your childhood friends at twenty-nine. They get married, have kids, move away, maybe even stop talking to you, but die? That's for later. I thought it was, at least.

The last time I saw Mark was at Walmart. It was Christmastime, and he was flipping through the DVD bin. I stopped and stared as he went through his options, thinking that maybe I should say hi or apologize for what happened between us. I couldn't get the words to come out, though. It was like there were too many rushing through at once, like a fire drill gone wrong or a bottleneck in traffic. He looked up before I settled on anything. I raised my hand, either asking for permission to speak or waving—I'm not sure of which—and he walked away. I don't know if he meant to buy a five-dollar copy of *Super Mario Bros.: The Movie*, but he kept it in his hands, a testament to either his love of '80s video games or his anger toward me.

I always planned on making things right with Mark. After the incident at Walmart, I told myself that it wasn't the right moment, just like how the other chances I had to apologize weren't. Now, it seems the right moment has come and gone.

Jabba, my basset hound, hops up next to me and licks the backs of my ears and what he can reach of my face. I roll over, desperate to avoid what I can of the drool, and drag my legs over the side of the bed.

On my way to the bathroom, I stumble across my girlfriend, Lauren's, chalkboard wall, where we're supposed to leave cute messages for one another. Most days, she leaves for work before I wake up and gets home after me, and a blog she follows told her that this would be a good way for us to stay in touch. It's more an accumulation of doodles than anything, but in the middle, she's left a note:

The grass is greener where you water it.
xoxoxo

I stare at it for a moment, admiring the fluidity of her letters and the way they hold true to lines that don't exist. Behind them, I can see the remnants of the last note she left, but I can't make out what it said. I can't remember either, so I turn and walk to the bathroom.

Instead of getting ready, I stare at myself in the mirror. Most mornings, I look like a bloated, melting version of my former self, and today is no exception. Twenty-nine hasn't been as kind to me as I'd prefer, and while there are hints of the former runner staring back from the mirror, those traits are long buried by an ever-growing sediment of fat and curling hair. I keep telling myself I'll work out, and I run when I'm able, but a steady diet of beer and takeout has done a number on me in a way my aging body can't beat.

For a second, I wonder if by staring at myself, I can will Mark back to life. It's stupid, I know, but between Mark's death and Lauren's work schedule, the chance to look into a pair of eyes is an encouraging addition to my morning. Despite this, I can't stop thinking about that last encounter with Mark. If I'd had the nerve, I would've apologized to him and made things right. I don't know why I assumed I'd have another chance, but somehow, in the cosmic way God has fucked this all up, Mark's dead, and I'm a dick.

My phone chimes, and I rush to grab it. I cross my fingers that it's Brian, but when I look at the screen, my stomach sinks into itself, causing what I'm sure is a black hole or a cosmic tremor in my gut.

It's a text from Amanda. My boss.

You coming in?

I tap my thumbs on the screen to type out my reply.

On my way.

I throw on a polo and a pair of khakis. I try not to rush, picking up Jabba's toys and giving him a belly rub before putting him in his crate. I want to stall a little longer, but, knowing the impending shitshow waiting to unleash itself at my office, I resign myself to my fate and hop in the car.

It takes me about half an hour to get to work. I brake at every yellow light to check Facebook and look for news on Mark, but there's nothing except recipe videos and pictures of people's kids. I check the newspaper's website and try calling Brian but find nothing.

Brian didn't mention last night how Mark died, just that he was dead. I asked, but he wouldn't tell. He said he hadn't heard yet, leaving me to obsess over all the things that could have gone wrong.

Seconds after I walk into work, Amanda barks my name. I head to her office.

"Good morning," I say, forcing a smile.

She stares at her monitor, fingers tapping away as she writes some email or another. "What's this about you asking Rose for help on a project?"

I bite my bottom lip, thinking instead about where Mark's obituary might be or when it will show up. "I don't know."

"I saw an email from you asking her for help."

Amanda checks our emails on a daily basis. She's a woman who takes the title "Associate Manager" way too seriously. I was supposed to be Amanda, actually. A year or so ago, I was lined up for the "Associate Manager" promotion, but the company had been sold and a restructuring had put someone new over the department. Before the sale, we partnered with local businesses to develop employee trainings. Now, we do the same, only it's across the country, and we more or less sell packaged trainings that we swap the logos on.

Either way, I'd spent a couple years working toward that promotion—part of the growing up I came to Louisville to do, I suppose—and after all my hard work, it had been pulled out from under my feet. You could say it's left me sour.

"Oh yeah," I say, "*that* project. What's up?"

I have no idea what she's talking about.

"You shouldn't be asking her for help. She has one of the higher workloads on the team."

"I just thought that since she used to work with the client, she'd have some valuable insight."

Amanda rolls her eyes. "She does, but the client's not worth it. They're only a Revenue Tier 4."

Since the aforementioned sale, my company ranks its clients on three criteria measured by four tiers each. If you're wondering what this looks like, I have no idea. Truth is, I don't care. All I can think about is that the last time Mark and I spoke, he thought I'd end up a teacher. Here I am in a corporate mind-suck instead, getting bitched out by a woman who took my job and can't even look at me.

I look down at the back of a picture frame on her desk. "According to the CIS—"

"I know what the CIS says. They're a Tier 4."

"Did you say that's a Revenue Tier 4? Or a Personnel Tier 4?" I ask, more to entertain myself than anything else. "I forget."

Amanda stops typing. "Revenue."

"I didn't know that."

Amanda's short, a feature her sprawling, polished desk highlights, and she has a round, toad-like face that gives her anger a comical glow. "It's in the CIS."

Like mega-corporations across the country, our business operates on several acronyms that make no sense but make us feel like we're important and efficient. Given that my company makes a profit exploiting mid-sized businesses by "helping them develop strategic ways to train, develop, and retain employees," we're most certainly not immune to this.

"Okay," I tell her, tapping my fingers on my iPhone and hoping it jostles to life with some news. "I'm going to sit down now."

"Why were you late?"

"Traffic."

She huffs, her cheeks puffy and red.

"Yeah," I say. "Crazy."

"Just get to work."

I smile and walk to my cube, running my fingertips along the curved walls on the way, taking in the reds and yellows that shout at one another and, at least according to an email from the CEO last year, should "inspire us to light our internal fires." It was one of his better gimmicks, sure, but now we're stuck with an elementary school palette for walls. It doesn't do much to make up for the gray-on-gray cubes they contain, either, eight-by-eight hellholes stacked into tight rows with nametags in each corner. It works, though, as evidenced by my coworkers huddled into theirs and over their keyboards, tapping away to change the futures of our clients.

When I get to my cube, I slouch into my chair, ignoring the blinking red light on my office phone that signals voicemails I should care about. I go to Facebook instead of checking them, hoping again for an update about Mark that, as far as I can tell, doesn't exist.

The thing about leaving home and never going back, it seems, is that it's impossible to get information from there when you need it. Resigned to this fate, I pick up my office phone and hit MESSAGES.

"Hi, Jack, it's Nelson. I know we talked about including a standardized pre-assessment in our new sexual harassment training, but I noticed that it hasn't been included in this year's launch. I remember us talking about what that would look like, but yeah. It's not there. When you're able, would you give me a ring?"

I hang up my phone and open my last email from Nelson, telling me that they're going to wait to launch the pre-assessment for another year. I click forward and add:

Hey Nelson,

Sorry I missed your call. Per your message below, you and your team made the decision to postpone the pre-assessment, which is why we didn't include it in any of your courses. If you have any questions about this, please don't hesitate to reach out.

Best,
Jack

My job title is Educational Support Representative, though since we were acquired by Confluence Training Solutions, I'm just my company's bitch as well as my clients'. I'm supposed to help our partners develop employee professional development opportunities, but due to the imaginary processes my company has made up and sold our clients on, my job is really to play a glorified game of he-said, she-said.

About sixty seconds after I hit send, my phone rings. There's a red light on it that blinks in short little bursts that remind me of an ambulance or police car, and I wonder whether Mark saw his ambulance before he died. I picture him on the sidewalk, lying on his back, huffing in air as sirens screech in the distance before his breaths get slower and—

"Hey, Jack?"

I spin in my chair, taking in the temporary surge of importance it gives me. Katie, a coworker of mine, is standing outside my cube, wearing a black sweater and khakis. Her head is cocked to the right as if she's a teacher waiting to see if I make a good decision.

"What's up?"

"Jesus," she says. "You look beat."

I take in a long breath and exhale, nodding. "It's been a morning."

"Sorry," she says. "I just had a question about—"

"A buddy of mine died."

It isn't until her mouth drops that I realize that Katie, a recent college graduate whose outside knowledge of me is limited to the Nick Hornby book on my desk and the Spider-Man poster in my cube, is the first person I've spoken with about this. Between Brian's brief call, Lauren's job, and my overall lack of a social network, I haven't had much of a chance to bring it up. And, while Katie isn't the ideal candidate, she's a warm body with the reaction I need.

She blinks a couple times, her long lashes batting together as her eyes move from one side to another. She starts to hike her thumb over her shoulder, then she brings it back, biting the curled-up knuckle before taking a step away.

"I'm so sorry," she says. "I'll come back later."

I run my hands over my eyes, pressing my palms into them. "No, I'm sorry," I say. "I can help."

"It's all good," she says, taking another step back. "I didn't mean to intrude."

"It's really no big—"

"I'll just ask Amanda," she says. "Sorry about your friend."

Before I can get another word out, she's gone.

My stomach tightens and my throat dries as I grapple with how stupid of a decision that was. I spin back around in my chair, feeling nowhere near as important or valuable as I did a minute ago, and am immediately greeted by my phone winking at me with its voicemail light. I pick it up off the receiver, press it to my ear, and listen to my next message, letting the words pour out from it as my head spins with what could have happened in the seven years since I ruined my friendship with Mark and left home.

THREE

I 've been at the house for two hours when Lauren walks in, drops her bag on the table, kisses me on the forehead, and walks to the kitchen.

"My boss is such a dick," she says. "He's never going to let me stop writing about this goddamn special election."

I rub my eyes, realizing I've been staring at a picture of us on the mantle for half an hour. "I think they all are," I tell her. "It's a boss prerequisite or something."

Lauren works for *The Gambit*, a left-wing alternative paper. After finishing her degree at the top of her class and being unemployed for six months following, it ended up being her best option. Despite her grades and her dad's connections, the market for new journalists didn't exist, and she took what she could get. She's looked for something new from time to time, even interviewed at a paper in New York and another in Denver, but nothing's stuck.

"It's different with Eric, though." She grabs a LaCroix, then cracks it open and arches her head back to take a sip. She sets the can on the counter without making a sound and looks past me, heading back toward her bag. "He's just so condescending. The man can't get his head out of his ass for one minute to think about anyone other than himself."

My phone, sitting next to her bag, starts to hum.

"Who's that?" I ask.

Lauren stops. "Brian."

"I need to answer it," I tell her. "It's important."

She steps closer to my phone. "So is this. We're trying to be better about supporting each other through these sorts of frustrations, remember? We agreed on no phones when we're talking."

I stare at it, torn between Lauren and Mark, uncertain of myself and the situation and everything that's happened over the course of the last eighteen hours. The feelings bubble up, making my stomach twist and my palm sweat, until I can't handle it anymore.

"Mark's dead," I tell her, jumping off the couch and reaching past her to grab my phone. Her eyes go wide before she bites her lower lip in a way that reminds me that she probably can't remember who Mark is.

"Hello?"

"Hey, dude," Brian says.

"Do you know what happened?"

Brian coughs. "I got a call from Harry last night. I talked to some friends from the ER up there, and he apparently got hit by a truck while biking home from downtown. It pretty much crushed him. Dude didn't stand a chance."

Brian's an ER doc, so he doesn't think twice about people getting killed. He clamshells chests open, forces tubes down people's throats, and does all sorts of procedures that make dealing with death effortless. "Why was he biking home?"

"I guess he lost his car when he lost his job."

"He had King's," I say. Mark lived for that place—it had been in his family since 1932, and he'd given up his shot at college after his dad told him he'd be taking it over. Mark wasn't crazy about it, but he was the sort of guy who did what your dad said because he said it, and he never looked back.

"Nah," Brian says. "His dad fired him a few months back for drinking on the job."

I close my eyes, trying to picture an unemployed Mark with a drinking problem. Mark never drank. He'd go to parties with us, sure, but he wouldn't touch alcohol. Said it would get in the way of school or work or whatever else he had going on in his life at the time. He had the keys to King's Frozen Custard, a Lafayette staple that, even though it wasn't a sexy job, was about as secure as it got back home.

Only, as it turns out, he had none of that after all.

When I open my eyes, Lauren's stepped closer, as if she wants to do something but has no idea what.

"You okay?" Brian asks. I'd almost forgotten I was on the phone.

"Yeah," I say, even though I'm not. "I'm fine. Is there anything I can do?"

"Not really," he says. "Not that I know of, at least. I'm going to run, though. I told Mom and Dad I'd update them too."

"Later, dude."

"Bye," he says.

I throw my phone onto a couch cushion.

Lauren sits next to me. "I'm sorry." The way she says this —like she forgot to take the trash out or buy dog food—makes me want to sink into the couch and never get up.

"Mark's dead," I say again. I know she knows this, but I don't have any other words. I'd hoped that Brian would tell me it was all a big joke, that Mark's alive and I could go home and catch up with him and say sorry for screwing him over all those years ago, but it's not.

"You went to school with him, right?"

"Yeah."

"What happened?"

"Pretty much crushed by a truck?" I ask, still trying to make sense of it.

"Shit," she says. "I'm so sorry, hon. I can't imagine." She comes over and rubs my shoulder. "You want to grab dinner or something? Would that help at all?"

I haven't eaten all day, but the thought of food makes me want to yack. All I can think about is that I should have gone home sooner, should have said something at Walmart or given him a call. I scramble for a solution, something I can do here and now to make things right, but I've got nothing. He's just gone.

"Can we just grab a drink?"

"Sure," she says. "Your pick."

Truth be told, I'm fine with drinking anywhere. Hell, if the Burger King down the road served booze, I'd probably drink there. But we settle on Mulligan's, a dive in town that's far from perfect but appropriately dark and littered with heads of animals I can only assume the owner shot and killed. When we walk in, they stare at me—a bear's head, a deer or two, and even a raccoon—and I half wonder if they're hanging out with Mark wherever Mark is. As if he's just sitting up in heaven or hell, chilling with dead animals from a shit bar in Louisville.

Lauren and I have been hanging at Mulligan's since we bought our house a year or so ago. When we first moved, it was the only place where we could afford to drink. PBRs run $2, a shot of whiskey about the same, and the mixed drinks, while a little pricier, are boozy enough to be worth it.

When we sit down at our table, Ruben, the resident cat, hops onto Lauren's side and nuzzles his head against her arm. "Two shots," she says, smiling at the bartender. "Your pick."

He brings them over quickly, as men often do for Lauren, and she slides one my way. "For Mark?" she asks. "Is that appropriate?"

It's hard to think past him getting fired for drinking on the job and how, if I'd gotten my shit together a little sooner, I might have been able to get home and help out. Assuming it would have made a difference, that is.

"I guess."

"Okay," she says, raising her glass. "For Mark."

We clink glasses and knock back our drinks, an action that inspires the bartender to bring another round. Three or four later, Lauren and I are sitting sideways in our booth, backs against the wall, twiddling each other's thumbs across the table while we watch tennis on the thirteen-inch TV across the bar.

"How did you and Mark meet again? You know, besides school."

"Seventh grade," I tell her. She nods, as if the story's coming back to her. "Kurt Klosterman was picking on me for reading comics, and Mark stood up for me. Knocked the kid out. He tried to play hero and disappear, but I wasn't going to let him, so I ran after him and invited him over."

"And you guys stopped talking why?"

Because I slept with Beth, Mark's girlfriend. I can't tell Lauren that, though. I didn't mean to keep it from her, but in the years we've been together, I've never had a reason to bring it up. Now, it seems too late to.

"The band," I tell her. "We didn't see eye to eye on it."

She smiles. "I always forget that my boyfriend used to be a rock star."

This isn't entirely the truth, but it isn't a lie either. In high school, Mark and I teamed up with my brother, Brian, and our friend Kenny to start The Jackals. We were pretty popular before I left. We played most every spot around town and even booked some of Lafayette's little festivals. For some reason—probably because she's never seen how small Lafayette is—Lauren's always been impressed with this. Besides the promotion that never was, it's one of the things she's probably most proud of.

I start to say something but stop when somebody steps up to our table. He's a tall guy, and he's wearing a polo that hugs his arms and chest in a way that makes him look like he's stepped out of an American Eagle ad. His blond hair practically shines in the dark bar, and it's perfectly combed up and over to one side in a way that highlights his tanned skin and square face.

"Lauren," he says. When he smiles, I picture his teeth sparkling.

"Jeff," she says, letting go of my hand and scooting herself up in her seat. "What are you doing here?"

He hikes his thumb over his shoulder, pointing to a table of equally muscled men across the bar. "Just grabbing a beer with some work friends. You?"

She blinks a couple times, then wipes her hair from her face. "Grabbing a drink with my boyfriend," she says. "This is Jack. Jack Dotson."

Jeff laughs, then scoops my hand up from the table and shakes it. "Like the guy from *Titanic*."

"Dotson," I say. "With a 'T.'"

He laughs again, then shrugs and looks toward Lauren, who lets out a little laugh too. "Close enough," he says. "Anyway, just wanted to say hi. You running this week?"

She nods, a small, brisk thing. "Yeah," she says. "I think so."

"Great," he says, taking a step back. "I won't keep you. Have a good one. And nice meeting you, Titanic," he adds.

When he's gone, I turn toward Lauren. "Who's that?"

"Jeff," she says. "I've told you about him. He organizes the run club, remember?"

The way she says this, like it's my job to keep track of her career and clubs and volunteer gigs, makes me feel like I don't try. Like I need to memorize her planner, keep an address book of everyone she's talked about, do something. Kind of like how I didn't try with Mark—didn't try to go home, make amends, apologize. Nothing. She'd say that this is me projecting my expectations of something else onto our relationship, and she's probably right. There's just the nagging feeling that I should have done something more for Mark, and I can't shake the disappointment.

"You ready to go?"

Lauren knocks back the last of her drink, then sets the glass on the table. "Yeah."

On the walk back, Lauren slips her arm through mine and rests her head on my shoulder. Moonlight shining down on us, it's hard not to think of when we first moved into our place, penniless, just two kids in an empty house with no idea what to do. It took us months to save up enough money to furnish the place well enough for a house-warming party, and by the time we did, most people didn't bring a gift since we'd lived there so long.

I probably should have invited Mark to that party.

"You could have told me earlier today," Lauren says. "It must have sucked holding that in all day."

I look away. "I tried to tell you last night, but you were asleep. You were gone by the time I woke up."

"Sorry," she says. "Things have just been crazy with work."

I kiss the top of her head, and she buries it into my shoulder. "I know. That's why I didn't call. And it's not the sort of thing you put in a text."

"Didn't Brian text you?"

"Yeah," I say, snorting a laugh, "but Brian's a dick."

When we open our front door, we're greeted by the familiar slap of Jabba's tail against his crate, groaning as he waits to get out.

Lauren sets her bag on the table. "It's your turn."

"I let him out earlier."

"Yeah," she adds, "but I let him out before we left."

I rest against the wall. "So I get all the shitty ones."

Lauren shrugs, then leans forward and kisses me on the nose. "I guess you do. I'll let him out in the morning."

When I open the crate, Jabba barrels through the house, stopping only to wag his tail at the back door until I open it. When I do, he explodes out and into the darkness, leaving me to stare at the porch steps. Looking at the top one, I think back to letting him out last night, sitting on that step, and reading Brian's text. As Jabba makes his way across the yard, I wish I could travel back in time and avoid having learned about all this. If this were a sci-fi movie, I'd make the trip and steal my phone from past me, only to bring it back to the present where it can't do any harm and Mark's still alive.

It wouldn't have worked that way, though. Brian would have found me by calling Lauren, or emailing me, or calling my office, and I'd be in some other version of this same shit-storm. It feels nice to think about a world where I could have done something, though.

At least that way, too, I would have gotten a full night of sleep.

Jabba trots up the stairs, wagging his tail behind him as he goes, and sniffs my toes before hopping through the open doorway and running to Lauren. When I walk inside, she's lying in bed in a '90s-era Green Day sweatshirt and a pair of my old pajama pants. Glasses on, hair falling over her shoulders, she looks every bit as captivating as she did the night we met at Fitzgerald's. Lauren's the kind of beautiful you get in fights for, and the thought of this makes it near impossible to put aside the inadequacy I've felt since long before she came around.

"You okay?"

I shake myself into reality. "Yeah. Just thinking."

"You look sad."

I nod, frustrated at the obvious but appreciative of the effort. "I am," I tell her. "It just sucks. You think you have a chance to apologize to someone, to make it right with them, and it just doesn't work out that way."

She pats on the bed. "Get some sleep."

I lie in bed and pull the comforter over myself, an invitation that sends Lauren to my side, running her fingers up and down my abdomen in a way that makes me want to kiss her. Before I can, though, my eyelids fall heavy against the light above our bed, and I'm out.

FOUR

When I wake up the next day, I'm thinking about Beth. Lauren's asleep next to me, lying on her back and breathing in quiet snores I've promised her aren't real, but I picture Beth. In my head, she's wrapped in a quilt, drinking a PBR and laughing because we've had sex. If I'm being honest, I don't remember if she had a PBR, or if she laughed. It makes for a pretty thought, though.

I wonder if Beth's heard about Mark's death. She's still back home in Lafayette—last I heard, at least—so I can only assume she has. I try to shake the image of her—the blonde hair over her shoulder, the way she side-eyed me when I told her I ought to leave, the condensation from her beer rolling down the can and onto her arm—but I can't. It forces its way through the thoughts in my head like the sunlight peeking through the blinds.

My phone rings, a loud, piercing thing that sends a bolt of pain to the front of my head and the backs of my eyes. Lauren pauses mid-snore and rolls over, and I reach over to grab it off the nightstand. My brother, Brian, is the only person who calls this early, another side effect of the doctor life he assumes everyone understands.

I slide my thumb across the screen and slap the phone against my cheek. "What?"

"Did I wake you up?" Brian asks.

"What do you think?"

In the background, his Tesla hums down the highway. We used to drive matching cars until he started residency and took out a student loan to buy his "doctor car," which I've never been able to match.

"I'm heading to Lafayette," he says. "I called Mark's folks to ask if they needed help with anything, and Mrs. King mentioned not knowing where to begin with everything he had at his place. I think they're swamped with the funeral arrangements. You want to meet me up there?"

I roll onto my back and stare at the ceiling fan. Its blades chop through the air in a blurry circle that reminds me of a helicopter. For a second, I wonder if a chopper came for Mark. Then again, he died in Lafayette, where you can drive from one side of town to the other in fifteen minutes, so I guess that wouldn't have been necessary.

I think back to the image of him screaming at me from across the couch, the sound of him and Beth yelling at one another when he found out about the affair. The optimism of knowing that I'd make things right one day, the flatlining of that optimism when I made my way to Louisville, and the brick it left in my gut when I found out he'd been pretty much crushed by a truck.

This, I realize, is my chance to show everyone how far I've come, make amends where I can, and, even though it might be too late, do something right by Mark. Be the adult I've been trying to be.

"Yeah," I tell him. "I'll do it. When's the funeral?"

"A couple weeks," he says. "I guess his parents—"

"Weeks?" I picture a rotting corpse, flies and sunken eyes, and my stomach churns. "Isn't that a little long?"

"Cremation," Brian says. "His parents have a lot of things they want to get together, too. I think they want to do what they can to do right by him. Send him out in style."

"Okay," I tell him. "I'll talk to my boss today." I try to picture Amanda's face when I ask for the time off, wondering what shade of red it will turn and what problem she'll make up to try to force me to stay. "Where are we crashing?"

"Mark's."

I prop myself up on an elbow. "What?"

"Where else would we stay?"

He's right. Our parents sold their place a couple years back when they retired to Florida, leaving us homeless in our hometown.

"It'll be fun," he says. "I have to go, though. I'm about to pull off the highway."

Not a reason to get off the phone. But whatever.

"Sounds good," I say, hanging up.

Jabba stretches, a move that's sure to evolve into cries, then barks, then tail-wagging pleas to go outside. I sneak out of bed, past Lauren's "grass is greener" message on the chalkboard wall, and into the bathroom to take a shower. I'm greeted by the sight of my ever-disappointing body in the mirror, a sad, aging thing with breasts where pecs used to be and hair creeping over the tops of my shoulders. Your late twenties aren't a time to panic, but the signs of the slow transition into middle-agedness are sometimes hard to swallow. Truth is, I know I'm not in *that* bad of shape. I'm no athlete, that's for sure, but I'm a far cry from others my age. I've seen it on Facebook and all that, jocks and assholes who thought they were immortal and could do whatever they wanted but turned out jobless and wrecked instead. Turns out, effortlessness sucks, and it brings with it fifty pounds after graduation.

Staring at the bulbous sack of fat spilling over my boxers, I realize I should probably shut up.

Mark was always athletic, but he wasn't an athlete. He enjoyed kickboxing, sure, but most of his strength came from the work he put in at King's. Lifting boxes, fixing equipment, hauling trash—all manner of things to help out and keep the place running. The one summer I worked with him, I thought I'd lose weight, but I gained ten pounds because I sat on my ass, took orders, and ate free custard instead.

The shower water's cold against my skin, shocking me awake. I raise my face to it and relax as it runs over the top of my head and down my chest and back.

"Hey there," comes a voice, and I jump and almost slip. Lauren laughs, and I turn around to find her head poking through the curtain, dark hair framing her face against the white-tiled walls. "You're up early."

"Couldn't sleep," I say. "Thinking about Mark."

The corner of one side of her mouth turns downward, as if she's trying to frown but can't. Or trying not to frown. I can't really tell.

"You need to shower?" I ask.

She smiles. "Later. You want coffee?"

I don't say anything. Truth is, I can't. I'm never up this early, so I don't know what to do. It's like being at a party but not knowing anyone, so you stand still against the wall and hope you'll fade into it and not have to deal with people ever again. Only I'm not at a party. I'm naked and fat and freezing and standing in front of my girlfriend.

"I'll make coffee," she says, snapping the curtain shut with a quick tug.

I guess I'll have coffee.

When I'm done, I cut the water and step out, once again greeted by my reflection in the mirror. My hair's slicked back in a way that makes me look like a mafia member or someone tough. For all my shortcomings, I haven't lost any hair, something I thank my dad—or my mom's dad or whoever you get that from—for on a regular basis. I run my fingers back through it, half expecting it to fall out and splurt onto the floor, and I smile when I see it still there.

I get dressed and step out to find Lauren sipping coffee at the table, Jabba wrapped around her feet. The way his basset skin folds over itself makes it look like he's melting into her.

"Who called?" she asks.

"Who do you think?"

She nods. "What did he want?"

"He's going to Lafayette. Trying to help take care of some of Mark's stuff. I guess his parents are overwhelmed with it all."

Her eyes widen. "You going?"

I walk into the kitchen and pour myself a cup of coffee. "I think so."

There's a pause, and I can almost picture her tilting her head to the side while she thinks of a response. "Really?"

As I walk back into the room, I take a slow, dramatic sip of my coffee, both for effect and caution against burning my tongue. "That okay?"

"You think it's a good idea for you to see your brother?"

I sit down across from her at the table, suddenly feeling like we're in some sort of detective drama. "Not really," I say, "but we'll deal."

"The last time you saw him was Christmas, and you called him Dr. Fuckface before throwing your present at him and making us leave."

I laugh, then remember that was around the time I ran into Mark at Walmart. "Like I said, we'll deal," I tell her. I set my coffee cup on the table. "I'm going to go to work."

Lauren raises an eyebrow. "Do you know how to get into the building early?"

I used to come in early, before the acquisition and all that, but it's been a while. "Of course," I say. "You just sell your soul to the demon at the door."

"You're a brat."

"They've made me this way," I say, kissing the top of her head before grabbing my keys and walking out the door.

When I get to work, the lights are off except for those few that shine up from desperate cubes, people either too young to know any better or too old to have any hope. It's a fine line to walk, and as I make my way to my desk, I wonder which side of it I fall on. This sends a grumble of regret into my gut, so I hang my head and stare at the ground instead.

"Jack?"

I keep walking, pretending I didn't hear, and settle into my chair just in time for Amanda to peak her round, red-cheeked head in. She's a short woman with curly dark hair, her face in a constant state of panic due to the pretend problems we solve for our clients.

"I'm surprised you knew how to get into the building this early," she says.

The sitcom audience in my head laughs, and despite the fact that a snarky reply creeps up in the back of my mind, I smile. "The early bird gets the worm."

"Well, Rob's your worm today."

Rob Duncan is Confluence's CEO. Like most aspects of the CEO job, I have no idea what he does besides host quarterly meetings and send motivational emails that are, in all truth, vaguely veiled excuses to share a TED Talk or tell us all about his fitness routine.

And, apparently, he wants to talk to me.

My eyebrows raise, more out of instinct than anything, and I'm certain that my face reveals the concern that's crept up in my chest. Despite how much this place has screwed me since it sold out, it's a paycheck, and I'm not much to anyone without it.

"Why?"

"I don't know," she says. Her mouth quivers while it struggles to contain her smile. "But he wants you in ASAP. You available?"

I knew I shouldn't have come in early.

"Do I have a choice?"

The corners of her lips break free, and she grins from ear to ear, looking like the Cheshire Cat in this deprecated, corporate version of Wonderland. "Good point. Probably not."

I force a smile of my own, lost of my normal wit while visions of homelessness and hunger swirl through my brain. Would Lauren stay with me? Could we keep the house? Where else could I be hired? The newspaper won't take me, she's made that much clear, and I don't have any more reputable contacts in town. For a second, I think about Mark, getting fired by his own dad only to get pretty much crushed by a truck. Who would let Jabba outside if that happened to me?

I push my chair back and stand up without saying goodbye, suddenly feeling underdressed and stupid in my Frightened Rabbit T-shirt and Old Navy khakis.

I make my way to the back corner of my floor, around the far west corner to the annex Rob's reserved for himself and his executive council. They used to be on the upper floor, but Rob listened to a podcast a year or so ago that talked about the importance of "corporate confluence," so he moved himself and the rest of the executive council down to our floor. I used to refer to them as the Council of Elrond, something that got me a laugh or two from time to time, but I stopped when Justin in IT started quizzing me on which of the higher-ups were which *Lord of the Rings* characters.

Linda, Rob's receptionist, looks up from her computer

when I turn the corner. She has brown hair speckled with gray streaks, and her glasses rest on the end of her nose in a way that makes them look like they're about to fall. "Hey, Jack," she says. "Rob will be glad you're here. He wasn't expecting you until later."

This should comfort me, but the reality is that, on the few occasions that I've been to Rob's office, I've always had to either wait or come back at a better time. That he planned on speaking with me, especially early in the day, makes matters worse, so I wipe my palms against my khakis before nodding toward his door. "So, I just walk in?"

She smiles. "Yup."

I slowly push the door open, creeping my head around the corner like people do when they enter haunted houses or in horror movies, only there's no ghost or killer, just Rob with one leg up on his desk, his head resting against his knee while he pulls on the bottom of his foot with both hands.

"Jack!" he says, smiling against the top of his knee cap. "I was just finishing my morning stretch. Take a seat."

I settle into the leather chair across from him, watching as he switches legs and pulls into the other foot. Rob's not a big man by any means—he's short and lean, like most runners are —but the circumstances unsettle me as if he were twice my size and pummeling my head against the concrete. Rob's a pacifist, though, having reminded us on multiple Wednesday Wake-Up emails that aggression isn't a solution.

"So," I say, my eyes scouring the bookshelves, papers, and diplomas, "how's the training?"

"Good," he says, nodding into his leg. "Have you ever run a marathon?"

"I haven't. I once watched all of the *Star Wars* movies back-to-back, though."

Rob laughs, and the muscles in my shoulders loosen. People don't fire people who make them laugh. "You should," he says. "It's cathartic. People say the distance is too long, but by the time you're five or six miles in, it's almost euphoric. The hormones change everything."

"I felt the same way right before Luke found out Vader was his father," I say. "My girlfriend didn't buy it, though."

Rob laughs again before exhaling and lifting his leg from the table. "You're a funny guy," he says. "Some people take this gig too seriously, but you have a way of keeping it light-hearted. Reminds me of my yoga instructor."

I don't know a lot about Rob, but, if I had to guess, I'd say he holds his yoga instructor higher than his children, parents, wife, dog—anyone, really. I sink into my chair a little and cross my legs, comfortable enough with my surroundings to let my guard down some. What if he's building me up before breaking my heart, though? The classic "it isn't you, it's me" argument? All at once, I'm in high school again, thinking over every word and movement as if the fate of the world hinges on when I scratch my ear or if I say the right thing to a girl. The questions spin through my head, making me feel like I've been out drinking, sloshing my thoughts and sending my vision swirling. As my armpits sweat, I sink further into my chair, not out of comfort but out of fear, knowing that I'm fired and homeless and lonely, all in the face of Mark being pretty much crushed by a truck and me never having had the balls to apologize to him.

"I'm going to die, just like Mark," I say.

Rob's eyes go wide. "What?" he says, sending everything into focus with a force that wrings my stomach.

I shake my head and swallow my anxiety. "What?"

"Who was Mark?" he asks.

The reality of what I've spit out hits me in the face, and I stare into Rob's incredulous eyes with a fear that makes me want to quit before he can fire me. "I'm so sorry. He was a friend of mine."

"Do you want to talk about it?"

In my terror, I feel my head shaking. "I think I'm okay."

"I can't imagine losing a friend that young," he says. "I can't imagine what you're going through. If there's anything you need from us, absolutely let us know. We want to help you crush it as you go through this hard time."

"Thanks, Rob," I tell him. "That really means a lot."

"I'm glad," he says. "Would you like to meet another time?"

Aside from the new job honeymoon phase, this is my life at Confluence. I throw myself into a bath of cynicism and sarcastic jokes, only for something to happen that gives me a pang of regret for all those comments in a fleeting glimmer of realization that what we do matters. That the people here aren't all that bad. That, truth be told, I was one decision away from getting that promotion I wanted. It's an abusive relationship, really, and one that I'm familiar enough with to realize which way the pendulum is swinging. So, despite the fact that Mark's death is settling over my thoughts like those slow, murky fogs in horror movies, I embrace this fleeting glimpse of pride for my company, knowing all too well that it'll soon be gone.

"I'm good," I say. "We can talk."

Rob smiles and leans forward, setting his arms on his desk like executives do, elbows out, forearms crossing one another in a way that frames the perfectly forced grin on his face. "Okay. If it's any consolation, I've kind of been there before. When I ran my last half marathon, I finished first, but they took my win away on a technicality with my timing chip. I was devastated."

And, it's gone.

"Enough tragedy, though," he says. "Let's talk good news."

I push myself up in my seat. "I'm not being fired?"

Rob's eyes shoot open in a way that, in a rare instance, shows surprise. "God no. Why would you be fired?"

I shrug, instantly aware of a dozen reasons but also aware, for once, that I should keep my mouth shut. "I don't know. I wasn't sure what to expect."

"Definitely not that," he says. "We've had our eye on you for a while. We want to promote you."

Had I been taking a drink, I would have spit it out. Instead, I sit up farther in my seat, as promoted people should. "What?"

"We're working on the development of a new strategic initiatives department. We're keeping it small for now—just a one-man department, reporting to me—but I think you're the one for the job. There's a lot to like about you, Jack. The college drop-out who moves to a new town to start his life over, pull himself up by his bootstraps. It's admirable."

"What is it?" I ask, my throat burning as if battling the lingering heartburn of a late-night slice of pizza. 'Strategic initiatives' is one of those phrases in business that's as substantive as a handful of water, so, despite my relief, I struggle to settle down.

"Keeping an eye on the market. Adapting our strategies so we're skating to the puck."

I chew on this for a second. "That's not the quote."

Rob tilts his head, eyes narrow. "What?"

"You're quoting Wayne Gretzky. The point of the quote is that you shouldn't skate to the puck, but to where it's going to be. If you skate to the puck, it's going to be somewhere else before you get there."

Rob nods, his head rocking like a cheap bobblehead from a baseball game. "And this is why you're the man for the job."

If I would have known that being able to quote Gretzky would be my way of moving up the corporate ladder, I wouldn't have wasted twenty-five grand on my unfinished secondary education degree.

"I suppose so."

"So, you'll take it?"

For no reason whatsoever, I lean back in my chair and cross my legs again, feeling like a confident badass out of *Mad Men*. You know, one of those guys with a tailored suit and a fedora and a cigarette dangling from his lip. Only I'm not one of those, because I'm wearing a T-shirt and khakis and you can't smoke in the workplace.

"Absolutely," I tell him, worried for a second that this promotion will disappear out from under me as quickly as the last one did. Then I remember my conversation with Brian, my commitment to Mark. "But there's a catch." I take in a breath, then exhale, trying to keep cool. Stay confident. "I was actually going to ask Amanda for some time off to attend my friend's funeral."

Rob's nodding, one elbow resting on his desk as he looks me over. "Have you been reading the Wednesday Wake-Ups?"

My instinct is to laugh, but I swallow it down. "Sorry. Which one?"

"March 27th," he says. Half a year ago. "Successful organizations don't limit themselves to when and where someone's working—they commit themselves to making sure each person is in a position that best utilizes his or her strengths. This can be admittedly difficult given paid time off policies, especially when we're client-facing like Amanda's team, but this set-back? You're going to have a hard time pushing our new department forward if your head's on your friend's death. Stay available in case of an emergency, but take the time you need."

The words make my heart flutter, like when a cheerleader asks the dorkiest kid in the class to dance, and I can't stop myself from nodding. I'm here. I did it. I'm the Director of Strategic Initiatives, and I'm going to make things right with everyone back home. Do right by Mark.

"Absolutely," I tell him. "I won't let you down."

"I know you won't," Rob says, standing from his desk in a

way that urges me to do the same. "Stay connected while you're out, okay?"

I shake his hard. "I can do that."

"Awesome. Have a good one, Jack."

I smile, forcing the corners of my lips up in a way that makes my face feel heavy. "Will do."

As I pull the door open, Rob stops me. "Hey, Jack?" he says, making me feel like my dad did when I screwed up in baseball and he wanted to explain what I did wrong. Rob's eyes are wide, and I can almost see his thoughts—the empathy, the pride, everything—forming in his head. "Keep crushing it."

I push my smile up higher and nod, trying my hardest to keep my mouth shut and accept that something good might be happening in the face of all this.

FIVE

When afternoon rolls around, I go to my car and hide. Everyone knows about my meeting with Rob, so it's easier to stay low and keep to myself. My morning's been a marathon of veiled small talk with people trying to get the pulse of things, but nobody's concerned about me. They're all looking out for themselves, as people do when there's a whiff of change, and I'm either an alliance worth having or a waste of time.

Mark used to make fun of me for not knowing anything about cars. One morning, during our senior year of high school, I called him and asked him to pick me up since I had a flat tire. He asked me why I didn't change it, and when I told him I didn't know how, the drubbing began. Nothing too harsh, but I spent the next few years being asked if I knew how to fill up my gas tank (yes), change a headlight (no), change my oil (no), and all other sorts of repairs (probably no).

My phone rings. I check the name to make sure it's not Brian, hoping to avoid the when-will-you-be-here? talk, then grab it off the passenger seat and pick up.

"Hey, hon," Lauren says.

"What's up?" I lean into my seat and stare at the concrete wall and the D3 location marker painted on it. I park here because of the *Mighty Ducks* movies, even though the third one sucks.

"Not much," she says. "I took the afternoon off. Thought you might want to grab lunch or something."

I tap my finger on the steering wheel and wait for the follow-up. Lauren doesn't take off work for anything, so after a few seconds of silence, I cave. "Really?"

"Yeah," she says. "When's your lunch?"

"I'm on it. I'm in my car."

She pauses, and I can picture her biting her lower lip, thinking over how to best respond. I consider telling her about the promotion, picture her lighting up and throwing her arms around me, but decide to wait.

"How about The Lodge?" she says.

The Lodge is a New York-style pizza place that opened a few months back. Next to my house, it's probably my favorite place to be. The pizza's cheap, the beer's cheaper, and the service is no-frills.

"That sounds awesome."

"Great," she says, and I can almost hear her smile. She's trying to be nice here, supporting me even though she'd rather be at work. "See you soon."

I get to The Lodge in just under ten minutes. When I turn into the lot, Lauren's leaning against her Jeep, dark hair whipping across her face as she stares down at her cell phone.

I park next to her and step out of my car. She slides her phone into her pocket, then gives me a quick hug and a kiss on the cheek. "You seemed bummed this morning. Thought a pizza date might do the trick."

"Thanks," I say. "What's the slice of the day?"

"Bacon and banana pepper."

I grab her hand, and we start walking toward the door. "That sounds awesome."

She walks through the door as I open it and leads me to a table near the bar. The Lodge is an old VFW joint brought back to life with a fresh set of white and dark red walls, a polished bar, and a handful of dart boards, TVs, and more. They've sprinkled the place with a collection of drawings—things people have scribbled on napkins, the backs of receipts, and anything else, really—that make it almost seem like a curated display. A kid's drawing of a pizza here, a picture of King Kong climbing a giant breadstick there. No rhyme or reason. Just character.

The place is mostly empty, though. There's nothing on TV at this point except for a pre-season look at Louisville's football team and some baseball highlights, which a few older men huddle around.

"How'd work go?" Lauren asks.

"All right," I tell her. "They offered me a promotion."

Her eyes pop open. "What?"

"Don't act too surprised."

Her head moves back and forth like some sort of creepy, dying toy. "I'm not," she says. "It's just that you—well, after last time, you've been kind of, I don't know. Disengaged. What's the promotion?"

I look down at the table and run my thumb across the grain of the wood. I guess there will be no lighting up, no jumping hugs into my arms or anything of the sort. Just surprise.

"Director of Strategic Initiatives," I tell her. I puff my chest some, sit up a little straighter. You know, sit how a director should.

"You take it?"

The bartender's voice echoes between us before I can respond. "You want any beers?"

"Two," Lauren says. "A PBR and a Bell's Two Hearted."

I smile. "Thanks. And, yeah."

"You excited?"

Over Lauren's shoulder, I notice a drawing of Spider-Man eating a slice of pizza. The '90s Spider-Man, with the giant white eyes, big spider on the chest, muscles so big he almost looks scary. The Spider-Man Mark and I grew up on.

"Yeah," I tell her, coming to. "It's a good opportunity to start over. Get a new set of legs now that I'm not under Amanda."

The bartender brings our beers. Lauren takes a drink from hers, holding the neck of the bottle between her fingers so casually that I half-worry it's going to fall out and shatter. Things like that don't happen to Lauren, though.

"That's fantastic, hon." She reaches across the table and squeezes my hand. "You really deserve this."

I take these words in, let them marinate in my conscious-ness. Even if it wasn't the response I wanted, after finding out about Mark, it's nice to have something to look forward to.

I point to the chalkboard menu on the wall. "Slice of the day?"

"God no," Lauren says. "Slice of pep."

I turn toward the bartender. "Slice of the day and a slice of pep?"

He nods and repeats my order to the kitchen.

Lauren leans forward and rests her elbows on the table. "So you're not going to Lafayette then, right?"

"What?"

Lauren opens her mouth, then closes it. She pushes herself up in her seat, shoulders square, before resting her hands in her lap. "This isn't an entry-level job you're working anymore," she says. "You can't just take a promotion and run."

My eyes narrow, and I can feel the grimace spreading across my face. Lauren has a knack for comments like this. She means well in her attempt to nudge me toward how she'd behave, but she doesn't always realize that, despite a few hiccups, I've accomplished a thing or two on my own.

"I already talked to Rob about it."

Lauren pulls her lips in tight, forming a thin line across her face. At one point, she was on some love language kick, and she told me that in moments like these, she's trying to gather her thoughts, and that I need to respect the way she processes things. "I mean, that was nice of him and all, but are you sure it's the best look after what happened last time?"

I pull the tab off the top of my PBR and set it on the table. She could be right, of course. Last time this happened, I was all but offered the position when the company reorganized and it disappeared. This time, though, I had actually been offered it. At least I think I was, right?

Lauren grabs the tab and flips it between her thumb and forefinger. She stares at it as it moves between her fingers, top to bottom, bottom to top. After about twenty of these, she sets it down. "What are you really going to accomplish if you go home?"

My mouth drops. "What?"

The bartender brings our pizza to the table, sliding our plates to each of us before turning away. Lauren grabs for the Parmesan and starts sprinkling some on her slice. "All you've ever told me is that everything fell apart. What are you really trying to accomplish?"

I stumble over thoughts, trying to figure out how we got from my promotion to here. "Are you saying I'm wasting my time?"

Lauren folds her slice in half and takes a bite. "I didn't say that," she says. "I just think it would be good for you to focus on what you have here. It's not like things have come easily for you at work. Maybe things are finally turning around."

I look down at my slice spilling over the plate, grease shimmering in the little light the place offers up.

"You're not mad, are you?"

I take a swig from my PBR. "No," I tell her. Sometimes, when she goes on like this, it's easier to go along with it. "I understand where you're coming from," I add, even though I don't, knowing now more than ever that I could use some support.

She reaches across the table, grabbing my hand again and squeezing it gently. "Thanks. Now, eat your pizza. This is the slice of the day, you know. Last chance."

I force a smile against the disappointment. "Yeah. Thanks."

"You really okay?"

I stop mid-bite and set my pizza back down on the plate. "I mean, not really. No. Not at all."

"What?"

"What do you expect me to say? My friend is dead, and all I want to do is go home and help my friends take care of some of his stuff. It's good enough for my boss, but not good enough for you?"

Lauren's frozen right before taking a bite, her slice resting on both hands, mouth open, eyes wide. Spider-Man's still behind her, making just about the same face. I don't know what Spider-Man's feeling, but Lauren's somewhere between confusion and anger—the raised eyebrows, the way she sets her slice back down without taking a bite—and I know she wants to snap back but won't. She's trying to be a good listener.

"I understand it's not an easy decision, but I think you need to—"

"Not easy? That's what you can come up with? It *was* easy. It was easy for me and Rob and anyone else who actually has a say until you stormed in and decided it wasn't good enough for you."

We sit in silence for a couple minutes. Lauren picks at her pizza, grabbing slices of pepperoni between her thumb and forefinger and popping them into her mouth, and I stare over her shoulder at the drawing of Spider-Man, wondering what Mark would have thought about this place if I ever would have invited him down here.

"Are you going to eat?" Lauren asks.

I push the plate toward the center of the table. "I'm good."

"Okay," she says. "I think I'm just going to work, then."

"Of course you are."

Lauren kisses me on the cheek on her way out the door, leaving me fuming. I can't see him, but the bartender's staring at me. That's what happens in situations like this—she fucks up, I get mad, and everyone thinks it's my fault. I want to say something to him, but truth is, he'd kick my ass. It'd be middle school all over again, a pummeling for no reason other than opening my mouth, and Mark wouldn't even be here to help me.

Loneliness creeps over me, covering me like a long shadow I can't get away from, and I fold my slice in half and take a bite, letting the greasiness envelope me like a sickness. I force another bite and slouch into my seat, and it hits me that I couldn't care less about whoever might walk in and what their opinion might be.

FIVE HOURS LATER, I've called into work, eaten three slices, drunk two pitchers of PBR, bought the now-full bar a round of shots, and watched two ESPN 30 for 30s (one on the XFL, and one on Reggie Miller). I'm right at that point where I think I'll get kicked out if I do anything stupid, so I've kept my mouth shut and stared at the Spider-Man on the wall instead. Comics are something living, with each panel relying on the next, and I can't help but feel sorry for this '90s-era Spider-Man stuck forever in an attempt to eat a goddamn slice of pizza.

I wonder if Mark has his old comics. I got him hooked on them. He was always a reader, so he wanted to know the back-stories, the alternate universes, the whole shebang. He had longboxes of them in his house—Beth hated them, but she'd never take them away—and he'd read them all backwards and forwards until he knew everything about them.

Mark can't have them, though. He can't have anything because he's not present to have anything. He had them and he's dead, and the comics are probably sitting where he left them, waiting for someone to do something with them.

I imagine picking up my phone, sliding my thumb across the screen, and calling Beth. Is her number even the same? In my head it is, and the phone gets to only half a ring before she picks up. Her voice is electric, bright as she tells me how long it's been, how much she's missed me and how sorry she is that we were never able to talk about what happened. She hints that she knows I'm drunk, and she asks where I am before I tell her that I'm at this cool little pizza place in Louisville, a place I think she'd love. I picture her holding her hand to her chest, like people in movies do when they're flattered, and I try to imagine what she's wearing. In my head, she's wearing the blue blink-182 T-shirt I made fun of her for once, and the only reason I know this is because she's told me because of course I'd call her on the day she's wearing it. I imagine asking her if I should come home, and, in my head, there's a pause. Then, an "of course" as she tells me that I'm being stupid, that every-thing's fine and that she can't wait to see me.

I imagine us talking for hours about what we've been up to and what we're going to do when I get to town. When I come to, though, it's been five minutes, and my phone's black. I look down at the table and run my finger around a ring of conden-sation, smearing the water in an ugly circle. Each wet lap my thumb makes around it muddles my thoughts a little further until Beth isn't happy to see me at all, until she's thrown away the blink-182 shirt and changed her number because I screwed everything up by sleeping with her and being a shitty friend and running away.

It's going to be okay, though, I tell myself. This is my chance to fix things.

I GET HOME at a quarter past ten. Lauren's on the couch when I walk in, reading a book in her sweatpants while her glasses rest on the middle of her nose. Jabba's on the other end of the couch, curled up in a white-and-brown ball, ears flopped over his eyes. The whole scene reminds me of when I'd sneak out late in high school and my dad would stay up waiting for me.

I take in a breath, then let it out slowly. "Hey."

Lauren closes her book, pages rattling off the tips of her thumbs as they meet in between the covers. She sets her glasses on the coffee table, then looks up at me. "Hi."

"I'm leaving in the morning."

She nods, and a strand of her hair falls in front of her face. She leaves it there. "You know I can't go with you, right?"

I should have figured.

"I'm sorry." She looks down at Jabba, then at a bowl of fruit, then down at her book. "I might be able to come up for the funeral, but I can't make it up for everything else. Eric just has me too busy at work right now."

"It's fine," I tell her. I don't know if I believe myself, but there's not much else to say. Our relationship counselor would be proud of me.

"I'm sorry about earlier too. That was pretty shitty of me. What you've done, what you've put up with at work and gone through the last couple days, it's pretty remarkable."

I look over her shoulder at a shelf on the wall behind her. It holds three plants, big and leafy and flowery, that Lauren's kept alive as long as we've lived here. Next to one of them sits a small Power Rangers action figure I snuck up there when we moved. Despite Lauren checking on those plants every day, it took her three months to notice it. As a reward, she said, I could keep it up there.

"Jack?"

I shake my head, coming to. "Sorry. Thanks," I tell her. "That means a lot."

Talking through this and trying to sort this mess of a situation out, all I can think about is that she might be right. That maybe I shouldn't take time off work, that I should stay here instead. Take care of myself. I can't shake the feeling, though, that I can do it. I can take some time off work, get back to Lafayette for a few days, sort things out with everyone there, then come back, get started on this new job, and live my life with Lauren. I look up at the Power Ranger next to her plants, though, frozen forever in a battle pose, and see everything I could lose if I screw this up.

SIX

When I pull into Mark's driveway, I turn off my car and unbuckle my seat belt.

The basement window's open. Eyes watering, teeth trembling, I try to picture what Mark's done with the place where I spent so many of my college weekends. Maybe it's the same—same shitty Walmart futon, hand-me-down Playstation 2, tattered Red Hot Chili Peppers posters. Maybe he burned it all the day after he found out about Beth and me. The questions circle through my head, crashing into and flipping over one another, and I'm tempted to pull out of the driveway and go back to Louisville. I can do this, though, I remind myself. Things have changed. I've changed. I owe it to Mark to help sort this all out.

The outside of the house is exactly as I remember it. Vines creep up the brick walls as if holding them together. The lawn's a splotch of different shades of green, islands of dirt speckled throughout like stepping stones across a creek, leading their way up to the front porch. There's a swing up there, probably the one Beth and I shared beers on the night we slept together. Only it's tattered now, some of the boards warped and curling upward as if they're trying to get away. One of the windows on the door has been replaced with plywood.

Mark hated this place. Said the owner couldn't give two shits about it. By now, I guess I thought he would have done something about it.

When I make my way up to the door, I notice a drawing in the middle of the plywood. It's the lightsaber fight from the end of *Empire*, Luke handless, Vader calm. Only it's not Luke and Vader, it's two basset hounds. They're dressed for the scene —the Vader basset in black armor, the Luke basset in that off-white jumper thing he wears—and I try to picture Mark drawing it. I run my thumb over the pen marks, feeling the indentations against the grain of the wood, but I've got nothing. I can't picture a Mark that existed within the last few years, so I turn the doorknob and head inside.

Beth's not supposed to be here. At least, Brian didn't mention she would be here. A bandanna keeps her hair back, and while I can't see it, I know her hair's shorter. She has a bottle of cleaner in one hand and a wad of paper towels in the other, and the sleeves of her flannel shirt are rolled up just enough to reveal a tattoo on her arm that I didn't know existed.

My bag rolls off my shoulder and lands in a heap next to the door. My palms start to sweat, and my breaths come a little faster. "What are you doing here?"

She narrows her eyes.

"I didn't expect to see you."

"I could say the same for you," she says. "Nobody expects the disappearing Jack Dotson to come home, you know."

"Well, I did," I say, shrugging. There are a million questions I want to ask her—questions about us and Mark and them—but I swallow them down, focusing on the here and now instead. "Where is everyone?"

"Brian's out running errands. Kenny's doing God-knows-what. How are you?"

"I'm good," I tell her. The house is darker than I remember. Tapestries hang over the windows, dangling from crooked nails and swooping over the tops of one another in dramatic fashion. Books and comics litter the tables, most sitting open atop paper plates and pizza boxes. In the corner is a picture of Mark and Beth, and I wonder how recently it was taken. Mark's hair is cropped short, and his shoulders are broad, arms thick. Beth's huddled up next to him, one hand on his chest. The same tattoo that creeps out from under her sleeve today is on her forearm, front and center. On Mark's is one that, at least from here, appears identical, and, for the first time, it hits me that they might have gotten back together.

Well, did get back together, by the look of things.

Beth walks over to the picture. She stares at it for a few seconds, running her thumb over the edge of the frame, then sets it facedown on the table.

"How are you?" I say.

"Good." She walks toward me, and I open my arms to hug her. Beth sidesteps me and picks up my bag, though. "You'll be in the basement," she adds, slinging it over her shoulder. "Thought it would be familiar."

Beth walks out of the room. I start to speak, but my throat catches and the words freeze. It's nice of her to take my bag, sure, but it doesn't do much to help me understand what's happening or why she's here. Why nobody told me about her and Mark. Why I still can't put together that Mark and Beth were, well, together. I don't know what I expected—to pack boxes, share some memories, maybe order out or something—but it wasn't this.

"You're sharing the futon with your brother," she yells from downstairs.

I'd forgotten how thin the floors are. It takes me back to my life in that basement six years ago, lying on the futon, trying to sleep while Beth and Mark talked about whatever it was they had going on. Some nights, they'd talk about trivial shit, like which one of them needed to sweep the kitchen or what bills they had to pay. Other nights, though, they'd talk about deep things, like where they'd want to go on their honeymoon (Mexico) or how many kids they thought they'd have (two). Those nights, I felt like an intruder for listening, and I probably was. There wasn't much else to listen to except for Brian's snores, though, so it was hard to turn off my ears.

I shake my head, trying to put those memories behind me. "Isn't there another room?"

"I'm upstairs," she shouts from the basement. "Kenny's in the spare room."

I walk over to the bookshelf, running my fingers over the spines and looking for some evidence of what their life was like here while conversing with what appears to be the floor. "Why does he get the spare room?"

Beth's feet creak on the steps as she makes her way back upstairs. "We knew he'd be here." She walks into the living room with a pizza box and throws it into one of the large trash cans she's strategically placed for cleanup. "You'll get by," she adds. She says this without looking at me, then disappears into the kitchen.

I start to ask her if she's mad, or if I did something wrong by coming, but the back door flies open, slamming against the wall with a force that sends the tapestries whipping through the air. "Brochacho!" Brian shouts, stepping past Beth to surround me in a hug. "You really came." He claps me on the back before turning to Beth. "And you guys finally get to reunite after your awkward hookup, huh?"

I take in a long breath through my nose. Brian's as smug as ever, smirking like he's drunk or in love. He's bigger than me— always has been—but if age has been unkind to me, it's been worse to him. His hairline has started to creep back and gray at the edges, so he keeps it trimmed short. He'd still wreck me in a fight, too, but he's not all muscle like he was in college. His T-shirt sleeves stretch tight around his arms, but they're less forgiving in his waist, where a roll of a belly has started spilling over his jeans. He doesn't look at himself and worry about these things, though. He has a six-figure salary to look forward to after residency, fancy dinners with even fancier people, a loft in downtown Indianapolis, and a car that draws the attention of everyone around him. He has nothing and everything all at once, and he couldn't care less.

A noise comes from the basement. It sounds like a broken doorbell, or maybe even a toy firetruck with dying batteries, but before any of us can question it, the basement door pops open and a cat pokes through, meowing as if he's been trying to get a hold of us for hours. He's a small guy, with thick, fading black fur and bright yellow eyes.

"What the hell is this?" Brian says.

Beth bites her lower lip. "That's Jack." The cat stops by Beth's feet and stares up at her. "Mark adopted him a year or so ago."

Brian's cheeks shine red beneath his beard, and he's working so hard to contain a grin that his face looks ready to explode. "Please tell us the story."

My stomach tightens into a thick knot, feeling like it's going to sink through my body and splatter on the floor.

"There's no story," Beth says.

Brian snorts half a giggle. "Come on. There has to be."

Jack meows, and Beth scoops him into her arms and rocks him like a baby. "If there is, I don't know it. Mark never told me anything. Just that he wanted him called Jack."

"Come on," Brian whines, slumping his shoulders. "It's got to be some sort of revenge after what you two did, right? Naming some mangy little thing like this after Jack?"

Beth forces a smile and walks downstairs.

"Good one," I tell him.

Brian shrugs. "What's she so pissed about?"

"Probably the hooking up bit you mentioned."

He narrows his eyes and tilts his head to the side. "Is it too soon to talk about you guys?"

I take in a breath and force myself to think through everything I want to say. It's something Lauren's tried to get me to do since the "Dr. Fuckface" Christmas, and now seems as good a time as any to give it a go. I'm here for Mark, after all. To make things right and get together with these people, even my brother. Mend some fences, I guess.

After working through "Are you shitting me?" and "How the fuck are you a doctor?", I settle on a response. Exhale.

"I don't know, man. Probably so."

"That sucks. How was the trip?"

And we're normal. I think to ask him about Beth, why she's here an how things worked out with Mark, then remember the thin floors. "Good. Yours? I thought you were getting here days ago."

"Got called in, ' he says. "I popped a drunk guy's ankle into place last night, though. That was pretty cool. I don't think he saw it coming."

I take a seat at the table. "Don't you have to ask for permission?"

"God no," he says. "That would be awful. Have you ever tried to tell a hammered dude that you need to pop his ankle into place? It's like telling a kid he can't have a piece of candy. They throw a fucking fit."

Listening to him, it's hard to picture a doctor. I can't get past it sometimes—the crassness, the lack of empathy—but it's true. There's a Brian Dotson, MD badge in his car, along with a Brian Dotson, MD flight suit for his helicopter shifts. There are embroidered Brian Dotson, MD fleeces, vests, business cards—anything you can put a name on, really. Sitting next to him, listening to him talk down about this patient and that one while he paces back and forth in his sweater and khakis that look so nice they almost smell like money, I can't help but feel small. Suddenly, my Wilco T-shirt and tattered jeans feel wrong. Dirty.

I push that back, though. I'm moving on up, making strides.

Brian pounds a fist on the table. "People are fucked up," he says. "That's why I do what I do. Have you heard from Kenny?"

I kick at a wadded napkin on the floor. "No. Beth doesn't know where he is, either. What's the plan, though?"

Brian opens the fridge and pulls out a beer. "What do you mean?"

My mouth falls open, and my eyes go from the empty takeout boxes to the sticky stains on the floor to eventually my brother. "Your plan? Us picking up the place and getting Mark's stuff together?"

"I don't know," he says, knocking back half his beer in a couple gulps. "Guess we'll figure it out."

My mind races back to my promotion, asking for time off at the worst possible moment, the moment when, on my last go-around, everything fell through my grasp. Lauren's voice echoes through my head, reminding me that this isn't an entry-level job anymore, that I ought to stay home and focus on work, and it hits me that I might have screwed up by coming here. That I put it all on the line for a pit of a house with no plan of attack so I could stay with a handful of people I don't get along with.

"You're kidding, right?"

Brian rolls his eyes and chugs the rest of his beer, then crunches the can in his fist and tosses it toward the trash. It misses. "What? No. How hard can it be?"

I run my hands down my face. "How the fuck are you a doctor?"

"What does that have to do with anything? At least I don't sit in a fucking cubicle all day."

I think to tell him about the promotion, that I'm about to have an office and a raise and all that, but it won't do any good. Brian's understanding of professional life outside of a hospital is nonexistent, so I walk toward the fridge and grab a beer of my own, then head toward the stairs to the basement.

"Hey, Jack?"

By the time I turn around, Brian's grabbed another beer. "What?"

"Could you get me your status report on the quality of that beer by five? I need it before I head out for the golf course this afternoon. Chop-chop."

I turn away before I say something stupid, then head downstairs.

The basement's the same as I remember it. Mark never finished it—the walls are as gray as a sidewalk, and the texture not much better—but he decorated it as if he had, with a bright red futon against the far wall and a TV across from it. The same old PS2 is hooked up, waiting to be brought to life with the push of a button. Posters hang haphazardly at varying angles, some overlapping each other, all signs of an early 2000s high school experience. The Red Hot Chili Peppers, *Smallville*, Tobey Maguire's *Spider-Man*—all staring at me, as if wondering what I'm doing here.

"Not much has changed since you lived down here," Beth says. She's bent over the far end of the futon, stretching a sheet over it. I can almost picture the lot of us. Mark and me on the futon, sharing a bowl of chips; Brian and Kenny sitting in front of the TV, yelling at each other over *Metal Gear Solid* or *Dragonball Z: Budokai*. Laughing. Smiling. We didn't even try back then; we just did things, became friends, and stayed friends because that's who we were. It's what we did. It was effortless. Yet here we are, years later, being pulled back together into some sort of awkward tumbleweed of emotion.

Well, except for Mark.

"You remember that we all but gave this space to you and Brian, right? That you two used to be inseparable?"

I lean against the stair railing. "Can we not? Things are different now."

"That's shit," Beth says, tucking a pillow under her chin while she slides a case up over it. "You guys just decided you were better off competing over everything."

"You don't know us."

She tosses the pillow down, then turns to look at me. "I think I do." Hand on her hip, face red, she stares me down as if challenging me to respond. I don't know how, though. She *does* know us. She did, at least, but that's different now. She knew us before this all fell apart, and between her attitude and Brian's shitty jokes, all I want is for her to drop the know-it-all act. I came here to help, for God's sake, to pack up boxes and clean the place up, maybe even rekindle a friendship or two, and all I am is the butt of a joke or the focus of a lecture.

I'd say this isn't going according to plan, but there apparently isn't one.

"I'm going to go," I tell her. "Get some fresh air or something."

Beth goes to the closet and pulls out a comforter, grabbing it in quick bursts like a cat tearing at a roll of toilet paper. "That's probably a good idea," she says, throwing it on the bed. Her voice is charged yet restrained, like a parent who's disappointed, and I have no idea how to respond.

"I'll come back later."

Beth says something as I make my way up the stairs. I should probably listen, but I can't, focusing instead on how terrible of an idea it was for me to come here and pondering how I can get back to Louisville as quickly as possible. Brian asks me if I want another beer, and I grab one from him and carry it with me on my way out, swinging the door shut behind me. I stop at the sound of a pattering on the ground, though, and turn to find Mark's plywood window pane facedown on the porch. I take a long swig of my beer, letting it fizzle and funnel down my throat, before throwing the can down in the yard and picking up the piece of wood. The indentations prick at my skin as I run my thumbs over the drawing one last time. Some part of me—the part of me that said it was a good idea to come here, I guess—tells me to fix it, but I swallow it down, toss the wood back to the ground, and leave.

SEVEN

I t takes me thirty-four minutes of driving—or two laps around Greater Lafayette—to come up with a plan. Not a plan to get out, and definitely not a plan to head back to Beth and Brian at the house, but a plan to fill the time until I can come up with a way to bring some structure to this shitshow.

My first thought is to call Lauren, but she's at work. So, I call the only person I have left, Kenny. It rings once before he picks up.

"What did you do?" he asks.

I roll my eyes, almost missing the turn onto his street. "Want to grab a drink?"

"That bad, huh?"

I park in front of his house. It's a brighter yellow than I remember, and he's painted the door orange, but its bones are as familiar as ever: the front window we used to look out, the garage door he wrecked his car through in high school, the bushes we used to sled off the roof into. "I'm pulling up to your place now."

Kenny laughs. "Do you know where I live?"

I roll down my window to check the house numbers—127 S. 23rd Street. "Yeah?"

"I moved two years ago."

Fuck.

I pull away just as someone starts opening the front door. "Well, where do you live now?"

"On Ferry. Head that way, and I'll meet you outside."

By the time I get near Kenny's street, I've backtracked half the route I took to get to his old place. You'd think I'd know the city well enough to get around it—I spent most of my life here, after all—but so much of it is gone. There are things that stick out, of course: names of streets, old sights, and even a few of the bars we visited in college. They're all missing pieces, though, like someone took little snippets away and rearranged everything in my head.

Kenny waves me down when I turn onto Ferry, and I pull over. If he hadn't waved, I wouldn't have recognized him. His hair, which used to be a curly black mop, is now cropped short, matching the beard that's grown over what were once baby cheeks. His glasses, which were thin frames, are now thick and black. The contrast is a stark one, as if someone took the guy I used to know and stuffed him through a Banana Republic catalog.

When Kenny gets in, he reaches over the armrest and takes a stab at hugging me. Like all car hugs, it's an awkward pretzel of arms, so I give him a pat on the shoulder.

"I can't believe you're here," he says.

"I've heard a lot of that," I tell him. "You cool with Stevie's?"

His eyes widen.

"What?"

"Nothing," he says. "Mark just hung out there a lot before, you know, everything happened. He was kind of a celebrity there."

This is the Mark who filled in a window with a piece of plywood and drew on it. The Mark who littered his house with pizza boxes, couldn't put away his books, and got fired for drinking on the job. The Mark I knew didn't do that. He fixed everything. He read everything he could get his hands on (and put it back where he found it). Shit, he probably didn't even know how to find Stevie's.

"Huh."

"Things have changed since you left, man."

We ride in silence until I turn into the lot. "At least it looks familiar."

Stevie's—short for Stevie's Down Under—is a dive in the bottom of an office building downtown. The only way in is through a dust- and trash-littered stairway at the back of the building. That is, unless you're Brian, who once kicked his way in through one of the sidewalk-level windows (spoiler alert: he's not welcome back).

The door sticks when we pull it open, just as it did years ago, and I'm immediately hit with the smell of tobacco and cheap beer. Light spills in through the small windows, illuminating the dust settling in the air, and, for the first time today, I feel at home.

"Jack Dotson?" comes a voice from the far side of the bar. It's dark enough that I can't see her, but the chill in my bones and the dryness overtaking my throat tells me it's Lisa, my ex-girlfriend from high school and my first year of college. Besides Mark, the most awkward falling out I've ever had with a person was her.

That's the thing about Lafayette. You can leave, but as soon as you come back, you're hit with bad thoughts and everyone you never wanted to see again. It's like finding a time capsule, only it's full of your worst memories and you dug it so far into the earth that you never expected to come across it again.

When Lisa and I broke up, she started a smear campaign

saying I was a chauvinist who didn't listen to her or take her seriously. It all started because I refused to move to New York with her so she could "launch her writing career." I didn't do this because I didn't support her, though. I did it because I was a year into my degree at Purdue and didn't want to transfer all that work to a college I probably couldn't get into in a city bigger than anywhere I ever wanted to live. The problem was, Lisa thought that if I believed in her enough, none of that would have mattered. That our three-year relationship should have meant more.

Anyway, as you might have guessed by now, she never moved, and we never gave it another shot because we probably weren't that good for one another.

I force a smile. Kenny laughs.

"Lisa."

She walks over from across the bar and stops a couple feet in front of me. Hands on her hips, head cocked to the side, she stares. She hasn't changed since we last saw one another. Short blonde hair, pale skin, gray-blue eyes—every bit the girl who edited my face onto a pig and posted it all over MySpace.

"It's good to see you," I say. I try to step around her, but she shuffles in front of me.

"What brings you to town?"

I come up with a handful of answers: doing right by Mark, making amends with Beth, helping sort out Mark's things. Doing the adult thing, I guess. I can't tell her any of this, though. Anyone but her.

"Just catching up."

She smirks, one side of her mouth curling up like she's some sort of supervillain. "You must feel like shit."

She's right, of course. She doesn't need to know that, though. "Why's that?"

Lisa crosses her arms in front of her chest. "Mark and Beth would have worked out if it weren't for you. Even after you left town and they got back together, things were ugly. You pretty much screwed up their relationship."

I don't know if it's the finger-pointing or the reminder that Beth and Mark got back together, but my stomach churns and my palms sweat in a way that makes me want to pass out.

"Okay, okay," Kenny says, putting a hand on my shoulder. "You two clearly haven't missed a beat." He pushes me forward, and I half fall, half walk into motion.

"Good seeing you, Lisa," I say.

"Glad you still have your little crew, Jack."

Kenny narrows his eyes and looks back over his shoulder. "I'm not his crew. Grow up."

My cheeks warm, and the feeling of being home all but disappears, replaced instead by a nothingness, a feeling that maybe I've been gone long enough that I've missed out on these people after all. That whatever I set out to accomplish here might be harder than I thought it would be.

Kenny pushes me into a chair at a table in the corner and pulls up a seat across from me. On the other side the room, Lisa's taken up her spot at the bar again. She's typing something, but I can't tell what. These pieces I come across—the state of Mark's house, Kenny's new place—keep piling up. That Mark and Beth got back together, and that he forgave her, is a bigger bite than I can deal with, though.

"You okay?" Kenny asks.

"Yeah."

He leans back in his chair, then runs his hand back through what's left of his once-shaggy hair. "You really haven't been around in a while. A lot's happened."

I signal for a beer from the bartender. "Things have been pretty crazy lately."

"Yeah?"

No.

"Work and stuff," I tell him.

Kenny's eyebrows peek up over the top of his glasses, and he nods. He knows I'm full of shit, but he's too nice to do anything about it. "Have you been over to the house yet?"

I nod and bite my lower lip. "It's a shitshow. I thought Brian had a plan?"

The bartender comes over, but instead of a beer, he's holding two shots.

"Two Homewreckers courtesy of Lisa."

I stare at the glass. "What's a Homewrecker?"

"Shot of Jack. An old regular named it, rest his soul."

Lisa's staring at us from the bar, lips spread wide in a grin.

"Thanks," I tell him.

"My pleasure."

Once the bartender leaves, Kenny leans forward and rests his elbows on the table. "Like I told you, Mark was kind of a celebrity here."

I pick up the shot glass and stare at the whiskey. It catches glimpses of light and swirls them around in little golden waves. "Why don't they hate her?"

"Who?"

"Beth."

Kenny taps his fingers on the table. "She stayed? What happened kind of tore her up, so when the two of them—"

I take the shot and slam the glass down on the table. "Never mind. I don't really want to hear about it." I do, of course. I want the ins and outs, the good and bad, so I know how my best friend—the guy who saved me from getting my ass kicked, helped me with my homework, got me my first job—turned into a drunk who named a cat and a shitty shot after me. Whether I can stomach that, though, is something else. "I want to hear about you, dude. How's work at Purdue?"

Kenny shakes his head. He starts to roll his eyes but stops, forcing an awkward blink out of it instead. "I'm not there anymore. Left to start my own business."

"IT work?"

"Food truck."

The response jolts me to attention. Not because it's bad—just unexpected. Kenny's worked in IT for as long as I can remember, and he had an interest in it going back to middle school. To picture him doing anything else is, well, I don't know. Impossible, I guess.

"What kind of food?"

"Specialty crepes. It's called Who Gives a Crepe?"

I laugh. It's a weird feeling, teeth bared, lips spread, but a sliver of humor on this shitshow of a day is refreshing. Lisa perks up at the sound and glares at me from over Kenny's shoulder.

"How long have you been doing it?"

"About two years." He looks down at the table, then over at the bar, before coming back to me. "I invited you to our grand opening."

As soon as he says it, the realization punches me in the balls and sends me scrambling for an excuse. I have nothing.

"I'm sorry."

He shrugs, but his eye twitches. "It's all good. Things are going well. We're getting ready to expand to two trucks, which is always cool, and we're pretty much booked on events for the next couple months."

Lisa slips out of her barstool and makes her way over to our table. Seeing her move gives me half a mind to run, but I'm not so confident that would help either of our situations. When she pulls up a seat next to Kenny, I kick back the neglected Homewrecker, hoping in some way that I can make things awkward enough that she'll leave.

"I thought you'd like that," she says.

"It's kind of fucked up."

"He liked it, though. Bought them for just about anyone who'd talk to him."

The thought of Mark sitting by himself at the bar, buying shots for company, ties a knot in my stomach. I look past Lisa's head at the stools, wondering which one he sat in and who he talked to. It's a far stretch from the Red Hot Chili Peppers and *Spider-Man* posters in his basement. It's dingier, darker—heavier, even, as if the weight of everything he'd been dealing with had pushed him underground and into a basement bar.

"What are you doing with Mark's things?"

Lisa never was good at subtleties.

Kenny stares ahead, either at the wall or outside one of the small windows. My friends never liked Lisa. I didn't understand it at the time—I was a kid in love, after all—but as the years have passed I've come to understand their dilemma. Lisa has no social tact, and not for a lack of understanding. She just doesn't care. At one point, she planned to propel this I-don't-give-a-shit attitude into a journalism career, but the problem was that she's just as shitty of a writer as she is a person.

"Well?"

"No clue," Kenny says, still staring forward.

Lisa rolls her eyes. "Really?"

It hits me that I have no idea either, so I say the first thing that comes to mind. "We'll probably just burn it."

I know I'm better than this, that it's a comment that Lauren would scoff at, not to mention one that isn't very "Director of Strategic Initiatives" about me, but given how today's gone, I don't have the energy for anything better.

"Do what?" Lisa spits.

Kenny shrugs.

"I can't believe you," she says. "It's like you never grow up."

Something—maybe everyone telling me to grow up, expecting me to know what to do, wanting me to walk into Lafayette like nothing's changed—snaps. Because I don't know. I don't know where Kenny lives, what drink specials are named after me, what's happened to everyone. I don't know Mark. Didn't know Mark. Don't even know how to think about Mark. I came here to help, though, and people won't stop shitting on me for it.

"Not grown up like you?" I say, over it. "How'd New York work out? Did your big adult move work out like you wanted it to?"

Lisa's jaw drops, and her eyes narrow in a way that widens her face. She looks at her drink, then down at me, and even though I know what's coming, I don't move.

It isn't the drink that shocks me, but the ice drilling my face —one cube to the eye, another to the top of my cheek—like frozen Nerf balls. Lisa's done this before—it's our thing at this point, really—but there's never been ice. She normally drinks beer.

"Piece of shit," she huffs. And with that, she's gone. A small price to pay, really.

Kenny hands me a napkin. "At least that hasn't changed, huh?"

I pat at my forehead and wipe across my mouth. Whiskey sour. "I suppose."

Kenny grabs a handful more and tosses them to me. I dab what I can off my face and shirt, but the stickiness lingers, and I know that I won't be forgetting it until I get a chance to shower. The way things are going, only God knows when that's going to happen.

I set the napkins in the middle of the table. Soaked in sour, they look like a soggy, dying neon mountain. I start to reach for them, but it hits me that I don't know what I'd do with them. When we were in college, Stevie's had a trash can by the door, but it's gone. The one next to the bathroom is gone too.

"Trash is behind the bar," Kenny says. "Or in the bathroom."

"Got it," I say. The pile of napkins starts to sink into itself, flattening out like it's melting. Between this and what happened at the house, I'm starting to wonder why I'm even here. "Nobody has any idea what we're doing, do they?"

Kenny grabs the pile of napkins. "Nope," he says. "But we're not going to figure it out here. Ready to head back?"

Fuck my life.

"I guess."

"You'll be fine." He gets up from his seat and holds up the napkins. "I'll throw these away, then we can head out. You want me to show you where the trash cans are?"

"I'm good," I tell him, and he walks toward the bathroom. I don't plan on coming back here anytime soon.

EIGHT

Someone's put the piece of plywood back up. Kenny knocks on the door a couple times, and it rattles, almost making the Luke and Vader bassets look like they're fighting and not frozen in time.

Kenny's about to knock for a third time when the knob rattles and the door swings open. On the other side is Beth, looking just as tired and irritated as she was when I left. Her eyeliner has smeared into dark clouds, and she's dangling a half-empty PBR from the fingers of her left hand. The other one stays wrapped around the doorknob as if she's ready to shut it in my face.

"Kenny," she says, smiling. "Thanks so much for coming."

"I'm sorry." I don't know why I say this, but between the eyeliner and the beer and the hand on the doorknob, my nerves have twisted into a knot that makes me feel like I'll burst if I don't do something. I don't know what I'm apologizing for, but between storming off earlier and running off for a few years before that, I guess I have a tab going.

She bites her lower lip, and her eyes move from one side to the other before settling on me. "Thanks?"

Brian's footsteps boom across the house, so I force a smile and wait for him to arrive. It's only a matter of seconds before he's at the door, one arm around Beth in a half hug. "What's up?"

Beth and Kenny turn toward me.

"Nothing," I tell him. "Just apologizing, I guess."

"Good. That was quite the stunt you pulled, brochacho." He points his beer toward the piece of plywood in the door. "I had to fix the fucking window."

"We're good," Beth says. "He apologized."

I still don't know what for, but it seems to have worked, so I'll take it.

Brian blinks a couple times, then takes a swig from his beer. "Why's it so fucking tense out here, then?"

I shrug.

"Well, I'm starving," he says. He pats Beth on the shoulder, then squeezes her into another half hug. "Who's up for dinner and board games?"

My stomach grumbles, having lived off an Egg McMuffin, a beer, and two shots of whiskey so far today, but it's squashed by the reminder that we're staying here. That this is it. Between finding out that Beth and Mark got back together and getting a drink thrown on me, I'd pretty much forgotten.

Beth raises an eyebrow. "Excuse me?"

"What?" Brian says.

Beth's face goes red. "Do you not realize why you're here? Your friend is dead. And while it would be great to have a bro-fest for the next few days, there's a lot that needs to get done. We have all this shit," she says, spreading her arms wide, "to find a place for."

It's quiet for a moment, none of us aware of how to break the silence. I expect to hear crickets chirp, maybe even see a tumbleweed flutter across the room. My mind races to come up with a solution, some line to break the ice and get everyone smiling, but it's all blanks. I was never the one to break these silences—not then, and certainly not now—so I stay put and keep my mouth shut.

Given that I'm just now on the upswing here, that's probably not a bad idea.

Brian hates when this happens. In his opinion, a room full of people, especially these people, should be talking. He looks from one of us to the next, probably placing bets against himself who will speak up. Unfortunately for Brian, he's not that patient. "So, what are we eating?"

"Takeout," Beth says. "Just order takeout."

Brian chugs the rest of his beer, craning his neck farther back with each gulp. When he finishes, he tosses the can onto the coffee table. "On it," he says. "Dinner's on me. Jack and I will pick it up."

"You're not driving," Beth says.

Brian tosses me his keys. "Jack's got it."

"I don't know how to drive a Tesla," I say. "We'll take the Prius."

Brian's eyes light up. "That'll take me back. You two," he adds, pointing at Kenny and Beth, "text me your orders within the next fifteen minutes. If I haven't heard from you, you get General Tso's." He claps me on the back, and I stumble forward. "You ready, broseph?"

No. "Yeah."

When my Prius hums to life, Brian's eyes widen. He raises his shoulders up as he studies the dash, looking as excited as a child going to Disney for the first time. "Dude, I missed this thing. These are such good cars."

"Why'd you get rid of yours?"

The car beeps as we start backing out of the driveway. "I don't know," he says. "It was pretty beat-up. Didn't look too good in the hospital garage, either. When you're parked next to imports and shit all day, it's hard to be the odd one out."

I always assumed Brian bought a nice car for the same reason other doctors do: to look like doctors. I hadn't really considered that peer pressure might be involved, that it might be the equivalent of some sort of high school status quo. When you're a teenager, you do everything for other people. You listen to pop radio to be with the "in" crowd. You wear a band's T-shirt because it's what a cute girl listens to. You take auto to look tough. Everything is for someone else, which is why it sucks. Despite trying to be you, you end up becoming a conglomeration of everything you love about everyone else, like some sort of Frankenstein who doesn't know what the hell he wants out of life. Turns out, it doesn't change much when you start to get older, either.

Maybe one of Brian's doctor friends drives a Tesla. And maybe another doctor used to drive a humble Prius (they were cool when I got one, you know) but was made fun of behind closed curtains. Maybe someone made fun of Brian's Prius. I don't know, but I suddenly feel like an asshole for assuming the worst of him.

The outside of Double Dragon China Buffet is exactly as I remember it. Brick walls, red neons, and a tattered, yellowing menu hanging in the window. The inside, though, is what gets me. Double Dragon was never a nice restaurant—it was acceptable, but never a place you'd take a date—but the buffet's closed, and the area in which the tables once sat is now full of three cots and a pile of children's toys. The lights are off on that side, I guess to hide the living quarters, but they remain on by the counter, where a waving gold cat statue greets us.

No one's texted us, so we order four General Tso's dinner specials and two orders of crab rangoon ("just in case," Brian tells me).

"That'll be $61.47," the cashier says.

Brian pats his back pocket a couple times. He pats his front pockets too, then he turns toward me and starts to open his mouth.

"You've got to be shitting me," I say.

"I'll get the next one."

"Oh yeah?" I ask, having abandoned my revelations from the trip here. "You doing that before or after you buy another Tesla?"

Brian scoffs. "That was a student loan."

"How much are you going to make when you finish residency?"

"Dude. Don't play the salary game."

"Six figures?"

Brian takes in a long breath.

"That's at least twice what I make, no matter what."

The poor cashier's probably terrified of us or ready to call the police, so I hand him my card and sign the receipt. It has a tip line, but I'm not sure what for given the state of the place. Either way, I add on ten bucks for good measure.

For those keeping score at home, this trip can now be summarized as follows:

1. I've arrived at and immediately stormed out of Mark's house.
2. I've had a drink thrown on me by my ex-girlfriend.
3. I've spent almost $75 at a crumbling Chinese restaurant.

I ought to make more lists. If I made more lists, I'd probably be more organized, and if I were more organized, I might have a Tesla and be able to get out of paying exorbitant restaurant bills. I'm half-tempted to make a list of all the things I'd be better at if I made lists, but by the time I decide to do so, our food is ready.

On our drive back, Brian's mellowed, so I take my chance

to ask the question that's been nagging me since I got here. Things have settled now, the tension's eased up to a tolerable level, and we're about to hit the ground running on getting Mark's place taken care of, so now seems as good a time as any.

"Did you know she and Mark got back together? That they were living together?"

"Yeah."

I didn't ask this expecting a "yeah." I asked it expecting an "oh really?" or an "I had no clue" or a "how did that happen?" The fact that it's a "yeah" throws me off, and for a second, I want to pull the car over. I know I shouldn't feel this way, that I should focus on being here and helping out and all that, but I can't shake the dirty, itching feeling crawling across my skin.

I look over. Brian's staring out the window. "You didn't think I'd want to know that?"

Brian takes in a long breath through his nose. It's as if the question has sobered him up and snapped him into doctor mode. "What good would it have done? You went through a lot of shit with those two, and by the time they were back together, you were already in Louisville. Plus, it's not like you would have come if you knew she was here. She has a lot going on. Their relationship was so on again, off again after what happened that it seemed best to keep quiet until I knew you needed to know."

I try to piece this together, but the nuggets of information don't fit. "What does that mean?"

"We'll talk later," he says, pointing up the street. "We're almost back."

As soon as we walk in the door, Kenny grabs the bag of food out of my hand.

"You get China nuggets?"

China nuggets is Kenny's admittedly racist and long-used term for sweet and sour chicken.

"We grabbed General Tso's. You didn't text us anything."

Kenny's shoulders sag as he stares into the bag. "Fucking hell," he says. "Beth said she'd text you."

Brian pulls his phone out of his back pocket. He stares at it for a second, then presses his thumb into the power button, only for a lonely, empty battery icon to appear on his screen.

"Shit."

Kenny sighs. "And you forgot yours," he tells me. "It's in the kitchen." He grabs a carton out of the bag and walks toward the living room.

Beth comes next, taking a carton of her own before turning on her heel and walking out, followed by Brian, who takes the second to last and an order of crab rangoon for the group. I grab the soggy, smashed, bottom carton for myself, cradling it in my hands like a bowl of soup or a desperate handful of water. It's warm and moist, and even though it feels like a wet diaper, my stomach grumbles at the thought of it.

We've all taken our spots: Brian's on the left side of the couch, with Kenny on the floor beside him. Beth's on the ottoman, legs crossed, while Mark's chair sits empty behind her. I can almost see him in it, arms behind his head, grinning as we debate *Stars Wars* or *Dragonball: Z* or some other stupid thing. He would have enjoyed a night like this.

I fall into my spot on the right side of the couch. "So, what's the plan?"

Ten bucks says no one agrees.

Beth looks up from her food. "I've got it taken care—"

"That's a good question," Brian says. Beth narrows her eyes, but he doesn't seem to notice. "We probably ought to talk about it."

Beth and Brian have always had a weird relationship. They met in college while working together at the park across from

King's. One day, as the story goes, Beth found Brian sleeping behind some bushes during his shift. She was going to tell their manager, but Brian offered her a map of his prime napping stations instead, and they pretty much hit it off from there. Not too unlike siblings, they've learned to bring out the worst in each other.

I guess I know a thing or two about how Brian has that effect.

"I already took care of it," Beth says. "Cleaners are coming—"

"I canceled that," Brian says. "Called them after Jack's little meltdown earlier."

I start to open my mouth, but it's too late.

"Brian," Beth says. She sets down her food and takes in a long breath, then exhales. "I paid for that."

"I'll pay you back. Anyway," he adds, "I thought this would be a good opportunity to get back on the same page. Mark meant a lot to all of us, and I'm sure we all thought things would go a lot differently than they have the past few years. I don't want to speak for him, but I think this is what he'd want."

"Well," Beth says, "the last time I spoke with him, he got hammered and referred to you as 'Dr. Asshole' since you bailed on Halloween. I'm not sure you're qualified to be making these decisions for him."

"Hey," I say, thinking of last Christmas. "I call him something like that too."

Beth rolls her eyes and shakes her head. "I can't believe I thought this was a good idea. This is a fucking mess."

"How so?" Brian says. He grabs a crab rangoon and tosses it into his mouth.

Kenny leans forward and sets his food on the coffee table. "Can't we just talk about what to do with his excess stuff? I think I have a plan."

Beth side-eyes Brian, whose face is a blank canvas. "Fine," she says.

"Let's hear it," Brian adds.

I've just shoveled a hot forkful of General Tso's into my mouth when I realize that everyone's staring at me. I chew through it as fast as I can, wincing against the heat, then swallow the scalding bite. "Let's do it," I say, thankful to finally get going on a plan of attack. "Where do we start?"

Jack meows from the next room over. His paws patter against the hardwood, sounding almost like a tiny horse trotting our way, until he appears in the doorway. He looks up at the lamp for a second, then hops onto the armrest, where he lies down.

"I guess there," Kenny says. "Anyone want a cat?"

"Condo won't allow it," Brian says.

"I don't know," Beth adds. There's a heaviness to her face that I can't read. "I don't know if I want him on my own, you know?"

It takes me a second to realize Kenny's staring at me.

"What?"

"You want him?"

I scoop up another forkful of General Tso's. Across the room, Jack stares at me, head cocked to the side. My gut reaction is no—hell no, honestly—and that I'd need to run it by Lauren, but there's something about the little guy that feels right. It might just be the name, or maybe even the regret or guilt or everything else I've felt over the last few days, but this might just be the chance I was looking for. An opportunity to do a little something right by Mark.

"Sure," I say, stuffing my food into my mouth.

"That cool with you?" Brian says, looking over at Beth. "You were his fiancée, after all."

Kenny's eyes widen. Beth bites her lower lip and looks down.

"Fuck," Brian whispers. "I wasn't supposed to say that."

I close my mouth, suddenly aware that it's fallen open, exposing a half-chewed mouthful of Chinese food. I don't know what I'm feeling. It isn't good or bad—just there, like a quiet, still sort of emptiness.

"You got engaged?" I say.

Beth smiles. It's a closed-lip sort of thing, but her eyes brighten.

"When? Where?"

"Forget I said it," Brian says. "Let's have a beer." He starts to stand up, but I put my arm out to keep him in his seat. It won't do anything if he decides he wants to move, but it's all I've got at this point. I don't care that they were engaged, it just —wow. I don't have words.

"It's fine, Brian," she says. "It's not something I really want to talk about, though," she adds, looking up at me.

"But what—"

"I think I'm just going to go to bed," Beth says. I start to speak, but before I can she's up and gone, her feet creaking across the old wooden floors before her door clicks shut.

I wipe my palms on my pants, drying the sweat from them in an attempt to look calm. "Why is everyone keeping shit from me?"

Brian sinks into his spot on the couch. "You just lost touch, man. It's not really anyone's fault. It just happened."

I'm nodding, but I wish I wasn't. I never meant to disappear. Isn't that what people do sometimes, though? You grow up somewhere, put twenty-something years of your life into it, and once there's nothing left for you, you move on and go someplace new. It isn't romantic, sure, but it doesn't mean I should be kept out of the loop, right?

I need to make a list for this.

I want to yell at Brian and Kenny for keeping this to themselves, yell at Mark for not telling me, yell at Beth for going back to him. I want to hate all of them because we could have gotten through this as a group and avoided it all. I don't hate them, though. Hearing it, I'm just sad. Sad for Beth. Sad that Mark's dead.

I push myself up off the couch. "You think I should go apologize?"

Brian holds his hands out, beckoning me back. Somehow, throughout all of this, I've become an animal in need of taming.

"I think you ought to call it a night. There's plenty of time to talk."

"Okay," I say, looking down. "I guess I'll head to bed."

I walk to the basement, and Jack follows me, apparently having gotten the memo that we're family now. I lie down on the futon, and he meows and crawls onto my chest. He rubs his face against mine a couple times, purring, and I let him, unaware of what else to do. I've never owned a cat before. Never wanted one, really. The chance to help out with something of Mark's—something that was named after me, at that—feels right, though. A bright spot on an otherwise mess of a trip.

The mattress feels like an old, flat pillow. The metal frame pushes through it, and it reeks of pot. I think back to lying on this mattress—well, sharing it with Brian—and listening to Beth and Mark talk. Even in the most mundane of times, I couldn't help but want that—someone to talk to, argue with about stupid shit, tell my goals to. I should have known then that I should get away, set out for myself, and find someone. I could have left it alone and let them move on with their lives. I could have never gotten close with Beth when Mark started working late. I could have kept to myself.

That's the thing about hindsight, though: it's a twisted, sloppy mess of extremes. Everything was either the best time of your life or the worst, and the longer time goes on, the harder it becomes to distinguish which is which. What you do have is the present, though, a chance to right the ship and make the most of our messes, so I scratch Jack behind the ear, roll onto my side, and go to sleep, determined to make tomorrow a little more productive.

NINE

There's no coffee in this house.

There's a brand-new coffee maker and an unopened package of filters, but not an ounce of coffee. I've searched the whole kitchen at this point—the cabinets, the pantry, even the silverware drawer—but found nothing. Mark used to drink coffee all the time. He'd make a pot before going into work, pour it into a massive thermos, and drink it over the course of the day. In what he left of his house, though, the only signs of that ever being a consideration are the couple things I've come across.

Maybe he tried to take it up again. Maybe he was trying to use it to cut back on drinking. Clearly, I have no idea.

Brian's snoring. The noises come through the floor in low, fluttering waves that fade off just in time for the next ones to arrive. Other than that, the house is silent, so I grab my keys off the counter and walk out the door. There's a gas station down the street—well, there used to be, at least—where I could get a cup.

I've barely made it off the front porch when I freeze, one

foot lingering midair above a step, stunned by what's in front of me.

My Prius is covered in toilet paper. Not just a casual teepee-ing, either—it's wrapped in what must be layers, making it look like some sort of mummified hybrid box. Tucked in between a couple layers on the windshield is a red envelope with my name written in big, thick black letters.

Cars drive by, one after another, seemingly unaware of the scene in the yard. It's as if this is commonplace in Lafayette, like every day someone's car is teepeed into a mummy and decorated with a single envelope. The town joke, I guess. I wait for someone to pop out of the bushes and throw an egg or laugh or call me an asshole, but everything stays still.

Maybe they're waiting for me to make a move. Maybe "they" aren't here at all. I walk up to my car and look from one side to the other, not sure what to expect but also not willing to write off anything.

I snatch the envelope and rip it open. To my disappointment, the only thing inside is a piece of paper. I expected an explosion, or at least one of those glitter bombs, but nothing flashy happens. Apparently, flash wasn't on the agenda.

In jagged, pasted letters from magazines, it reads:

Jack Dotson,

Mark wouldn't want you at his funeral. On his behalf, we're asking you to leave immediately. You can agree to this by leaving his house and not returning.

Should you choose to stay, consequences will follow. Consider this your only warning.

I look from the letter to the car, still expecting something to happen. Fireworks. A tackle. Anything, really. Another car drives by, and the gust makes the toilet paper flutter, as if it's trying to run away but can't, so I fold the letter in half and stuff it in my pocket. My instinct is to rip the paper off and get my coffee— it's too early to deal with this shit, much less without caffeine— but I can't do it. Maybe there's a sign, some sort of mark the mummifier left, or maybe I just want someone else to acknowledge what's going on. Whatever that is, I'll figure it out later.

Kenny might know who it is. Beth would have a better idea. It's the crack of dawn and everyone's asleep, though, so I head inside and take a seat next to Mark's comic books. I don't know what Beth or Brian or whoever has planned, but I'm assuming we'll have to start going through Mark's stuff at some point, and his boxes of comics seem as good a place to start as any. I grab a handful out and start making two piles: one to keep, and one to donate. Mark would struggle not to keep all of them; he loved every piece of every story arc and wouldn't put one over the other. Mark's dead, though, so I guess I'll do what I can.

I'm about to set an old *X-Men* title in the donate pile when I hear a meow from across the room. Jack, sure enough, is pattering across the hardwood in slow, clunky steps, headed my way. He hops into my lap when he gets to me and starts rubbing his head on the *X-Men* book, almost knocking it out of my hand before I can set it where I want.

I pick him up and set him on the floor. "Stop, dude."

He meows and hops back up, so I toss the *X-Men* book in the donate pile and move onto the next one. *Hulk*, discard. Another *Hulk*, discard. *Thor*, keep. An *X-Men* variant cover, keep. Jack chimes in every once in a while, headbutting a comic in one direction or another, and I let him. After all, he knew Mark more recently than I did.

Jabba's going to hate this cat. He's a king-of-the-house kind of dog, one who isn't going to take kindly to another four-legged creature headbutting its way into his business. I'm trying to work my way through this, how I'm going to introduce Jack to Jabba and Lauren, when I spot *the* comic. The one Mark and I discussed over pops, ice cream, coffee. The one we spent hours and nights arguing over. *Amazing Spider-Man* #121.

One thing most people don't realize about Spider-Man (at least before Mark Webb's *Amazing Spider-Man 2* came out) is that way before Peter Parker fell for Mary Jane Watson, he loved a girl name Gwen Stacy. Spider-Man enthusiasts will tell you she was the love of his life, and that he only ended up with Mary Jane because of the friendship that developed between the two of them after Gwen died. These enthusiasts will also tell you that Peter was responsible for her death.

See, early in Spider-Man's career, the Green Goblin captured Gwen (knowing she was Peter's love interest) and threw her off a bridge before Spider-Man's eyes. In an attempt to save her, Spider-Man shot a string of webbing, which connected with her back before she hit the ground. It's a terrible scene, really. Spider-Man jumps to her all proud, thinking he's saved her, only to get down there and find out she died anyway. At first glance, it's easy to assume that the fall killed her—probably a result of a heart attack or some other scare—and that Spider-Man got to her too late. When you examine the art in the panel, though, it becomes clear that Spider-Man's web snapped Gwen's neck. See, in the panel where the web hits, there's a small "snap" by it, making it pretty apparent that the webbing itself, not the throw, killed her.

I run my fingers over the cover, and I can see Mark hovering over those panels, dissecting every detail of the scene. He wasn't the type to believe that Spider-Man failed. To Mark, these heroes didn't screw up like you and me. They were larger than life, gods who committed to their cause, saved the girl, and received the key to the city. They were, well, super. The thing about that Spider-Man story is that he tried to save a girl and killed her in the process. He never had a chance to apologize or make it right, and Mark hated that.

My phone buzzes in my pocket, and I pull it out. Lauren's smiling face is staring at me from the screen. I freeze for a couple seconds, already struggling to explain the amount I spent at Double Dragon or the letter I just received, and decide to slide it back into my pocket.

Jack meows and jumps out of my lap, knocking the comic out of my hands. I look down at the cover—a bright yellow thing, Spider-Man swinging across it, his spider sense telling him someone's going to die—then push myself up and follow Jack down the hall and up the stairs. I might have missed my chance to get on good terms with Mark, but that doesn't mean I've blown my chance with everyone else.

I knock on Beth's door.

"Yeah?" she says, not opening it.

"It's me."

Her footsteps make their way across the floor, creaking as she gets closer, and eventually stop. She pulls the door open a couple inches, leaning her head on it in a way that lets me see only a sliver of her face. Behind her, blankets are pinned up over her windows, leaving the room dark.

"Can I come in?"

She blinks. "I think this is okay."

"I'm sorry," I say. "For prodding. It's none of my business."

"It's fine." She sighs, leaning into the door, and I can almost feel the weight on her shoulders. "I get that there's stuff between us that we never tackled, but this isn't the time. I just can't."

There are a lot of things I'd like to say, questions about the engagement and if she ever thought about me, but she's right. "Yeah," I say, swallowing them down. "That's fair."

She pauses, eyes wide in surprise, as if she thought I would have made the wrong decision. "Thanks."

"No problem," I tell her. I pull the letter out of my pocket and hold it up. "If it makes you feel any better, though, someone's out to get me."

She'd started closing the door, but she stops. "What?"

I hand her the letter. "See for yourself."

She opens the door and unfolds the letter so quickly I expect it to rip. "Jesus Christ."

"Any idea who it is?"

"None." she says. Her eyes move from one side to the other, scanning the words. "Is this a joke?"

I shrug. "It sounds like something I'd expect out of this place. The Society for Advocates of Mark, a trashy group that meets at the diner on Teal Road every Sunday for brunch and collaging threatening letters. They wear monogramed S.A.M. hoodies and everything."

Beth looks up, so I stop. "Mark didn't have a lot of friends after you guys." She pauses, and the words punch me in the stomach. "He drank with people and stuff, but I can't imagine any of them doing it. It's kind of hard telling with you, though. People weren't all that thrilled with you after everything went down."

This doesn't help.

She folds the letter back up and hands it to me. "Kenny might know. Is he up?"

"Not yet." I put the letter back in my pocket and force a smile. "I'll check with him later, though. And sorry to wake you up—I wasn't really thinking. Just wanted to say sorry."

She smiles, the edges of her lips held up by little more than willpower, but it's something. "Thanks."

"I'm going to sort through some more of his comics. See if there's anything we can get rid of."

She nods, and her arms twitch in a way that makes me

think for a second that she's going to hug me. I look for a ring on her left hand, but there's nothing. Just the faint tan line of where one once was. "I'll be down in a few," she says, stuffing her hands in her pockets. "I just want to hang out in here for a while."

"No worries," I tell her, and she closes the door.

On my way downstairs, I try to call Lauren back. The phone rings on and on, just like it has the last couple times I've tried calling, before going to her voicemail. I hang up without leaving a message. By the time I make it to the couch, though, my phone screen's lit up with a fresh text. *At breakfast with a coworker. Can't wait to hear how your trip's going! xoxo*

Three dots appear on my screen—you know, the three that show up when someone's typing—then disappear. I wait for another message to arrive, then wait for the dots to show back up, but, after thirty seconds or so, realize nothing's coming. I create a reminder to call her tonight, and just after I save it, Jack walks back into the room, meowing as if he's determined it's time for everyone else to wake up. I can't say I blame him for it. Between the wood-paneled walls, the mid 2000s décor, and the pulled-shut blinds, it's a lonely place to sit by yourself.

I reach down to pet him, and he hisses and bats at my hand before running away. Today's going to be great.

TEN

"You can't leave," Brian says.

I start to open my mouth, but he swipes S.A.M.'s note out of my hand before I can say anything. His eyes scan it from left to right, wide and frantic, as he paces from one side of the basement to the other. I try to picture him doing this in the hospital as he runs through the different ways he could save a person's life, but between his tattered *Star Wars* sweatpants and his beer-stained T-shirt, I can't get the image to come through.

"You show this to Kenny?"

"Didn't have time," I say. Kenny left a couple hours ago to take his food truck downtown. I tried to say something, but he got ready in a fell swoop, throwing on his Who Gives a Crepe? shirt while juggling a Diet Coke in one hand and a banana in the other. By the time I had a chance to mention it, he was on his way out the door, apologizing and muttering a quick "see you later."

Brian makes his way back across the basement, then stops and hands me the letter. "Whoever this is can't run you out of town. They're just fucking with you."

I haven't said I'm leaving town because I'm not sure that's the plan. The thought's crossed my mind, but there's still work to be done. Sure, offering to give Jack a home is nice, but other than that, all I've done is buy everyone takeout and organize half a pile of comic books. Not exactly what I had in mind when I agreed to come up here.

Then again, neither was getting a threatening letter from a mysterious sender.

"We'll see," I say, folding the note in half and slipping it into my back pocket. "I'm not really here to start shit."

"Fuck it." Brian storms over to his suitcase. He flips open the top and starts digging through it, tossing shirts out until he finds one he likes. "Let's go see him."

"Who?"

"Kenny."

"He looked pretty busy this—"

"He has people," Brian says, his voice muffled as he pulls his T-shirt over his head. He replaces it with an Indiana University School of Medicine polo. "He can take a few minutes to help sort this shit out."

I hadn't planned on going out to investigate. My two experiences leaving the house so far have ended with a drink being thrown on me and a seventy-five-dollar Chinese food bill landing on my tab, so I feel like staying put. There's the fact that I've been here for a day already, too, with almost nothing to show for it while my new job and my girlfriend wait for me back home.

This S.A.M. business, which has found me despite these efforts to stay in, has struck a nerve with Brian more than I could have anticipated. And, as much as I hate to say it, watching him storm around in an attempt to keep me here pulls at my heartstrings a little.

God, Lauren would love this.

Brian's halfway up the stairs, his hair matted in random,

splotchy patches like a dying lawn. His bright red med school polo, though, is tucked into his ripped *Star Wars* sweatpants. If I were any worse of a brother, I'd let him run out in this, but, in the spirit of friendship and us all taking another stab at things, I figure this is the least I can do.

"You planning on changing into some real pants?"

"Fuck," he murmurs, shuffling back down the stairs.

"I'll meet you up there."

He says something in return, but he's head-first in the suitcase again and I don't catch it. Upstairs, I find Beth sitting at the kitchen table. She's wearing an oversized blue sweater and a pair of yellow flannel pajama pants, leafing through Mark's old copy of *The Silmarillion* and sipping a cup of coffee. Jack's curled up in her lap, resting his head on her thigh.

"Where'd you get coffee?"

Beth looks down at the steaming cup. "Above the fridge. Mark didn't like leaving it out. Said he didn't want to be tempted by it."

I think back to Stevie's, about how he knew the bartender, named a drink after me, and lost his job because of his alcoholism. A cup of coffee would have done him some good, it seems. Now that I think about it, though, there hasn't been a drop of alcohol in the house that we didn't bring in.

"Your brother okay down there?"

"I think so. He's pretty worked up over this S.A.M. business."

"You're really leaning into the S.A.M. moniker, eh?"

I shrug. "I thought it was clever."

The sound of footsteps booms below us, echoing around the house like a troll chasing a chicken.

"Like I said," I say. "He's pretty worked up."

"I know how he can be," she says, cradling the coffee mug in her hands. "He'll calm down in a minute." She takes a sip, then sets the mug down. "S.A.M. scaring you out of town, then?"

I stand there for what feels like a solid minute, mouth hanging open, trying to sort out what to say. Beth tucks one leg under the other, careful not to disrupt the cat, and looks up at me. I try to imagine what she's thinking. Whether she wants me to stay. If this morning was a turning point for us.

"I don't know. I don't think so."

She nods a couple times. "I wouldn't blame you if you did. This whole situation's kind of fucked, you know?"

"Yeah, it is," comes Brian's voice. He's standing at the top of the stairs, huffing in breaths. His sweatpants are replaced with a pair of what I think are chinos. He's tucked his polo into these now and covered his hair with one of Mark's old Cubs hats, making him look like a salesman who's about to take a client out to the range and push a new deal on him. "You ready?"

"What are you doing?" Beth asks.

Brian shrugs. "Seeing what Kenny knows. Want to come with?"

Beth raises her eyebrows. "Too much to do here," she says. "If I come across anything that solves your mystery, though, I'll let you know."

"Thanks," Brian says. "Come on, brochacho," he adds, waving me toward the back door. "I'll drive."

The ride to Who Gives a Crepe? is silent, both because of the lack of conversation and the Tesla's electric motor. Brian's gripping the steering wheel, his knuckles white as I only assume his brain runs through the possibilities of who could be involved in the Society for Advocates for Mark. I've been trying to sort through the same thing, but I've got nothing. Having left when I did, I don't know who Mark was close with, much less who liked him enough that they'd start a secret society to avenge him. To be honest, it sounds like the sort of stunt I would have pulled back in the day. Maybe it's some sort of *X-Men: Days of Future Past* thing, where future me is traveling back in time to stop present me from sticking around town so that I can avoid enslavement or torture or God knows what else.

Kenny's set up at Digbee Plaza, a public space downtown that's dedicated to one of Lafayette's former mayors. The scene is a far cry from what I expected. The truck is nice enough, painted bright blue with swirling red letters outlined in white. The flags of Indiana and France hang by either side of the window, billowing gently in the little bit of wind offered up. The truck isn't the surprise, though. Of course Kenny would do up the truck. It's the line of people at the window, stretching back ten or so deep. Others are huddled nearby, some munching on crepes, others looking at the menu from afar, all engulfed in what Kenny's apparently created.

"Christ," I say as we step out of the car, "is he always this slammed?"

"As far as I know," Brian says. "The guy's figured something out, that's for sure."

I start to make my way to the back of the line, but Brian grabs my arm and pulls me in the other direction. I almost stumble over, looking like a cartoon character getting pulled off stage with a cane, only to recover in time to fall into place beside him.

"What the hell?"

"We don't have to wait," Brian says, looking ahead. "We ought to get some sort of perk for knowing the guy, right?"

Glancing at the folks waiting to order, I'd guess that each of these people knows Kenny a little better than I do at this point. Prior to yesterday, I didn't even know Who Gives a Crepe? existed.

Brian circles around to the back of the truck, then bangs on the back door three times. There's nothing for a couple seconds save for the murmuring and awkward glances of folks in line, but sure enough, the sound of a lock popping up comes from inside, and the door swings outward. Kenny's standing on the other side of it, a red hat backwards on his head and a white apron tied around his waist. Behind him, some kid is cooking on a sort of round griddle, using paddles and some other tools I don't recognize.

"You have a second?" Brian asks.

Kenny looks over his shoulder, sweat beading on his forehead. "Not really."

"It's important."

Kenny's mouth falls open, and he blinks a couple times as his eyes dart from Brian to me and back to Brian again. "I have a meeting in ten minutes. Can it be quick?"

"You got it, K-Dog."

Kenny shakes his head and unties his apron. He hangs it on a hook on the back door before giving the kid a couple last-minute instructions and hopping out. He leads us to a picnic table on the other side of the plaza, then sits down across from us, hands together like he's conducting some sort of business meeting.

"What's up?" he asks.

"Show him," Brian says, nodding at me. The subtle way he does this makes me feel like we're about to make some sort of high-price deal that the cops could bust at any minute. Like we're not just a handful of awkward twenty-something dudes trying to figure out who teepeed my car.

I slip the note out of my back pocket and toss it on the table. Kenny's eyes narrow, and he scrunches his mouth to the side as he picks it up. "What's this?"

"Read it," Brian says. "Some fuckers messing with Jack."

Kenny's eyes widen as they make their way across the letter. "This real?"

"As far as I know," I say. "Whoever did it teepeed my car and left that with it."

"Shit," he says, handing the note back. "Any idea who?"

I fold the note in half and slip it into my pocket. "We were hoping you might know."

Kenny looks over my shoulder, into the distance. His eyes are blank, his brow furrowed as his head moves slowly back and forth. "Not really," he says. "I mean, word got around about what happened, and Mark started talking quite a bit of shit when he started drinking and all that. I hate to say it, but a lot of people blamed you for how things turned out with him."

"Anyone in particular?" Brian asks.

Kenny shakes his head again. "Not really. It——" He stops for a second, then sighs. "It was the talk of the town there for a while. Kind of hard to pin just one person down."

Like a needle in a haystack, I guess, only every piece of hay is out to get you too.

Brian takes in a long breath, then sighs and rests his arms on the table. "Damn."

"I'll keep thinking about it," Kenny says, "but I'm not——"

"Jack?"

I turn to my right, and my eyes widen in horror to find Mark's dad at the head of the table. He's a thick, athletic man, with leathery skin that's covered in waves of black hair. He's grown a beard since I last saw him, inky but speckled with gray, but he's wearing his same old hat, a tattered, fading thing with a melting cone of vanilla, chocolate, and strawberry embroidered on top. Behind his glasses, his eyes shine red, bloodshot, and below them, his skin is dark and sagging.

"Mr. King," I say, shoving myself up so quickly that I almost trip over the bench. "It's so good to see you," I add, holding out my hand.

Mark's dad pulls his lips in tight and casts a look a Kenny. "Didn't think you'd make it."

"How—uh, how . . ." I stuff my unshaken hand into my

pocket and try again. "How are you and Mrs. King holding up?"

"Okay," he says, setting a notebook on the table. "It's funny that I'd run into you. I was just listening to those songs you guys recorded way back when. The ones you were going to release after the big show downtown."

Kenny and Brian both look down. The summer before I moved, The Jackals had finally booked Dancing in the Streets, a music festival that takes over Lafayette for a weekend every year. It feels stupid now, but if you're a musician in Lafayette, Indiana, it's the gig to get. We were going to use it to debut an album, but I slept with Beth and ran to Louisville before it could ever happen. Judging by the looks on Brian's and Kenny's faces, it looks like they didn't attempt it without me.

"It's a shame that didn't work out," Mr. King says. His eyes are locked on mine like a bouncer telling a kid with a fake ID that he can't get into the bar.

"Yeah," I say, stuffing my other hand in my pocket. "It really is."

The silence hangs over us for a few seconds, lingering in the air like a heavy fog. I try to come up with something to say, but I draw nothing but blanks. I could apologize for the show, but that seems pointless now. I could ask about Mrs. King, but I already did that.

God, I don't fucking know.

"I can finish up with these two later," Kenny says. He turns toward Brian and me. "That cool with you guys?"

I look from Kenny to Mr. King. "You guys are meeting?"

"King's Frozen Custard and Who Gives a Crepe? team up pretty often," Kenny says. "Apparently, Purdue's just recruited some French kid for the basketball team. He's a pretty big deal, so we were going to see what we can come up with to celebrate the occasion. Kid's supposed to be a star."

"Huh," I mutter, stepping backward while Mark's dad

slides into my place at the table. "Guess I didn't realize Lafayette did that sort of stuff."

Kenny pulls a pen out of his pocket and opens his notebook. "Food specials?"

"Just food trucks and collaborations and all that. Didn't know that was a thing here."

Kenny's eyes narrow. "It's not like we're in the middle of nowhere."

"Yeah, I just—"

"Come on, brochacho," Brian says, putting a hand on my shoulder. "Let's let these guys do business."

I start to turn, but a thought hits me. "Mr. King?"

Mark's dad looks up. "Yeah?"

"Do you have any idea why Mark would name his cat after me?"

"Who told you that?"

I shrug. "Just thought it made sense. Jack and Jack, you know?" I kick at a piece of gum on the pavement. "I guess it doesn't matter. Kenny said he needs a home, so I'm taking him back to Louisville. Just thought I'd see if you knew anything."

Mr. King narrows his eyes. His thick, furry eyebrows almost meet, looking like a rat sleeping on his forehead. "What?"

I take a step backward. "I don't have—"

Mr. King swallows. "I'm sorry," he says. "I just know how much Mark loved that little guy. It's nice of you to take him in."

Kenny clears his throat. "We really ought to get to this," he says, tapping his notebook. "Talk later?"

WHEN WE GET BACK to the car, Brian locks the doors. "Well, that was useless."

"Yeah," I mutter, looking out the window at the specks of

Kenny and Mark's dad talking in the distance. "Mr. King seem weird to you?"

Brian turns on the car, which hums to life. "You mean for a dude who just lost his son?"

"Something just seemed—"

"It isn't him," Brian says, pulling out of his parking space. "You think a fifty-something-year-old man teepeed your car?"

I curl in my lower lip and chew on it for a second. Mr. King has every right to be mad; he raised me as his own, letting me stay over countless nights, taking me on vacations with his family, and feeding me meals, and I screwed his son over. The motivation's there, but the reality? Brian's probably right.

"Don't sweat it," Brian says. "We'll sort this out."

I take in a breath and sigh, looking out the window at the people walking down the sidewalk and wondering which one of them it could be. From what Kenny said, it could be any of them. Maybe the whole city's against me, conspiring to kick me out of town or drag me through hell or both, all in the name of justice for its favorite son.

It's only been a day, but it feels like I've been here a week. Something tells me, too, that it isn't going to get any easier from here on out.

ELEVEN

Mark's desk is a haphazard collection of comics, inkless pens, and notebooks. There are drawings scattered across it, some of comic book characters and some of dogs, some taped down and some ripped in half, none having a hint as to why they were created or what they mean. Not to me, at least.

After getting back from Who Gives a Crepe?, I started helping Beth get Mark's belongings together. I didn't want to, but it beat trying to figure out why Mark would name a cat after me and digging into this S.A.M. mystery. So, I spent the day organizing comics into keep or donate piles, picking up trash around the house, and packing books into boxes while Beth called around town finding places we would be able to donate some odds and ends to. Brian helped for a little while, but when Kenny got home, they moved to the basement to "go through things" as Brian called it, meaning they played X-Box and drank beer.

Once Beth and I decided to call it a day, she asked if I wanted to take a look through Mark's desk and see if I could find any clues about who S.A.M. might be. I've been sitting here for an hour, leafing through the notebooks, drawings, and comics, but there's nothing useful. There's a ton of info on what Mark needed to order for King's two years ago, what bills he needed to pay last January, and what he needed to do around the house, but not a single clue about someone he was close with.

So far, the most interesting thing I've found is a framed Jackals poster commemorating the Dancing in the Streets show that never happened. Across the top, in thick, jagged letters like something straight out of a '90s comic book, it says:

THE JACKALS ALBUM RELEASE SHOW

The poster itself is four versions of Marvel's Jackal villain, a green-skinned monster with pointed ears, sharp teeth, and bright white eyes. There's one for each member of the band: Jackal Kenny on the drums, sporting his then-trademark curly black hair; Jackal Brian on the bass, wearing a tucked-in flannel and a pair of khakis; Jackal Mark, doing his best Freddie Mercury with a half-broken mic stand clutched in his hands; and Jackal me, well, looking just like the villain from the comics, wearing a brown loincloth and sporting a menacing, full-toothed grin while playing the guitar. The bottom of the poster, in smaller, jagged letters, reads:

DANCING IN THE STREETS
JULY 28, 2007 9:00 P.M.
COURTHOUSE SQUARE
LAFAYETTE, IN
BE THERE.

I never saw this poster. We'd talked about posters, sure, but the posters we'd planned on were simple things with an edgy Microsoft Word font and a black-and-white photo of us rehearsing. We didn't have the budget to hire someone to mock one up for us. And if we had, I would have asked for my Jackal to have some form of distinguishing characteristic, not look like the psychopath who had it out for Spider-Man because he had a crush on his girl.

I pick up the frame and hold it closer. In the bottom, right-hand corner, in tiny, Arial letters, it says:

© 2011

I flip the frame over and pry the little staples up, pricking my forefinger and stabbing myself under my thumbnail in the process, and pull it apart to find a note on the back.

Mark,

You're always talking about how cool this show would have been, so I thought I'd get you something to remember it by.

Happy birthday!

Lisa

Holy shit.

It's her. Bugging me at the bar, wanting to know what was going on with Mark's things. She knew him. They were friends. They probably bonded at Stevie's over how much the two of them hated me, how much of a backstabbing asshole I was. The shit she said about me in college, the things she posted on MySpace—those were just the opening acts for her grand performance, the Society for Advocates of Mark, an organization dedicated to fucking me over.

I grab the poster and the pieces of the frame and hurry out of the room. Beth says something as I make my way across the house, but I don't catch it. I can't tell her this, anyway. What if Mark and Lisa were sleeping together? What if he cheated on Beth to get back at her? I head downstairs instead, to where Mark and Kenny are "going through things."

And, well, they've gone through things all right. The room

looks like it's been plucked out of the house, shaken like a snow globe, and put back in place. The futon mattress has been flipped onto the floor, the TV is on its side, and the closets have apparently vomited their contents onto what little floor space remains. The Red Hot Chili Peppers poster is folded over itself, clinging to the wall with what little tape it has left, but a perfect pyramid of empty beer cans has appeared on the coffee table, so I guess it isn't all that bad.

I grab a beer out of the minifridge and knock on the wall. "Guys," I huff, cracking it open. "I know who S.A.M. is."

Brian comes out of the closet, shirtless, with a duffel bag draped over his shoulder. His gut spills over his waistband, a far cry from the way he looked when we used to stay here, and his chest is full of dark, curly hair. "No time for that. We found the old laser tag gear," he says. "We're going to Riehle Park for a round or two. You're in."

Kenny comes tripping out of the closet next. He stumbles over a box of old Playstation games and catches himself on the doorframe. "It'll be awesome."

The last time we played laser tag at the park was years ago, and the night ended with us getting frisked by a handful of police officers who cornered us at the water park. We weren't arrested, but the memory of the officer's hands making their way up and down my legs makes the prospect of another round less than appealing.

"I don't think so." I hold the frame and poster up and shake it, like doing so will catch their attention. "Are you listening to me?"

"I get it," Brian says, "but you need to chill the hell out. You've been wired up about this S.A.M. shit all day. Plus, there are only two of us without you. We can't play teams."

The handle of a laser rifle pokes out of the top of the duffel bag. The four of us used to play laser tag over the summers—me and Mark versus Kenny and Brian. We even made a circuit of it, playing one match at Riehle Park, another at Armstrong Park, and a couple in the woods behind the elementary school. Mark and I could normally squeak out a win in the woods, but Kenny and Brian almost always took the other matches. It drove Mark crazy. He'd look up the park maps and try to come up with a plan of attack, but it was never enough. Kenny and Brian always had some trick or another up their sleeve.

I take a sip of my beer. "Do a solo battle," I say, setting the poster on the table. "We used to do them all the time."

"Those suck," Brian says, tossing me a laser rifle. Against my better judgment I catch it, blood rushing through my fingertips as I grip the trigger. Gun in hand, the appeal is different—I'm hit with memories of sprinting across the park, diving behind bushes, the thrill of seeing Brian's vest explode in red lights whenever I hit him—but the emptiness that follows is like a punch to the stomach. For every sprint, there was Mark, covering me. For every dive behind a bush, the anticipation of waiting for him. For every hit on Brian, a high five.

And now, instead of that, I have Lisa trying to fuck me over.

I toss the gun to the floor. "I don't really want to, guys."

"Come on," Brian says. "Quit being a bitch."

"Who's on my team?"

The room goes silent. Brian, shirtless, huffing in air, stares at the gun I tossed aside. Kenny leans back against the wall.

Brian reaches into the duffel bag and grabs a target vest, which he tosses to me. "We'll do it for Mark. Sort of an *in memoriam* thing."

I drape the vest around my neck, resigned to the fact that these two couldn't give two shits about Lisa being S.A.M. "Fine. But I'm not playing alone."

"You and Kenny, then."

Kenny looks up, eyes wide. "Wait, what?"

"What's wrong with me?" I say.

Kenny grew up playing *Goldeneye* and *Halo*, so he takes things like laser tag more seriously than he should. "You don't know what you're doing," he says. "I'd rather have someone with more experience."

"So you pick the doctor?"

He shrugs. "I can't risk it. What if your cubicle's made you weak?"

I'm not sure what it is about the term "weak" that sends a man's blood boiling, but I suddenly want nothing more than to kick both of their asses. I swallow back my irritation with a quick swig of my beer. "We'll see."

"You've pissed him off," Brian says, rolling with laughter. "He's going to come after you with his stapler now."

I pick up a pillow and throw it at him, knocking his beer from his hands and spilling it across the concrete floor. "Let's go, fuckers. You're with me, Kenny."

Brian grabs one of the duffle bags and fills it with beers from the minifridge. When he's done, he throws it and the gear over his shoulder and grabs his car keys from his pocket, dangling them between his thumb and forefinger. "You guys done arguing and ready to actually do something?"

Kenny nods, and I do the same. "Who's driving?"

"You are," Brian says.

I hold up my beer in an attempt to get out of this, but Brian grabs it out of my hand, chugs it, and tosses the empty can to the ground.

"We've been drinking all day, dude. You had, like, half a beer."

I haven't brought myself to unmummify my car, and Kenny and Brian refuse to let me until they've had a chance to examine it, so the Tesla's our only option. It's not as awkward as I thought it would be. The drive is smooth, so smooth that I forget to keep track of how fast I'm going, but otherwise comfortable. We get to the park in what feels like a snap, pulling up right after the sun's gone. For all intents and purposes, the park's ours.

Riehle Park's a massive, sprawling thing with playgrounds littered across it. They're age-specific, some big, some small, with little paths leading from one to the other. In the middle is a hill, though, with the playground for those who are, as we're reminded, "twelve and up." We make our way to the top of it, then climb to the cove at the top of the slide, where Brian throws down his duffel bag. From here, you can see the whole park. To the north, the stone amphitheater, to the south, the pool (or, what used to be the pool—it's a water park now), and in between it all, islands of playgrounds, sprouting up to various heights like a mismatched garden.

Brian hands each of us a beer. He cracks his open, and the two of us follow suit, holding them up in toast.

"Gentlemen," Brian says, "the game is laser tag. We play by traditional rules—"

"Hold on a minute," I say.

Brian narrows his eyes. I reach into the duffle bag for another beer, crack it open, and hold it up with my free hand. "One for Mark."

Brian nods and starts to smile. "Good call. Anyway," he resumes, "traditional rules."

"Not European rules?" Kenny asks.

Mark would have laughed at that.

"Shut up," Brian says. "We'll play to seven kills. Each time you're shot, your vest will go off, and you'll have a thirty-second window before you're vulnerable again. When you're dead, you return here until the game's over, at which point the winning team is bought a victory beer by the losers. Are we clear?"

Kenny and I nod in agreement, and Brian tips his beer toward us. "Cheers, fellas. For Mark."

I hold up both beers and tap them against Kenny's and Brian's, who start drinking. Holding two, I'm not sure what to do, so I tap them together, start chugging one, and start pouring the other out. I've never poured one out for someone before, but I expected it to feel better. Like he was here, you know? Instead, I'm just wasting a beer, which I don't think helps anyone.

When I finish, I drop the cans and drape a vest around my neck, wrapping the straps around my chest and snapping them into place behind my back. Once they're secured, I grab my rifle from the bag, feeling once again the surge of power it gave me the first time, and slide the power buttons on each into place.

Once everyone's ready, Brian grabs the timer from the bag and holds his thumb over the button, looking like a terrorist about to flatten the park with a bomb. "You have five minutes to get to your location, at which point your vest will beep and the game will start."

"You know we've all played this before, right?" Kenny asks.

"It's been a while," Brian says, feigning disgust. "This is a gentleman's game, and the rules need to be discussed like gentlemen. Are we ready?"

Neither of us say anything.

"Game on, fuckers!" His thumb compresses on the button, and our vests flash in the darkness.

Out of habits I thought were dead, I grab the bar above the slide and throw myself down, my lower back squeaking against the plastic as I squint my eyes against the chilling air. When I reach the bottom, Kenny's waiting for me, his rifle single-handedly pointed upward like a character out of a Schwarzenegger movie.

"We're going east."

I stand up, wanting to hold my gun like him but knowing I can't pull off the look. "Shouldn't we track Brian?"

"That's how we lose," Kenny says. "Don't you remember anything? We stay together and find a base, then make him find us. There's a bench over there that will give one of us cover fire if we're in danger."

Kenny turns and starts jogging across the park. I run up behind him like a kid chasing his dad. "So, what do we do when we get there?"

Kenny looks back over his shoulder. "There are some bushes by the ten and under playground. We'll hang out there and wait for him to come out. Then, when he does, we have them for cover and the playground if we need it. Plenty of options."

I catch a glimpse at the side of his face as he leads us toward his bushes. "How do you know this so well?"

"Brian and I still play from time to time when he makes it back home. It's been a while, but we do it for old time's sake. Mark would even come out sometimes, believe it or not." He points to a shadowy mass with his rifle. "Here. There's a free space in the middle that we can use for cover."

Our vests beep, signaling that the game has started, so we jog to the bushes and climb through them until we reach a small, barren space in the middle. It's covered on all sides, providing cover against nearby lines of sight, with enough room for the two us to sit side by side.

"Won't Brian know you're here, then?"

"I doubt it," Kenny says, setting his rifle down next to him. "It's been long enough that he won't think anything of it."

"Mark used to study the shit out of the place," I tell him. "He was obsessed with beating you guys."

Kenny raises his eyebrows. "You screw it up for him or something?"

Before I can say anything, my phone rings. Given the circumstance, I might as well have waved my arms in the air.

"What the fuck?" Kenny barks.

"Sorry," I say, patting my pockets in an attempt to find it. I finally do, sliding it out of my pocket and pressing the mute button on the side.

It's the reminder I set to call Lauren.

"Hold on," I whisper.

"Put your phone away."

"Just one sec—"

"Put. It. Away."

I slide my finger across the screen, hit Lauren's name, and press the phone into the side of my face so hard that I think it'll become a part of me. It rings a few times, and all I can think about is how many times we've missed each other's calls, how often we've failed to talk over the last two days.

The ringing stops, replaced by a clattering, like the phone's been dropped.

"Hello?" Lauren says. Her breaths are heavy as they hit the receiver.

"You okay?"

"Yeah," she says, calming down. "Just didn't expect you to call. Why are you whispering?"

"We're playing laser tag," I tell her, probably sounding stupider than I feel. "I'm hiding."

There's a pause, and I picture her narrowing her eyes. "So you're really in mourning, huh?"

"I guess. They asked me to play."

Kenny elbows me in the side. "Get off the fucking phone."

"Shut up."

"What?" Lauren asks.

"Nothing. Sorry. Talking to someone else."

"Uh-huh," she murmurs. "Why don't we do this another time?"

"When?"

"We'll figure it out," she says. "Love you."

"Love you too."

As soon as I push my phone back into my pocket, Kenny snaps. "You really are the fucking worst at this. Who was that?"

I wipe my palms on my jeans. "My girlfriend."

"You tell her about Jack yet?"

Fuck. I'd forgotten about him. "No."

"How do you think she'll take it?"

I set my gun on the ground and lean back, bracing myself with my hands against the dirt. "I don't know. We've never talked about a cat."

"You know," he says. "I could probably find him another home. See if Mark's parents want him or something."

"Yeah?"

Kenny shrugs. "Couldn't hurt."

I mull it over for a second. This is the sort of thing you make a list for, but I don't have time for that.

"I think I'm okay," I tell him. "I've taken a liking to the guy. He's weird."

"You're going to head back to Louisville with a cat your girlfriend's never met?"

"Sure," I tell him, starting to push myself up. "What's the worst that can—"

"What are you doing?" he says, putting a hand on my shoulder and pushing me down.

"Looking for Brian."

"You're not ruining this."

I turn my shoulder, causing him to lose his grip, and push myself upward. "I just want to see if he's—"

Kenny's eyes fall to my chest, and it isn't until it's too late that I see a red dot on me. I drop, knowing I'm too slow but unsure of what else to do, and before I hit the ground, my vest is flashing red and beginning a countdown back to zero.

"You motherfucker," Kenny says, rising just enough to peer over the edge of the bush. "You gave us away."

"What?"

Kenny ignores this, pulling his rifle up to his side and over the edge of his hideout. Eyes level with the top, he looks more like a war hero than a laser tag combatant, and for a minute I wonder if he knows I'm even here.

"You still run?"

"What?"

"Do you run?"

I peer up over the edge of the bushes, as if doing so will tell me where he got the question. It doesn't. "Sometimes?"

"Good enough," he says. "Run, dipshit."

Before I can say anything, he puts a boot to my back and kicks me out of the bushes. I tumble out, and before I can push myself up, another red dot starts dancing around me. I roll to the side before it can settle and grab my gun, which Kenny's tossed out as well, and without another thought I'm on my feet, sprinting across the open park while a zigzagging red laser tries to focus on me long enough for a shot. As soon as one creeps down my chest I drop or turn away, desperate to avoid it.

As I make my way toward a new set of bushes, I'm tripped. The ground hits my chest like a hammer, sending the air out of me and making me feel like my ribs have imploded. I roll over, gasping for breath, but Brian's on top of me, pointing his laser rifle at my chest and laughing, his breath reeking of beer and excitement. Before he can pull the trigger, his vest explodes, and, as if it were a real bullet, he flies backward, screaming obscenities and spitting as he lands. As soon as he does the counter begins, and I push myself up and crouch behind a nearby trash can.

Brian's on the ground, staring upward as his vest makes its way back down to zero. When it hits five, he props himself onto his knees, and as it makes its way from three, to two, to one, he jumps to his feet and starts surveying the area.

"Come on, fucker!" he says.

As soon as he turns his head, I hop up and fire a shot at his chest, sending his vest into a sea of red as it starts its countdown again. He remains on his feet this time and throws his arms up in resignation.

"Really?" he says. "That's low."

I step out from behind the trash can and shrug. "You shouldn't have tackled me."

Before either of us can make a move, I'm jerked backward, Kenny's hand firm on the back of my shirt as I'm dragged God-knows-where. We don't get far, though, before flashes of red and blue appear around the perimeter of the park and Kenny drops me. The back of my head strikes the ground, sending a dull pain through my jaw, but I know better than to lie there.

"Not again," Kenny says.

I rub the back of my head. "You could have been gentler, you know."

"I think you'll be okay."

Brian jogs up to us. The opening and closing of doors prompts us into action, so we run, making our way quietly across the grass as flashlights skim across areas nearby. We hunker down as low as we can, looking like something out of *Rambo* or *Predator*, and my thighs burn as a reminder of how I was in better shape before thirty started creeping up on me. When the Tesla comes into sight, we pick up our pace, and just as I start to make out the handle on my door, a flashlight erupts in our faces, sending my eyes squinting and causing one of my friends to bump into me.

"What the fuck?" Brian yells.

"Freeze!"

"Are we being detained?"

I rub my eyes, waiting for things to come into focus.

"Sir—"

"Are we being detained?"

Brian must have gotten this from a YouTube video.

"Sir, I need you to—"

"Officer, are we being detained or not?"

Kenny's voice chimes in from behind me, and I realize that he was the one who ran into me. "Jesus, dude," he says, "just stop."

Brian doesn't, though. "Officer, are we being detained?"

The officer rolls his eyes. Before he can say anything, Brian's thrown his laser rifle at him, knocking the radio off his shoulder and sending him backward.

"Run!"

"Jesus Christ," Kenny says. "I'm going to jail."

"No time for that," Brian says, running past us. Before we can argue it, we're running after him, the cop cursing at us as we make our way back into the darkness. Brian turns abruptly, leading me to believe that he's done this on a couple occasions now, and it isn't long before I realize that we're headed toward the amphitheater.

As we cross the walking bridge and make our way down the steps, I realize that I'm not filled with the terror I associate with this memory, but with an excitement that I think I last felt right here. I haven't run from the cops since then—hell, I haven't encountered the cops since then—but, being here, I want nothing more than to stay away from them so I can get back to my game, have a few beers, and spend time with my friends.

We find a tree near the back of the amphitheater like we used to and make our way to the top. We step on each branch carefully, testing its strength against our weight, and try to remain as quiet as possible. In the distance, officers holler, shining their lights back and forth like half a dozen little lighthouses. While we know they won't shine them over here—they never do—my heart lunges into my throat whenever it appears one's coming our way

Brian jumps onto the top of the amphitheater first, followed by Kenny and finally me. Out of instinct more than anything else, we crawl behind a half wall and put our backs to it. Our sight of the officers is gone, the only signs of their existence being the slowing shouts and the bursts of light that momentarily make an appearance from behind us. Our view looks out over Goose Island, named by Brian after his favorite beers and the geese that hang out on it. It's a small island, with only room for a gazebo and seating for a dozen or so, but surrounded by a small pond where a hundred or so geese make their home. There's one bridge, a simple enter and exit from the other side of the park, that's most often used for marriage proposals or first dates.

"You remember when Mark tried to jump from here into the water?" Brian says.

Kenny nods. "He broke his leg, right?"

"It was his arm," I tell them, coughing up a laugh. "He broke his leg diving into the gravel pit."

There's a pause. The silence hangs in the air for a few seconds, thick and lingering like smoke taking over a room. I picture Mark next to us, his dark hair invisible in the night as he turns his head and peers out over the edge of the amphitheater. He's smiling, laughing but trying not to, as we keep hidden and try to figure out what to do next.

"You think he hated us when he died?" Brian asks.

My picture of Mark disappears, replaced by him screaming at me from across the couch. "Yeah."

The two of them turn toward me.

"I mean, not all of us. Me, though."

We sit in silence, unsure of how to tackle the topic. The

sounds of the officers have faded, the wisps of light less frequent, but before they disappear entirely, Brian peeps up.

"He probably did. But you don't need to beat yourself up over it."

Without another word, we're done, each staring off at Goose Island and thinking about God knows what. I try to shake the image of him screaming at me, but it sticks, accompanied by the growing terror that there are things back at his house that I have to help out with and take care of, answers I'm going to learn that I might not want to. I remind myself that I'm here to do some good by Mark, though, and that tonight might just have been a good start.

When the sound of the officers finally dies, we make our way back down the tree, through the park, and, finally, to the car to call it a night.

TWELVE

Someone knocks on the door, four or five of them in quick succession, making the house sound like it's going to fall down.

"Jesus Christ," Brian murmurs. He's lying on the futon next to me, taking up about two-thirds of it while I keep a sliver for myself. He pulls a pillow from underneath my head and puts it over his. "Who the fuck knocks this early?"

I sit up, wondering the same thing, and get out of bed. Jack's staring at me from the corner of the room. His orange eyes shine through the shadows. I force one foot up a step, then the other, then again, before finally making it to the top. Beth, holding a half-empty cup of coffee, is already on her way to the door.

"Wait," I say.

She stops. "What?"

"Let me get it."

She raises an eyebrow, and, for the first time since I arrived, I get the impression that she's warming up to me being around. I'm mildly hungover on account of the post-laser tag beers we had when we got back, though, so I could be misreading this.

"Why?" she asks.

"I doubt it's good."

"Why's that?"

"I don't know." In my head, I see the police lights and hear the chattering officers from last night. "Just my gut." I walk past her and toward the front of the house.

"You smell like beer."

"It was that kind of night," I say, pulling the door open.

The officer standing in the doorway doesn't seem amused. He's much taller than I, and while most men are, the way he looks down at me makes me want to clear my throat and stand in the corner of the room.

"May I come in?"

I read online once that it's a bad idea to let a police officer into your home. I don't worry about the police too often, especially given that I'm a middle-class white man and all, but there's enough police brutality in the world for me to think you should trust them as little as possible.

"I don't think that's a good idea."

Beth steps toward the door. "Oh please, Jack," she says. "It isn't a big deal."

The officer nods. "Your girlfriend's a little more welcoming than you are."

Beth looks up at me, and I shake my head. "She's not my girlfriend."

"Your loss," the officer says. The comment gives me pause, and my mind drifts back to the night she and I had together.

"So, may I come in?"

"No."

Beth sighs loudly enough for both of us to look at her. She turns and walks back into the kitchen.

"She's a keeper," the officer says.

I look over my shoulder in time to catch her disappear. "She's not my girlfriend," I repeat.

The officer laughs without laughing, his chest puffing as his amusement makes its way up and through his nostrils. "I'm looking for a Brian Dotson. We received a tip that he might be here. You know him?"

The fact that I *do* know him and that this isn't a fluke or mistake or routine bullshit police visit makes my throat tighten. Standing underneath this hulk of a man, I want nothing more than to run away. I remind myself that I'm not here to run away, though I'm here to be with my friends and help out Mark, so I straighten up and look the officer in the eye.

"What's it—"

A hand claps down on my shoulder, and I jump.

"Can I help you, Officer?" Brian asks. He's shirtless again, wearing only a pair of Batman pajama pants. I'm starting to believe he buys his sleepwear in the kids' section.

The officer looks him up and down, eyebrows raised. "I'm looking for a Brian Dotson. You seen him?"

"Doctor."

"Excuse me?"

"Doctor Brian Dotson."

"Well," the officer says, "have you seen a Doctor Brian Dotson?"

Brian smiles. The light shimmers off his teeth, making him look like something out of a sitcom. "That's me."

The officer narrows his eyes and holds up Brian's duffel bag in one hand. Brian's driver's license is wedged between his fingers. Somewhere between not letting him in and watching Beth leave, I must have missed this. "These were found in Riehle Park last night. Some folks called in complaining about a disturbance, and when some fellow officers and I went and examined it, one of them was assaulted. Given what we have here, it seems either you or your friends might know something about it."

At this point, my throat has constricted so much that the

vomit bubbling in my stomach wouldn't even make it out if I threw up. Pits sweating, fingers twitching, I look anywhere but up, comforted only by Brian's hand still on my shoulder. I can't get arrested. Not in this town, the one where I'm trying to rebuild some bridges. What if word gets back home? Will Rob take back the promotion? Will Lauren give me another one of her talks? Brian's grip hasn't loosened—if anything, it's tightened—and for a moment I wonder if the two of them have conspired against me.

When Brian lets go, I almost collapse.

"Thank you so much, Officer," he says, reaching forward and grabbing his things. "I was mugged yesterday by a group of kids. They took my bag."

The officer raises an eyebrow. "You don't look like you were mugged."

"It's a little bit of a rough thing to show." Brian pulls one leg of his Batman pajama pants up to his thigh. Purple and black spots have developed across it like craters on a moon painted in watercolor. A bruise, more likely than not, from when he tackled me.

The officer reaches out to touch the bruises, and Brian pulls his pant leg down, shutting him out like a girl with a pushy prom date. "Sorry," Brian says, stepping backward. "I'm tender."

"I think—"

"Look," Brian interrupts, "I appreciate you going out of the way to somehow find me here, but I'm a grown man who works stupid shifts to take care of the sick and dying in my community, and I had my ass handed to me by a bunch of kids who wanted to buy a case of shitty beer and cause problems in the park. I really just want to get some sleep. Is that okay?"

The officer looks from side to side, as if some evidence is hiding in between the bricks of the front porch. After a few seconds of silence, his eyes settle at his feet. "Sorry for the trouble," he says. "If you see anything"—he digs in his pocket and pulls out a card, which he hands to Brian—"just give me a call. We'd appreciate the help."

Brian takes the card. "Will do."

The officer nods, then turns and walks away, and Brian slams the door. "Jesus Christ. What a fuck."

I exhale, feeling like I've lost twenty pounds. "You familiar with this routine?"

He flashes me a grin, then turns and heads back toward the basement. "A little. Haven't gotten a ticket since I finished med school."

"Don't you think they'll catch on?" I holler.

He retreats back to the basement with a confidence that makes me jealous, leaving me standing alone in my pajamas in my dead friend's living room.

"He always had a way with words, didn't he?" Beth says. She's leaning against the kitchen doorway, a half-empty coffee cup still in between her hands. Her hair's down, like it used to be, though it isn't as long as it was back then. It brushes the tops of her shoulders, and for the first time I notice that it isn't as curly as it once was. It's almost like the shit she's dealt with over the years has weighed her down and sapped her of her energy so deeply that even her hair doesn't have the strength it used to.

"You could say that."

Another knock at the door. Beth and I look at each other, then it, so I grab the handle and pull it back open.

It's the officer again. In his hands is a small box.

"This was at the end of the drive," he says. "Figured the mailman put it in the wrong spot since the mailbox is up here and all."

He hands me the box, which is addressed to me.

"Thanks."

He nods. "Might want to clean that car off, too, you know,"

he adds, hiking his thumb over his shoulder. "That could get nasty if you let it sit for too long."

My Prius is in the driveway. It rained while we were asleep, and the tight layers of toilet paper have turned into thick, heavy clumps that cling to the sides like gray mats of hair.

"Thanks."

He leans to the side, looking past me and at Beth. "You two have a good day."

I close the door and toss the box onto the couch. Beth sits next to it and sets her coffee on the table. "What do you think it is?"

"No clue," I tell her. "Everyone who knows I'm here is here."

"Your girlfriend?"

I pause, remembering our call last night. Was that the first time we'd spoken since I've been up here? I flip back through the blurry memories of the last few days, unable to come to a conclusion, and make a mental note to call her later.

"Maybe. She might not know the address, though."

Beth looks down. "Are you going to open it?"

This is the most interested Beth's been in me since I arrived. I have half a mind to ask her what's going on, but I know that would blow up in my face, so I decide to roll with it and open the box. The handwriting is nothing I recognize. The letters are big and blocky, as if they were written by someone who only writes in straight lines.

I grab a set of keys off the table and wiggle them into the side of the box. Jack jumps on my lap and starts nudging it too, rubbing his cheeks on the closest corner and purring. I'm about halfway through cutting the packaging tape when the box explodes in a cloud of shimmering whites and blues. Jack darts off, and I drop it—more out of instinct than anything else, I guess—and look down.

I'm covered in dicks. They're all around me, tiny, glittery

dicks, blue and white, sparkling in what little light's coming through the blinds.

Beth smirks. She looks happier than I've seen her look since I got here, and, for a few seconds, I almost think getting covered in dicks is worth it.

"Did you do this?"

She laughs, shaking her head. A few dicks dangle from her hair.

In the bottom of the box is an envelope. In blocky, cut-out magazine letters, it says:

JACK DOTSON
EAT A DICK

And it hits me.

"S.A.M."

"Sam who?"

"S.A.M.—The Society for Advocates of Mark."

Beth leans over and peers into the box, then grabs the letter and rips it open. Her eyes scan it for a few seconds, moving from one side of her head to another, before she hands it to me.

It reads:

Jack Dotson,

We told you that consequences would follow. You and your friends did a nice job of running from the police last night, but we promise you things won't get easier if you choose to stay. You have no right in Mark's home, much less at his funeral.

This is your last warning to leave. He wouldn't have wanted you there, nor do you deserve to be there.

At the bottom of the box is a stack of photos. There's me, Kenny, and Brian with our beers on the playground; me sliding down, beer in one hand, gun in the other, my gut exposed by my shirt being pulled up against the plastic; me and Kenny, sneaking into the bushes. All sorts of moments from last night, moments I never expected anyone to see. Moments that, under reasonable circumstances, no one would have seen. Reasonable circumstances assuming it's normal for three grown men to play laser tag in a public park, I guess.

Beth leans forward, resting her elbows on her knees. "You want to grab a cup of coffee and figure this out? A change of scenery might be nice."

I don't know if it's a good idea to go out for coffee with Beth. The last time we were alone was when I arrived, and we got in a fight, and the time before that, we slept together and ruined Mark's life. Things seem different now, though, and she seems to be about the only person interested in helping me figure this out.

"That would be great."

We go to our rooms to change out of our pajamas. When I come back, she's sitting by the door, tying her shoes, and on the table next to her is a picture of her and Mark. Mark's heavier than I remember, and Beth's hair is longer, like it used to be. I can't tell where it was taken, but they're smiling, heads leaning against one another's like something out of a couple's photoshoot.

Beth looks up. She sees me staring at the photo, then forces a smile. "Anniversary shoot."

There's a moment of silence, so I stare at the ground. I'm right on top of a blotch of something or another on the rug—I'm not sure what—that might have happened when I was actually welcome here. I want to place it, but I can't. It could have happened anytime.

When I look up, Beth is staring at me. "I'm sorry," she says.

Beth's not an apologizer. She stews, letting the details of whatever she's dealing with wash over her, then makes a judgment once everything's settled. It's an aggravating thing, really, since the timeline is all hers. Sometimes, like now, it takes so long that you forget what she might have done wrong in the first place.

"What?"

"I'm sorry," she repeats. "I know this has probably been hard for you."

I shrug. It's a quick, casual thing—a flip of the shoulders, really—in an attempt to look cooler than I feel. I want to tell her that it has been hard, that I haven't known what to do or what I'm supposed to say or feel, but I shut it up and keep it to myself. We can sort that out later. "Don't worry about it," I tell her. "Grabbing coffee would be nice, though."

THIRTEEN

Beth's eyes widen when we pull into the parking lot. "Starbucks? Really?"

I pull the Tesla into a spot. It was a quiet ride—I'm coming to learn that trips in the Tesla are—until this.

"What's wrong with Starbucks?"

She turns to look out the window. "Nothing. I thought it might be a little plain for you. We don't have anything fair trade or organic around here, you know."

There was an article on *Thrillist* once—or maybe it was *Buzzfeed*—that listed Louisville as one of the best coffee destinations in America. Brian called me the day it came out, harping on me about how I'd moved three hours away from home to live near a bunch of hipster coffee joints. He posted it on Facebook, Twitter, Instagram—everywhere he could, really, to make fun of me for drinking only Americanos and lattes. Given how desperately he latched onto this joke, I can only assume that this is where Beth's gotten the idea that I wouldn't touch Starbucks. There's a lot of good coffee in Louisville, but there's also a lot of shitty coffee. I don't even care much for good coffee, but it's not like I was going to drive Beth to a gas station for a cup. You don't impress anyone with gas station coffee.

"I drink Starbucks all the time," I tell her. This isn't true. I drink office coffee, which, knowing Confluence and its attempts to be Louisville's trendy, hip workplace, might be from the organic, fair trade roastery downtown.

She smiles, her lips just barely parting, as I turn off the car. "Uh-huh."

We open our doors in sync and head inside. It's what I'd expect out of a Starbucks: black and khaki, with business-people in suits and students picking away at keyboards while hipsters sit in corners and thumb through tattered copies of something like Kerouac or Thoreau.

A high school-looking kid with thick-framed glasses and short hair stares us down from across the register. He looks more the type to scoff at Starbucks than work there—hell, if he were older, I'd think he wrote the *Thrillist* article—and I wonder for a minute if he's incognito, working to bring the man down from within.

"Hi," he says. "What can I get you?"

I nod toward Beth.

"Skinny venti caramel latte, no whip."

He enters the order, then looks up at me.

"Small black coffee."

Beth bats at my arm, embarrassed, but the barista grins. It's a subtle thing, the corner of his lip creeping up like a parent trying not to laugh at his kid's bad joke.

"One skinny venti caramel latte, no whip, and one tall Pike Place. Correct?"

Before I can answer, Beth puts a hand on my arm. It's the first time she's touched me—really touched me—since I returned, and even though my sleeve separates us, it distracts me while she pulls out her card.

"No, no, no," I say, pulling my arm away despite my desire

not to. "I got it."

"I can pay for this."

"Don't worry about it," I tell her, reaching for my wallet. "I got it."

The barista looks back and forth at us, his eyes wide behind his thick-framed glasses. Beads of sweat form on his forehead in a palpable nervousness that's sure to send him running as soon as we're gone. Before he can, though, I reach my arm over the register, dangling my card before his face like it's gold or something he'd actually want. Unfortunately for me, it isn't.

Beth pushes my arm down. "Look"—she narrows her eyes to read his name tag—"Steven. Let me pay for this."

Steven grabs her card and swipes it, due to either Beth's intensity or a desire to see us gone. What cred I'd earned as a result of my order has now disappeared, leaving me the bum who just had his dead friend's fiancée pay for his coffee.

We sit at a table near the window while Steven makes our drinks. The silence hangs in between us, awkward and thick, so I tap my thumbs on the table to kill some time while I come up with something to say. Do I apologize for trying to pay? Say thanks? Make small talk?

I've got to stop overthinking this.

Beth pulls the letter from S.A.M. out of her purse and tosses it between us. It sits there for a moment, silent, the cut-out magazine letters making us look like something out of a shitty sitcom or detective show.

"So," she says.

"So."

She inhales slowly, as if taking a drag from a cigarette, and nods. "It's not Lisa."

"What?" She might as well have told me the sky isn't blue or water isn't wet. "Of course it's Lisa."

Beth pulls her phone out of her purse. She swipes her thumb across the screen in a couple different directions until she gets to what she's looking for, at which point she sets it on the table and slides it to me.

"She couldn't have taken those photos. She was in Indianapolis."

Sure enough, there's an Instagram post of Lisa's from last night. She's holding a cocktail in one hand and the set list from some concert she was attending in the other, and she's smiling, teeth bared, cheeks rosy, as if she knows I've been stumped. The location tag is The Rogue, a little venue near downtown Indy. After reading this, I ignore her caption, turn the phone around, and slide it back across the table.

"So she had someone follow us."

Beth raises an eyebrow. "You really think she'd do that?"

I shrug as if it's an obvious and reasonable thing to accuse someone of. "Of course."

"And that she, a grown woman, would send you an exploding box of glitter penises?"

I hesitate. For everything Lisa's done—the way she bashed me in college, even the way she threw her drink on me the other night—she's never been one to resort to cheap EAT A DICK jokes. It's something I would have resorted to back in the day, to be honest, and I can almost picture her, eyes narrow, looking down her nose and shaking her head at me.

Fuck.

Beth smiles, scooting to the edge of her seat and suddenly aware that she's made her point. "So, it's probably someone else. Someone from work, if I had to guess."

"I thought he wasn't working?"

She closes her eyes for a second, and I'm suddenly aware that I should let her run this show.

"From King's."

"They all loved me."

"Loved. With a 'd.' Past tense."

I have nothing to say to this, so I keep my mouth shut.

"There's a kid named Henry. He came to Mark's dad a year or so ago looking for a job so he could get off probation, and Mark's dad said no. Mark talked him into it, though, pretty much saving the kid's ass, and Henry worshiped the ground Mark walked on because of it. Anyway, when Mark was fired by his dad, Henry came over to our place with this idea to send Mark's dad a glitter bomb." Beth pauses, smiling as the realization washes over me. "Kind of seems like a natural fit, no?"

I take in a breath, slowing myself down as I mull over the information. "But what's he got against me?"

Beth leans forward and sets her elbows on the table. A strand of hair falls out from behind her ear as she leans in. "The same thing most people do," she says. "Mark didn't like you."

I feel myself laughing—chest rumbling, nose sniffling little bursts of air like fireworks—though I know I shouldn't. "There's got to be someone in this shitty town who still likes me, right?"

When Beth blinks, her eyes go from peaceful to irritated. Brows narrowed, eyelids sharp, it's like I'm a kid about to get yelled at, and for a minute, I want Steven to hurry the fuck up with my coffee.

"Do you really have to do that?"

"Do what?" I shake my head as if doing so will undo whatever I've done wrong. "It was a joke."

"You make little jabs like that all the time. Calling Lafayette a shithole, making fun of the local bars, cracking jokes about everyone who lives here—you're always talking down on it. What did Lafayette ever do to you?"

"Skinny venti caramel latte and a tall Pike Place?"

We turn at once, as if choreographed, and Steven jumps, sending coffee hopping out of my cup and onto the plastic lid. He looks down, then up, as if hoping I wouldn't notice.

I go to the counter and grab the drinks. "Thanks."

Steven forces a smile and scurries to the register.

When I get back to the table, I hand Beth her coffee. She raises the cup to her face and closes her eyes, smelling the flavor as it seeps through the lid and into the air. The look of unmasked satisfaction that smooths her features reminds me of how she looked the night we slept together. Worriless. Happy. It's a feeling that contrasted the panic that had started to well up in me, the snowball of anxiety and fear and shame that would tumble out of control until I skipped town and settled down in Louisville. I envied her for it. In some respects, I still do.

"I wasn't anything until I got out of Lafayette, you know."

Beth's eyes snap open. She stares at me for a moment, her forehead crinkling as she thinks about what I've said. "What do you think you are now?"

Beth has a way of making dickish questions sound fair, a quality that's more frustrating now than it was when we were younger, when the most pressing questions were whether to buy Keystone Light or Burnett's Vodka.

The thing is, I don't know how to answer her. I have adult things now—a salary, a house, a long-term girlfriend, even a cat and a dog—but I'm not sure if they add up to anything. I've accomplished things, though. I've been approved for a mortgage. I'm the Director of Strategic Initiatives at one of Louisville's fastest-growing companies. I've even gotten a tax break for purchasing an environmentally friendly vehicle. Whatever these are, they're a far cry from placing second in the county track meet and finishing first in Artie's Pizza's "two pie challenge," which, as far as I can remember, are all I ever pulled off here.

I shrug. "An adult?"

Beth sets the cup back on the table and slides deeper into her seat. "Jesus Christ, Jack," she says. "You don't even know."

FOURTEEN

W hen we get back from Starbucks, I hop out of the car and run inside.

"What are you doing?" Beth hollers.

"I have a plan."

The rest of our coffee date was uneventful. I didn't see much value in arguing the merits of my adulthood, and there wasn't much else to say about Lisa and Henry and whoever S.A.M. could be, so we sat in silence, interrupted only by the occasional attempt at small talk, until we called it quits and left.

By the time Beth catches up, I'm wrist-deep in my package from S.A.M., digging through it and gathering up as much glitter as possible. Beth's eyes go immediately to the pieces I've spilled on the coffee table, and she freezes halfway through hanging her purse on the coat rack, one arm up as the strap dangles above the hook.

"I think you ought to slow down for a second."

"I'm going to King's."

She drops her purse on the hook and points toward the box. "And what's that for?"

I grip the handful of glitter and stuff it in my pockets. Most of it makes it in, but a couple renegades tumble over the side and somersault through the air before landing on the hardwood and winking up at me. "I'm going to bait him."

I came up with the plan on the way home from Starbucks. I go to King's, track down this Henry kid, order a cone, and when he gives me the total, I reach into my pocket to pay only for—whoops?—a bunch of glitter dicks to pop out and flutter all over the place. If Henry reacts, he was in on it. If he doesn't, we move on to the next suspect, whoever the hell that is.

Beth nods, but it's a slow thing, like she's forcing herself to admit that this could work. Or, forcing herself to admit that her twenty-nine-year-old friend is going to walk into a family restaurant and spill a handful of glitter dicks on the floor.

"You want to go with?"

Beth's head stops. She starts to talk a couple times, her lips parting in a small sliver before falling back into place. "I don't think that's a good idea."

"Why not?"

"Are you answering to Mark's dad when he sees us together?"

"Don't worry, brochacho," comes a voice from the basement. "If you need backup, we got you."

I look down, expecting the floor to open up into a view of the room below. Then I picture Brian sprawled out on the futon in his pajamas, probably shirtless, playing X-Box with Kenny or drinking a beer, and thank God that the view doesn't exist.

Brian's footsteps boom up the stairs, and it's only a matter of seconds before he huffs his way into the living room. He's wearing a pair of blue jeans and one of Mark's old Red Hot Chili Peppers T-shirts, which hugs him in all the places I imagine it didn't hug Mark. "Where we headed?"

"I'm going to King's. Beth says some kid there might be S.A.M."

"Who?" Kenny pokes his head up over Brian's shoulder.

"Henry," Beth says.

Kenny shoves his way past Brian, squirming through one limb at a time while my brother, oblivious, nods and stares off.

"What about Lisa?" Brian asks.

"She was in Indy last night," Beth says.

"Anyway," I say, "I'm going to check out this Henry kid. See if I can bait him into giving me a hint."

Kenny raises an eyebrow. "How are you pulling that off?"

"I have a plan," I tell him. I'd rather not pull the glitter out of my pocket again.

"Sounds good," Brian says. "Then we fuck him up, right?"

I want to say yes, that of course we'll fuck him up, but our odds of pulling that off are slim. There's the whole issue of a counter being between us, not to mention the assault thing.

No, there will be no fucking up. This will be a reconnaissance mission.

"I think I'm going to go on this one alone," I say. "Just scope things out." I start flipping through the notes in my head, trying to come up with a counterargument for whatever Brian's going to throw my way, but he shrugs before I can come up with anything.

"You want to get back to *Halo*?" Brian says, turning toward Kenny.

Kenny's eyes dart toward me, then back to my brother. "Sure." And, without another word, the two of them disappear back down the stairs to continue reliving their college years.

"Well," Beth says, stepping away from the coat rack. "Good luck."

"Thanks."

She sits on the couch. She doesn't fall into it like Mark did or how Brian and Kenny and I do. Instead, she lowers herself onto it, as if to not disturb the cushions. "He has long hair, by the way."

"What?"

"Henry. He has long hair. He'll probably be wearing a red bandanna to keep it out of his face."

"Oh." Of course I didn't know what Henry looked like. I've never met the kid. "Thanks."

She smiles, and her dimples form small parentheses on either side of her lips. "No problem," she says. "Go get 'em."

WHEN I DECIDED to come home, King's Frozen Custard was the last place I planned on visiting. It's pretty dead this time of year, with summer having given way to autumn and cooler temperatures, but there's still a patchwork collection of folks huddled around tables. King's doesn't have any indoor seating; instead, it has a long patio that stretches out from the front of the building like the deck of a ship. It's covered with a massive awning, a blue-and-white-striped thing that arches over the length of it, and at the back is a building no bigger than a one-bedroom house, painted white with a counter and four windows facing the patio. Overlooking everything, in big, blue neon lights outlined in red, shines the King family name.

I've parked Brian's Tesla across the street. The lot's empty except for two or three cars, but I didn't want to draw attention to myself by cruising in on this silent, electric beast. I tried to peel some of the toilet paper off my Prius before I left, but just as the officer warned me, it was now stuck to the exterior in fat, flaky clumps I didn't have time to deal with.

I pat my pocket to make sure the glitter's still there. A few blue-and-white dicks poof out of it, swirling into the no-man's land between the edge of the seat and the center console, but I leave them there and get out of the car. As I make my way across the street and up to the patio, my nerves tempt me to stuff my hands in my pockets, but I pin them to my sides instead. I need it to be one fluid moment when I go to pull some cash out. Stuffing them in there now could screw that up.

At the window on the edge of the patio, a blonde girl wearing a visor smiles and sets down her magazine. At the window next to her, leaning against the counter and sipping out of a foam 32-ounce cup, is Henry. I assume it's him, at least. He's wearing a long-sleeved neon green shirt, and his messy brown hair is pinned around his head by a folded-over red bandanna. His eyes are blank as he stares out over the patio, and his cheeks sink in every few seconds as he drinks from his soda.

"Welcome to King's Frozen Custard," the girl says. Her voice is energetic, electric even, but I walk right past her and step up to Henry's window.

"Hey, man," I say.

Henry's eyes practically creak as they make their way up to mine. He takes a long drink of his pop, making a narrow fish face in the process, before finally pulling the straw out of his mouth and setting his cup somewhere below the counter.

"What can I get you?" he asks. His voice is low, monotone, as if he barely has the energy for words.

"Jeez," I say, sighing and looking up at the menu. "I can't pick. You guys have so many choices."

I don't know why I'm drawing this out. It's either the nerves or the stupidity of the situation or maybe a combination of the two, but I can't settle on something, choosing instead to rock back on my heels and puff my cheeks full of air.

"What kinds of dessert do you like?" the girl asks, leaning over the register.

"I don't know," I tell her. "I like lots of desserts, to be honest."

"You could always go with a classic," she says. "Maybe chocolate or vanilla?"

Behind her, Henry's eyes gloss over as he stares past me and at the patio. He's either high or stupid, maybe both, and I can't imagine the guy being aware enough to pull off what S.A.M. has done.

Surely Mark and this kid weren't friends. Mark was passionate about this place. He spent more nights here than with his girlfriend, researched trends on sundaes, even took time to explain to people the difference between ice cream and frozen custard. This fuck, he couldn't care less about any of that.

"You know what?" I say. "I'll take a small chocolate ice cream cone." I picture Mark twitching at me calling it ice cream.

Henry blinks a couple times, then leans forward and starts punching the order into his register. "Anything else?"

Fucking asshole.

"Actually, could I make that a frozen custard instead? Not really feeling ice cream today."

The kid's jaw drops, and the tips of his yellowed teeth peek out from between his lips. His hand hovers over the register, and he taps his fingertips on a couple buttons, pretending to press them.

"Actually, sir," Henry's coworker says, standing on her tiptoes and hovering over Henry's shoulder, "we only serve frozen custard here. It's been the same family recipe since 1932."

"Oh," I say, trying to look at her and not lose sight of Henry. "That's perfect, then. A small—"

"That's $2.32," Henry says.

"Of course," I say, stuffing my hand in my pocket. Before I can pull it out, though, a slap comes down on my shoulder. My hand darts up, bringing with it a cloud of tiny, glittery dicks that make their way up and slowly down. For a second, I think to use them like a smoke bomb and disappear like people do in ninja movies, but they hit the ground before I can, shimmering and reflecting little dick-shaped slices of the sun up from the concrete.

Behind the counter, Henry's eyebrows rise in wide arcs that show more emotion than I thought possible. "Mr. King," he says, his voice suddenly perking up. "What can I do for you?"

Mark's dad taps his fingertips on my collarbone. "Jack," he says, ignoring his employee, "I have to say, I didn't think I'd see you up here."

"We were just showing him the menu," Henry says.

Mr. King lets go and gives me a couple pats on the back. "Oh, Jack knows the menu. Worked here how long—two years?"

"Just a summer" I say, looking down. I stuff my hands in my pockets. "With Mark."

"Jack was best friends with Mark," Mr. King tells the cashiers. "They had a little falling out, though."

Henry nods. "Mark told me about that," he says, pointing toward me. "You slept with—"

"Don't talk about it." Mark's dad spits the words out. His eyes narrow, and his right fist balls up. A moment of silence passes, and Mr. King, perhaps realizing his reaction, forces a smile and uncurls his fingers. "It happened a long time ago. And now, Jack's been nice enough to come up from Louisville and . . ." He trails off, eyes on the glitter. "Help out, I guess."

"Sorry about that," I say, squatting down and doing my best to brush the glitter off the concrete and into my hand. A few pieces get there, but most upend on one another and wedge themselves into cracks.

"We'll get it," Mr. King says. "Unless, of course, you needed that."

I shoot back up. "No, of course not. It was from a party."

Mr. King leans against the counter, nodding. Behind him, Henry smirks.

"I didn't realize you were partying over there," Mark's dad says.

"We aren't," I say, spitting up any words that come to my head. "It was a party in Louisville. Last week."

"Well," he says, "it looks like you've made quite a life for yourself there."

I force a smile and look to Henry and his coworker. The girl's turned to wipe the counters, but Henry shrugs, still grinning. "It's pretty nice."

"You excited about the addition to the household?" Mr. King adds.

I scurry through the notes in my head again, trying to figure out what he's talking about. Is Lauren pregnant? Did she post something on Facebook I haven't noticed? Thinking back on all the calls I've missed, I choke on my thoughts and come up empty.

"What?"

"Jack," he says, smiling. For a second, his face is Mark's when he'd win a bet or beat me at a video game.

"Yeah?"

Mr. King laughs. "The cat."

"Oh yeah." I sigh, pushing my thoughts on Lauren back into the ugly closet they came from. "Yeah. I guess he's coming to Louisville."

"Mark loved that little guy," he says, looking past me. "He'd bring him up here sometimes. We'd fight backwards and forwards about it—it's a health code violation, obviously—but Mark wouldn't give up. Said the guy was his spirit animal, that he wanted him here with him. That cat meant the world to my son."

With S.A.M. showing up, I'd almost forgotten about Jack. I open my mouth to speak, then stop, unsure of how to work out what I want what to say. After a few seconds, I force it out. "Do you—are you sure you don't know why he's named after me?"

Mr. King's eyes lock on mine. "Do you not want him?"

"No," I tell him. "It's not that at all. I just don't understand why Mark would name a cat after me. It kind of makes me feel like I have to take him."

For a moment, Mark's dad is silent. He blinks a couple times, slow things that make me wonder if he's even registered what I've said. "Hard telling," he says. "Nobody's saying you have to take him, though."

"I didn't mean it like that," I murmur, shuffling my feet, suddenly ashamed. "I kind of like the little guy."

"It could have been a 'fuck you,'" he adds, shrugging. "For what you did, you know. Either way, I guess you'll be taking him back to Louisville soon, right? Hard to believe you're sticking around town much longer."

I picture the clunky notes from S.A.M. telling me in various degrees of mystery and aggression that I need to leave. "I think I'm going to stick around for a while, actually," I say, looking over Mr. King and at Henry, who appears to laugh.

Mr. King raises an eyebrow. "Really?"

"Just trying to help out at the house and all."

He blinks again, nodding and staring me down. "Well then," he says, "I guess I'll leave you to it." He turns toward Henry, whose eyes are now focused on the counter, looking suddenly oblivious to everything that's going on. "Didn't mean to interrupt you two."

"That's $2.32," Henry repeats. For a second, I have no idea what he's talking about. Then the order comes back to me, the plan, and I pat my pocket and panic.

"Shit," I whisper. I look up at Henry, whose eyelids are half-draped over his eyes. "I forgot my money."

Henry's mouth falls open again. His eyes go from me to Mr. King and linger there before a hand comes back down on my shoulder.

"It's on me," Mr. King says. "Jack has his hands full right now. Can't fault the guy for being overwhelmed."

I force a laugh and smile, trying to picture what Mark's dad thinks I have my hands full with. "Thanks," I say, and Henry hands me a small strawberry cone. It crosses my mind to correct him and get the chocolate I asked for, but it's probably best to get out before things get worse.

Mark's dad gives my shoulder another squeeze, but he's looking at Henry. "Anytime," he says. "It's important that we be there for one another when things get difficult."

FIFTEEN

I'm sitting on Mark's front porch, petting Jack and drinking a beer with my brother. It's been two days since my failed attempt at tricking Henry (or buying a cone, for that matter), so I've decided to focus my attention on something other than playing Batman. We've just finished loading about a dozen boxes of Mark's belongings into the back of Kenny's truck, which he and Beth are driving to Mr. and Mrs. King's place.

It's quiet out here. It's always quiet in Lafayette, but the sounds of the leaves rustling in the trees, the hum of the occasional car going down Mark's street, the slurps whenever one of us takes a drink of our beer—it's peaceful. It almost feels like home, and, for a moment, I'm not even sure I know where home is. It should be Louisville, but all I have there is work, a girlfriend who doesn't seem to want to get a hold of me, and a house in a neighborhood the realtor said is up-and-coming. Good things, sure, but things that I'm starting to realize might not be everything.

I pull my phone out of my pocket, and Jack purrs and starts rubbing his cheeks on it. He's done this to just about everything I've had near him: comics, remotes, pizza boxes. According to someone on the internet, it's a possession thing, so I've decided to let him roll with it and claim whatever he wants.

Through the headbutts I open my messages. My texts with Lauren are all the same, each of us taking turns giving some excuse or another for why we can't talk. She's either in a meeting, out to dinner with her editors, or working on an assignment. I'm either packing, grabbing a bite with the guys, or running around the park playing laser tag. I type out a text to tell her I miss her, and, for a second, I wonder if she's missing me, staring at our conversation and lighting up when she sees that I'm typing. There's no way of knowing this, though, so I hit send and put my phone back in my pocket.

Brian hasn't opened his mouth for a good ten minutes, which might be a record. After Kenny and Beth left, we tried to figure out our next steps with S.A.M., but we didn't get anywhere. Lisa's still written off on account of being out of town, and Henry, well, we don't know what to do with him. Truth is, we've hit dead end after dead end. Given Henry's smirking over Mr. King's shoulder, I'd assume it's him, but what is there to do? March up to the window of King's and accuse him? Call the cops? Send a glitter bomb back?

There's the issue of the person he could be working with too. Henry doesn't strike me as the type to be able to pull this off alone, but where would we start looking for his accomplices? According to Kenny, you could line up just about everyone in town and take your pick. Not that *everyone* hates me, he said, but enough do that he's having a hard time figuring out who all S.A.M. could be. Things quieted down when I left for Louisville, he told me, but no one ever forgave me for screwing over Mark.

Whoever it is, it's been quiet enough since the glitter bomb, which is exactly why it doesn't surprise me when the sound of squealing tires screeches around the corner and onto Mark's street.

"You hear that?" Brian asks.

In the distance, the thumping of drums and the low grind of an electric guitar grows louder. Jack jumps off my lap and runs inside.

"I have a bad feeling about this."

"It's probably just some punk," Brian says. "Driving around like an asshole, blasting his music. Kids do shit like that all the time."

Brian's refused to accept that S.A.M. is serious. He insists that they'll stop, that they're full of shit and can be waited out regardless of who they are, and that, eventually, they'll just go away. I like his argument, at least the part where nobody hates me so much that they'd let this go on forever, but I don't exactly believe it.

The music grows louder as the car gets nearer. The driver is listening to Rage Against the Machine, and Zach de la Rocha is screaming "Fuck you, I won't do what you tell me" on repeat. I haven't listened to Rage in ages; Mark and I would listen to them while playing video games sometimes. Mark, though, might be another story. For a second, I picture him in the car, head bobbing, blasting the music and charging down the street. Maybe he set this all up, faked his death and every-thing to get back at me. That doesn't seem like him, though. He'd be less dramatic than that. I guess I don't really know what does seem like him, though, a realization that's grown increasingly frustrating since I arrived.

The music's coming from a baby-blue P.T. Cruiser that comes to a stop in front of Mark's house. It sits there while the last "Fuck you, I won't do what you tell me" comes out and the song ends in a handful of quick, aggressive thumps. Then, silence, though it's different this time. There's still the wind and the leaves and all that, and the car hums along with it all while the driver sits behind tinted windows. It isn't peaceful, though. It's still, threatening, like we're in a Western movie, all frozen while a tumbleweed skitters across the screen. Only we're in Indiana, so the closest thing to a tumbleweed is an old McDonald's bag, which, strangely enough, is stuck in one of the bushes in Mark's front yard.

The passenger's window slides down. Behind it is a small guy in giant aviators and a black ski mask.

"Jack Dotson," he says. His voice isn't high pitched, but it isn't mature either. It has the squeak you might except out of the car when its brakes start to go out in a few years.

I don't know what you're supposed to do when a P.T. Cruiser rolls up in front of you blasting Rage Against the Machine, so I wave.

"Despite everything we've said, you've continued to ignore us."

My phone vibrates against my leg. I pull it out of my pocket, and the screen shows Lauren's face, smiling at me from across our table at Mulligan's.

"We've tried to be reasonable—"

Brian sets down his beer and stands up. "Reasonable?" he yells. "What the fuck is your definition of reasonable?"

In the distance, I think I hear a stick break, maybe Jack running away to get backup, or just running away to save himself. Can't say I blame him.

"This isn't about that," the man says. His voice cracks when he says this, sounding like a hiccup in a record, and I realize he isn't a man at all. He's a kid, and he has no idea what the hell he's doing.

"You don't get to come home and make yourself feel better, Jack," he says. His words spill out louder, faster, sounding like he can't get them out quickly enough. "You ignored us. You didn't believe us. So, this is what you get."

There's another noise, a foot crunching its way through the

leaves, and a thump in the air. Before I can put it all together, Brian's falling backward, his chest oozing red, his eyes wide as he collapses into his chair. I sit there, frozen, as the crimson drips down his shirt in thick, slow streams. He runs his fingers through the mess, smearing it into his clothing, then balls them in a fist and sits back up. My stomach churns and bubbles as I take it all in, and I want to yell or cry or do anything, but all I can do is quiver. Before I even consider anything else, though, a dozen guys in paintball gear come out from the back of the house and point their guns at us. They look like something out of a sci-fi movie with their shimmering orange goggles and black bodysuits, and for a second, I wonder if I've fallen asleep and into a nightmare.

Behind them, the kid in the car waves. "Sorry you got roped into this, Brian. Bye, boys."

The engine growls as much as a four-cylinder can, sounding more like an angry go-kart, and the tires of the P.T. Cruiser squeak more than squeal. As soon as it's off, though, the paintballs come. I roll out of my chair and hit the ground, but not before one slams into my neck, exploding in blue and sending an ache and a lump into my throat that almost makes me feel like I'm choking. I curl up behind the half-wall on the front porch, and Brian's done the same. Above us, the front of the house gets peppered in small explosions of red, blue, and yellow, making it look like a cross between a Jackson Pollock painting and an elementary school art project.

I put my hands behind my head in an effort to ball up. "What do we do?"

Brian peers above the half-wall, narrowly avoiding a paintball to the face. "Wait."

My phone vibrates again. It's Lauren. I swipe across the screen and press it to my cheek.

"Hey!" she says. I can almost hear her smile. Then, a pause. "What's that noise?"

"It's complicated," I tell her. "Now's not really a good time."

"Oh, well, I can—"

I stop listening when my brother pushes himself up and leaps off the porch to charge at the paintballers. He's yelling like William Wallace in *Braveheart*, charging ahead as explosions of color erupt all over him.

"I have to go," I blurt, and I hear a final, distant "Jack" as I hang up and stuff my phone in my pocket. I chance a look inside to make sure Jack's safe, then I'm over the wall and running too, only the paintballers have dispersed, darting in all sorts of directions as if they expected us to just sit there and let them shoot at us.

"Get the fat one," Brian yells, pointing at one of them running out of the yard. He's at the back of the group, sure, but I wouldn't call him fat. Big, though. Maybe chunky. Either way, Brian's after him, face red, eyes narrow, and the poor kid doesn't make it to the sidewalk before my brother's in the air, grabbing a handful of his shirt and pulling him to the ground in a tangle of limbs and grunts. Beyond them, a taller, lankier kid turns around. When he does, a fountain of long brown hair flops out from underneath his ski mask.

"Henry," I tell Brian, patting him on the back. "I think that's him."

Brian's too caught up in his prey, though. He's ripped the paintball mask off. The kid's face is so white it practically shines against the grass, and his skin is peppered in thick, red pimples.

"Who are you?" Brian yells. His voice is low, almost like a growl, as if he's doing his best Batman.

The kid's response is a mixture of sobs and squeals. He's squeezed his eyes shut, though a few tears manage to squeak out, and I realize that he has no idea what's going except that a guy twice his age is interrogating him like something out of a crime thriller. Brian, covered in paint and sweat and dirt, looks everything the part of a maniac.

"Let him go," I say. "He doesn't know anything."

The kid squeaks what I think is an agreement. Brian doesn't seem to hear this, though, as he's too caught up in shaking the kid by his collar.

"Who sent you?" he barks.

"I-I don't know," the kid cries. "A guy just a-asked a few of us if we'd p-paintball a house for some money. I swear I don't know who."

"Jesus Christ," Brian says. He lets go of the kid's shirt, and he falls to the ground with a thump and a groan. The kid wiggles out from under Brian, then pushes himself up and starts running down the street. He makes it about half a block before tripping on a sewer and tumbling down again, sniffling and coughing away his tears. After one final push up, he looks over his shoulder, realizes we aren't coming after him, and starts walking.

"That was excessive," I say.

Brian swipes his hands up and down his sleeves and the front of his shirt, wiping leaves and grass clippings off his clothes. "No shit," he says. "Who the fuck has a house paintballed?"

I want to tell him that it was the tackling of the kid, the balled-up fists full of shirt, and the Batman yelling that was excessive, but he wouldn't care. Hell, it's not like he's wrong, either. Who *does* find an arsenal of high schoolers to shoot up a place with paintballs? Better yet, why would they hire an idiot like Henry?

My phone rings again, and Brian rolls his eyes. I swipe my thumb across the screen without looking at it and press the phone to my face. "Look, I really can't—"

"Jack," comes a voice, but it isn't Lauren. It's Rob, my company's CEO. "Long time no see. You have a minute?"

SIXTEEN

I've just finished packing my bags when Beth and Kenny get home.

"Jack? Brian? You guys all right?"

Brian, who's been washing paint off his face for the better part of half an hour, yells back at them. "S.A.M.," he says. Apparently, we're at the point now where that's all that's needed.

Rob asked me if I can come in first thing tomorrow to discuss the Director of Strategic Initiatives gig. He reminded me that we "haven't stayed connected" and that it's been over a week since we've talked, and all I can think about is how that means it's been over a week since I found out Mark died. Nevertheless, I told him I'd be there, because that's what you do when your CEO asks you to come in and discuss your new promotion.

I'm hit with momentary panic from time to time, worrying that what Lauren suggested—that by coming here, I'd screw it all up—is true, then remember to slow down. Breathe. Rob was cool with this, and he hasn't reached out before today.

I grab a couple shirts off the floor and sniff them to see if they need washed. They smell good enough, but one is covered in grass stains from our night at the park, and the other has a fading yellow stain near the collar that looks like beer, so I stuff both in my bag, zip it up, and throw it over my shoulder. Mark's place doesn't have a washer or dryer, so even if this talk with Rob doesn't go well, at least I can do some laundry while I'm home.

Worst-case scenario, I guess there's a small victory in that.

I start to walk upstairs, then pause and turn around. The basement's as dingy as ever. Light creeps in from the two windows near the ceiling and shines across the room in fat stripes that make it look like a prison cell. In between them are clothes, sheets, empty beer cans, a few half-packed boxes, and our laser tag equipment. As much as the grossness of it makes my stomach churn, I'm sad to leave it. My bed's more comfortable, sure, and Lauren would never let the house turn into this, but this place, the posters, the grossness, the behemoth of a tube TV, it feels like home.

This is a strange feeling, liking life in Lafayette, so I shake it out of my head, turn back around, and walk upstairs. When I get there, Brian, Kenny, and Beth are all in the kitchen, and they turn to look at me as if they coordinated the movement. Their eyes are wide, and a nervous lump develops in my throat, making me suddenly feel like I'm about to be interrogated.

And, of course, the questions come.

"What happened to your neck?" Kenny asks.

"What are you doing?" Beth follows.

I hold my fingers to where the paintball smacked me. I'd forgotten I was hit. The skin's warm, and touching it starts a new trickle of aches. "S.A.M.," I tell them. "And, I have to go."

"We're going with," Brian says. He does this the way he does everything, matter-of-factly, like he's Captain America or Cyclops or maybe even the President of the United States.

The room goes silent. Kenny shrugs and leans back against

the counter. Beth's mouth hangs open, and her eyes dart from Brian to me, and back to Brian, before she sets her purse down and folds her arms across her chest.

"What the hell is going on?" she asks. Her face is red, and I can't tell if she's angry, worried, or both. "And why's the house covered in paint?"

I start to speak, but before I can, Brian lifts his hand, hushing me and making me feel like a kid in trouble at school. "S.A.M. came and paintballed the house. Kids led by that Henry guy. We tried to get information out of them, but we couldn't. Then Jack here got a call from his CEO about some promotion he's gotten, so he has to go back to Louisville, and we're going with him."

"Seriously?" Kenny asks. I can't tell if he's talking about the paintballing or the promotion. "Congratulations."

I force a smile, wishing he would have been surprised about the paintballing and not my ability to move up the corporate ladder. "Thanks."

"We can't just leave," Beth says. "We have things to do."

Brian grins, as if he's been waiting for her to argue this. "We're ahead of schedule."

"That doesn't matter," she says.

"It does, though, because we were supposed to take things to Goodwill tomorrow, which we've already done, and the movers aren't coming to pick up some of the furniture until Friday. So, basically, we can run down to Louisville today, Jack can do his thing tomorrow, we can celebrate his first achievement as an adult tomorrow night, and we can come back Friday morning."

Beth's eyes narrow as she attempts to come up with a counterargument.

"I really can go by myself," I say.

"Shut up," Brian says. "You ran away to Louisville once

and didn't come back for years. God knows how long you'll be gone this time."

As if this is all it takes, Beth nods. "Okay," she says. "But we have to be back on Friday."

I swallow the lump in my throat. Louisville's been, well, *my* place for years. It's where I went to get away from this, where I went to start over. To bring everyone else there—these people, especially—seems sacrilegious, weird, like two parts of my life that shouldn't be together are colliding and there's nothing I can do to stop them.

"Mark hated that you left," Beth says. "The least I can do is make sure you don't do it again. Plus, you need someone to celebrate this promotion with, right?" She smiles, a full thing, lips spread, teeth shining, eyes wide. Brian's smiling, too, leaning against the wall, probably reveling in how another plan of his has fallen into place. And Kenny, he's not smiling, but he looks happy enough, and it hits me that for the first time in years, I have these people who care, these people who support me and want to tackle life with me. This isn't like back then, when I screwed up and wanted to run away. That wasn't them at all—it was me.

This isn't a jab at anyone or anything in Louisville, but these people know me. They know my mistakes, my strengths, the embarrassing bits of my life that not everyone does, and despite the bad, they care. They want to ride along. And it's that—the friendship, the camaraderie, the interest in something that means nothing to them—that means everything to me. I can show them my life, the one I've built with Lauren, the one I shouldn't have shut them out of. And maybe, just maybe, that isn't so bad after all.

Before I can say anything, I realize that I'm smiling as well. And to them, at least, it seems like that's enough.

SEVENTEEN

Lauren's car sits in front of our house. This shouldn't mean anything, but Lauren always drives herself to work, and that's where she's supposed to be. I could call her and check, but that doesn't matter because she's not there. She's here. Her car is, at least, because we're parked behind it. At first, I thought it was another green Jeep, then I realized that there aren't many people who drive green Jeeps. To make matters worse, there are even fewer people who drive green Jeeps with a basset hound sticker on the rear windshield.

The Tesla is running but silent. Brian insisted we all take it, because I guess that's what you do when you own a Tesla. The whole ride was silent. Brian attempted a game at one point, asking us to take turns finding consecutive letters of the alphabet on billboards, license plates, and road signs, but, after three rounds, we fell quiet again. In my attempt to avoid worrying about whatever Rob wants to discuss, I found it easier to stare out at the flatness of Indiana and the cornfields that stretch into oblivion.

Brian taps his thumbs on the steering wheel. "Maybe her car's broken down?"

"Her car never breaks down," I say, staring at the basset hound sticker. It's not that I think Brian's wrong. She could have gotten a ride or even taken an Uber, but, given the week-long game of phone tag we've been playing, it feels wrong, like something's turned on its head since I left.

"Are we going in?" Kenny asks.

"Yeah," I say. "Sorry."

As soon as the car door shuts, Jabba's baritone bark erupts from the backyard. It's only a matter of seconds before he runs up to the corner of the fence, wagging his white-tipped tail. His eyes are as wide as a basset's can be, excited, and his barks turn into low, grumbling howls that announce to the neighborhood that I'm home.

"You got a dog?" Brian asks.

"I did," I tell him. "Let me check with her before we barge in. I thought the place would be empty."

I thought about bringing Jack along, to introduce him to Jabba and all, but the logistics didn't work out. I don't have a litter box here—I don't have anything a cat needs, really—and I figured it wasn't worth the risk of something going wrong. Plus, once I get around to telling her, Lauren will probably pull up a few blogs preaching how to best integrate a dog and cat in a single household.

The three of them nod. Beth walks up to the fence to pet Jabba, and Brian and Kenny get back into the car, waiting as I walk up to the house. I reach into my pocket to grab my keys, then stop. I pause for a few seconds, running my fingers up and down the rivets, then leave them where they are and grab the doorknob. To my surprise—or maybe not at this point—it twists.

The house is just as I remember it, and it's as much of a contrast to Mark's as I could imagine. Our photo collage hangs above the couch, each frame polished, clean, and highlighting dozens of smiling versions of Lauren and me glistening beneath glass. The walls are white, practically shining in the little bit of sun coming in the windows. Everything from the orange chevron rug to the IKEA sectional is exactly as I left it, as if it's all just been waiting on me to return.

There's moaning, the squeak of a bed, and the rest comes into focus. Lauren's bra slung over one of the chairs at the dining room table. A pair of slacks wadded up at the foot of the chalk board wall, which still reads, *the grass is greener where you water it. xoxoxo.* I follow these things back to the spare room—the red blouse Lauren wore on our first dinner in Louisville, the undershirt of some guy I'm only assuming is better looking than me—where I find my girlfriend, naked, straddling someone who isn't me. Her dark hair runs down her back next to the small eyes of Dr. T.J. Eckleburg that she has tattooed on her right shoulder. I held her hand when she got that tattoo. I even read *Gatsby* to her on the ride to the parlor to calm her down. When the needle first hit her shoulder, she squeezed my hand so hard that her nails left little white half-moons imprinted in the side of my palm.

I want to say something because you're supposed to say something in these situations, but the words don't come together. It's like they're floating around my brain, coming close to falling into sentences, only to drift away or dissolve as they get near one another. It doesn't matter, though, because when Lauren moans and says his name—Jeff—she shakes her head to get some of her hair out of her face and catches a glimpse of me. When she does, the bed erupts in a tangle of screams and blankets as she and Jeff attempt to cover up. She says my name, but it's not like she said his. His name was a breath, like when you sink into the couch at the end of a long day. My name, it's a sharp, exhausting thing that comes out more like a bark or when you stub your toe.

I want to yell or punch a hole in the wall or throw Jeff through the window, but all I can do is run my fingers across the spot on my forehead where Mark hit me with a soda can when he found out about Beth and me. I picture him lunging at me from across the couch, spitting my name while Beth holds him back and begs him not to, and Beth, staring at me, her blue eyes glistening as they fill with tears and she tells me to get out. I remember not knowing what to do, just knowing that I wanted to do something, so I listened to her and left.

And just like then, I leave. Lauren's crying, and Jeff's saying something, but it's all muffled, like I've stuffed my head in a pillow, and I follow the trail of discarded clothes all the way back to the living room, where Brian, Kenny, and Beth are waiting for me. They couldn't look more different. Brian's face is as calm as ever, and, for a second, I wonder if this is how he looks when someone comes into the ER with a broken leg or a gunshot wound. Kenny's staring at the ground, hands stuffed in his pockets, probably wishing he never came here. Beth's biting her lower lip, and her eyes are glazed over like they were all those years ago.

Brian sighs, a heavy thing that makes his shoulders sag. I half expect a joke, but he puts an arm around my shoulder and pulls me close.

"There are some nice hotels downtown," I tell him. "I don't think this is going to work out."

EIGHTEEN

I'm sitting in the lobby of the executive annex at Confluence Training Solutions, slumped into the same chair where I sat a few years ago when I first interviewed for the job. The walls were white then, but they're yellow now. They shine in a way that makes the front of my head throb, and I'm half convinced I'd be better off curling into a ball on the floor and dying.

After leaving my house yesterday, Brian booked us all a couple rooms at the Marriott downtown. He also bought a bottle of bourbon, the effects of which are lingering in my body, causing the backs of my eyes to ache as I wish away my hangover. We stayed up talking about Lafayette and the things we have to get done before the funeral. We also talked about Mark, about getting Chinese food together, watching the *Spider-Man* trilogy in eight-hour-long marathons, and staying up until 4:00 a.m. trying to figure out why Spider-Man had to build web-shooters in the original comics, only to have organic ones in the movies. We didn't talk about Lauren, though. That stayed quiet, a taboo thing we apparently went through together and willed out of existence.

And now I'm here, staring at Confluence's bright primary-colored walls, completely unprepared for what might be the biggest meeting of my professional life. Whatever Lauren did, I've decided to box it up and store it in the back of my head until this is over. There's the occasional snippet, though—the sound of her saying Jeff's name, the way her hair fell over her tattoo—that creeps up, forcing me to swallow it all back down. I think about all the times she couldn't talk, and I wonder if she was screwing him then too.

If you can't tell, I'm not very good at this boxing it up and storing it in the back of my head thing.

Linda, Rob's receptionist, is sitting behind her desk. Her gray-streaked hair falls to about her shoulders, and her bangs are cut straight across her forehead. Linda didn't have bangs when I saw her a couple weeks ago, so I make a note to compliment her on them before I go in.

"You know," Linda says, not looking up from her computer, "I was starting to wonder if we'd ever hear from you."

The sound of her fingers tapping the keyboard pierces my head. It's a sound I've never thought of before, but somehow, in the way hangovers screw with you, it's all I can focus on.

"Yeah," I say, wincing. "It's been a weird week."

She smiles, still staring at her screen.

"I like your haircut," I tell her. "The bangs are nice."

The tapping stops, and Linda looks up. Her lips bunch to one side, as if she's thinking about how to tell me just how stupid I am. "It's been about a year," she says. "But thank you."

"Oh. Sorry."

There are a few seconds of silence as we try to figure out where else we can take our conversation. Before we come to a conclusion, though, Linda's phone rings, and, for a second, I think my head's going to explode. She picks it up, mutters a couple "uh-huhs," then hangs up.

"Rob's ready to see you," she says.

My stomach twists, giving me the sudden urge to throw up. The first time Rob and I talked, I was at work. I didn't have time to dwell on it. This time, though, I've had time for it to stew, for every terrible possibility to come to the surface and imprint itself in my mind. Maybe he's changed his mind. Maybe Amanda talked him out of it. Maybe he knows I'm such an idiot that my girlfriend's fucking another guy.

When I get to Rob's office, he's wearing running shorts and a neon tank top. A crumpled sweat band lays on his desk in a heap, and next to it is a small box, which I immediately recognize as my belongings, including (but not limited to):

1. A Spider-Man bobblehead
2. Three years' worth of service anniversary certificates
3. A toothbrush (in packaging)
4. A copy of Ernest Cline's *Ready Player One*

I begin to wonder just what's happening. Maybe Rob doesn't want to discuss the promotion at all. Maybe I'm being straight-up fired. Maybe this was all a ploy to get me to come down. Maybe Amanda's sitting at her desk cackling, her round cheeks bright red from the joy of finally getting rid of me.

"Jack," he says, his voice as energetic as ever. "So glad you're here. How was your week with the boys?"

"It wasn't quite that." I narrow my eyes and scan the room for a hint of what's going on. "One of the boys is dead."

Rob leans back in his chair. "Sorry about that—forgot about him altogether. How was the funeral?"

"Haven't been yet."

Anyone else would have dropped it by now, but Rob isn't what I'd call a people person. He can talk to people in the sense that he has words and knows how to use them, but understanding the nuances of what people say and how to respond to them is a different issue altogether. "What have you been up to, then?"

A few memories montage through my brain. Laser tag at Riehle Park. Sorting comics with Jack. Talking with Beth at Starbucks.

"I don't really know. Just being home, I guess."

"Well, we're glad to have you back. I want to talk about the job, though."

I want to swallow, but there's nothing there. My mouth is dry, like someone suddenly stuffed a fan in it and turned it all the way up.

"Director of Strategic Initiatives," he says, falling back into his leather chair. It squeaks against the skin on the back of his thighs, and suddenly, I'm thinking about Lauren and the skin she showed Jeff. About the sex they had.

"We talked about it before you left," he adds.

I shake my head, hoping that doing so will bring everything into focus. "I'm thrilled for it, but I guess I'm a little confused. Why's my stuff in here?"

Rob starts to smile, then freezes. "I had your cube cleaned out while we looked for an office for you. Unfortunately, though, we're going to have to rescind the offer."

I choke back the vomit or nerves or whatever it is that suddenly wants to come up. "What?"

"We've been trying to get a hold of you all week. A client of yours had a question about a sexual harassment training you were developing for him, and no one was able to answer it except for you—looks like the client notes were missing. Email and phone have been silent on your front despite our attempts to get in touch. As much as I think you have the right personality for the job, I need someone a little more reliable."

I pull my phone out of my back pocket. "I haven't gotten anything," I say, swiping through apps until I get to my mail.

"I don't have any notifications," I add when I arrive at my inbox. Only my work account isn't there. I stare at the screen, empty of words, and shake my phone a couple times as if doing so will make the account pop back up. "I-I don't know what happened. My email's not on my phone anymore."

Rob looks down and nods. "You're welcome to stay in your old position if you'd like. I just don't think an advancement is the best idea for you right now."

"I swear it wasn't me," I tell him, swiping to my settings in hopes of a lifeline. I scramble to come up with an explanation, flipping through everything that could have made this happen. "This wasn't on purpose. These people have been out to get me. They paintballed me and called the cops and covered my car in toilet paper, and something must have just—"

"That sounds tough," Rob says, still nodding. "I'm sorry you're going through that. I need to know if you'd like to remain in your current position, though. We'd need you back first thing tomorrow."

I clench my jaw and take in a breath, picturing everything back home. Kenny's food truck at Digbee Plaza. Beth's smile at the glitter bomb. Brian's Batman voice when he tackled the paintballer. Behind all of them, though, is the thick, lingering disappointment in the back of my head that Lauren was right all along, that I'd screw this up if I went home. That I'd screw everything up.

"Is that really it?"

"Yeah," he says. "I'm sorry, Jack."

I want to say yes, to grab the shitty life preserver he's thrown my way and get to shore, but I can't. I can't work for Amanda again, can't go back to that after thinking I'd worked my way out. Can't face Lauren with the news that I've blown it again. There's also my life back in Lafayette. Brian, Beth, Kenny—Mark. Everything I've thrown so much toward this last week. And, whether it was for good or not, the energy's there. The time is spent.

"I think I'm moving," I say. Rob's eyes widen, and my jaw drops.

This idea's come out of nowhere.

"Where?"

"Back home. To Lafayette."

"I guess that's your decision, then," he says. He pushes his chair back from his desk, then stands up, his skin squeaking against the leather again. Without breaking eye contact, he walks around it and up to me, and he hugs me. He's still nodding, wiping sweat onto my shoulder, and I pat him on the back a couple times, hoping it'll make him stop.

"Thanks for everything you've done at Confluence, Jack. Good luck back home."

As soon as I step out the front door, I exhale. The chilly downtown air hits me all at once, and I'm forced to recognize the beads of sweat resting in my hairline, the moistness of Rob's post-workout filth on my shirt, the goosebumps traveling up and down my arms. I quit my job. Apparently, I'm moving.

"Jack!"

Beth is smiling. Her pale skin shines against the red brick of the wall behind her. Her hair is down, and she's wearing the same red flannel she wore the day I got back to Lafayette. A couple golden strands cling to it near her right shoulder, but she either doesn't notice them or doesn't care. It only takes her eyes a couple seconds to notice the box of belongings under my arm, though, the bat signal of a corporate walk of shame, and her smile disappears.

She types out a quick message on her phone, then stuffs it in her purse and walks up to me, stopping close enough that, if we both leaned in, we could kiss.

"Hey," I say.

"What happened? I just texted the guys—they were excited to hear how it went."

"They rescinded the offer," I tell her. "I guess they'd been trying to get a hold of me, and I missed it. Said they needed someone more reliable."

She tilts her head. "You want to talk about it?"

I start to answer, but my phone rings. Unknown Caller.

"One second," I tell her, swiping across the screen. "Hello?"

"Jack Dotson," comes a voice. It's low, muffled, almost robotic, reminding me of a Storm Trooper. "Do you wish you would have listened to us yet?"

My fingers grip the phone. "Who is this?"

"You have an opportunity to stay away now. Forget the funeral, and this can all end."

Click.

NINETEEN

I'm standing in line to get into Paul's Bar and Ranch, or PBR, a place that has nothing to do with the beer and everything to do with professional bull riding (and Paul, I guess, whoever the hell he is). Brian insisted we come here to talk through S.A.M.'s latest act. I suggested a handful of quiet places instead—a little brewery near downtown and a dive bar near the University of Louisville—but he saw reviews of PBR on Google and couldn't look back. Not good reviews, mind you. It has two and a half stars, but the promises of assless chaps, country music, and, of course, bull riding, were too hard for him to turn down.

I thought about telling Brian no, that I didn't want to go out, but he would have pitched a fit. I'm not even sure at this point that I want to figure out who S.A.M. is. In the hours since I walked out of Confluence for the last time, all I've been able to think about is how Lauren warned me that this might happen, how, even though I had this golden opportunity to go home and do right by Mark, I also had an opportunity to advance my career and, in hindsight, save my relationship. I've spent my afternoon running through what-ifs one after the other, picturing things from a corner office to nice suits to dinners at fancy restaurants with Lauren, but I'm always left with the same emptiness that those opportunities are gone. That they're what-ifs for a reason, and they exist because I screwed up.

PBR is one of a slew of bars on 3rd Street Express! (their exclamation, not mine), a block that's been converted from being functional to being filled with trashy bars where tourists and early twenty-somethings can get hammered and spend a lot of money doing it. There's PBR, the country bar; 4th & Inches, the sports bar; Whiskey Neat, your standard Kentucky bourbon lounge; and a confusing mix of restaurants such as Applebee's and Guy Fieri's Smokehouse. We could have gone to any of these, but it really doesn't matter. 3rd Street Express! is garbage.

We're all here, though, ready to knock one back and get to the bottom of whatever's blown up since I came home. Brian's put on a flannel shirt he bought at Goodwill in an attempt to look like, as he put it, "something out of a Rascal Flatts music video." It's brown and blue and baggy on the arms while tight around his waist, making him look more like a soccer dad than a country boy. Beth's wearing the same flannel from earlier, though it isn't odd or out of place like Brian's.

Kenny, though, is wasted, wearing his blue Who Gives a Crepe? T-shirt, complete with a We do! on the back. When Beth and I got back to the Marriott earlier, we found him slumped against the hotel bar talking with some business-woman who looked desperate to get away. Brian told us he'd gone down there to make a few calls and order some things he needed for the truck, but by the time we arrived, it didn't look like he'd done anything but drink. His eyes were heavy, and his body had practically melted into the bar as if it were the only thing keeping him up. Fortunate for us, he sobered up a little before we left and is (fingers crossed) in good enough shape to get into the bar.

It takes us half an hour to get to the front of the line, and when we do, Brian pays our covers and we step inside. The walls of the place are a light wood, covered with a collection of cow skulls and barrel heads with "PBR" branded into them. It's dark save for the lights behind the bar and the neon beer signs sprinkled throughout, and people are packed in tight, bumping shoulders while they attempt what I can only assume is conversation. Brian leads the way through this, parting the crowd using some skill set unknown to me, until we get to the bar.

Brian's lips move, but I can't hear what he says. I do know, though, that he's not asking any of us what we want to drink. The bartender points back toward the shelves of bourbon behind him, and Brian nods and pulls out his wallet, sliding a few bills across it. The bartender's a young guy with a narrow, carefully shaved line of hair across his jawline and tribal tattoos creeping out of the neck of his shirt, and he looks like he could kill us if he wanted to. Only he's smiling, grabbing a bottle of bourbon, and pouring it into four rocks glasses, which he hands to Brian, who hands them back to Beth, who hands the remainders to Kenny, and then, finally, me.

Brian turns around and mouths something, but the hum of people chattering and the boom of country music obliterate his words before they can get to me. I shrug, and he mouths it again, and I shrug again, until he finally rolls his eyes and takes two steps in my direction.

"Where's the bull?" he shouts.

I want to tell him I don't know, but the unfortunate reality is that I've been here before. Lauren's coworkers come here for drinks sometimes, and, on occasion or two, I've been dragged along. I point over Brian's shoulder, toward a turn in the wall that leads to the other side of the bar, and he sets off again, waving for us to follow. Kenny does, stumbling a little, and I turn to Beth, who nods for me to lead the way.

I've only made it a couple steps before a hand wraps around my forearm. The fingers are cool against my skin, and they slide down it until they're in mine, intertwined and tight.

I turn around to find Beth looking up at me. "Don't lose me," she mouths.

My first thought is to let go, but I don't want to. Her palm is soft, and her fingers fit in between mine like they were meant to be there all along. I think to ask her what she's doing. She couldn't hear me if I did, though, and to be honest, I'm not sure I want to do that, either. After a day like today, it feels good to be held.

When we turn the corner, the room brightens. It's quieter here, the sound more manageable. In the middle of it is the bull, shining in a couple spotlights and surrounded by a sea of padding for everyone who gets thrown off. About ten feet out from every side is a barrier to keep people away, and, against the far wall is a raised line of big, round, black leather booths that my brother can't stop staring at. Above each is a picture of a man I assume is important. They're all in bright gold frames, polished with name plates below them and lights above them.

"What are we doing?" I shout.

Brian and Kenny turn around, and their eyes go directly to my hand, still holding Beth's. I let go, suddenly aware that they might not be as casual about this as I am, but it's too late. Kenny's eyes narrow, and his cheeks redden.

"I got us one of those booths," Brian says, hiking a thumb over his shoulder. "The Gary Shoulders one, whatever that means. You can look out over the bull and laugh at all the idiots trying to ride it."

Beth raises an eyebrow. "How much did that cost?"

Kenny murmurs something I can't hear.

"Don't worry about it," Brian says. "Figured it would be quieter up there anyway."

"The places I suggested were quiet," I say.

Brian shrugs.

We make our way around the bull and through the rest of the crowd until we get to a small set of stairs being manned by a security guard. Brian shows him a card, either an ID or something they gave him at the bar, and the guard lifts a chain and lets us pass. Brian walks past a few booths, then takes a couple steps past the Gary Shoulders one and points into it with his arms, looking more like a butler than a doctor. Above him, Gary Shoulders' portrait looks over the crowd. He's wearing a white cowboy hat and a blue shirt with thick white vertical stripes. He's not smiling, though. He's attempting it, I think, but his mouth just hangs open, curling barely upward at the corners.

Brian slides into the booth, followed by Beth. I start to follow her, but a hand comes down on my shoulder, fingers clamping into my collar bone.

"What was that?" Kenny spits. He sounds sinister, threatening.

I open my mouth to speak, but before I can, he lets go and slaps me on the back. "Forget it," he says, and I stumble into the booth. I slide up next to Beth, who smiles. In the middle of the table sits a bucket with a bottle of champagne.

Brian grins, lips spread ear to ear. He holds up his glass of whiskey, and everyone else does the same. "To showing these fuckers what's up," he says, and we clank our glasses and drink.

I set mine down and crack a smile of my own, but I don't know why. Between Kenny's attitude, the crowd, and the music, I never would have imagined myself enjoying something like this, but here I am. "Thanks," I say, and I realize that I don't have to yell anymore. "For helping," I add. "You guys are good friends."

Brian grabs the bottle of champagne out of the middle of the table. He pops the cork, which bounces off the ceiling and back down, and Beth jumps. Brian laughs at this and pours five glasses, handing us each one and setting another at the end of the table. I stare at it for a moment, absorbed in the bubbles making their way to the top and disappearing, until I realize who it's for.

"He wouldn't have wanted these guys fucking with you," Brian says. "Figured he deserves a spot at the table."

Beth blinks, then smiles, adding nothing. Her eyes are glossed over, and for a second, I think she's going to cry. Instead, she nods. "So, what are we going to do?"

Below us, people clap as someone gets ready to mount the bull. The noise is a stark contrast to up here, where the awkward quiet hangs over us. Our eyes move from one set to the next, waiting for someone to step up, and it's starting to seem like no one will when Kenny finishes his champagne in one long chug and sets his glass on the table.

"What do you say, Jack?" he asks.

"I really don't know." I pull my phone out of my pocket and open my blocked contacts, which is full of an assortment of Confleunce numbers, then toss it on the table. I haven't taken much time to think about this. Paintballs and glitter bombs are one thing, but managing to get into my phone is some next level trickery that, between losing my girlfriend, my promotion, and essentially my life here, I haven't had time to wrap my head around. "Whoever it was managed to turn off my work email and block my company from reaching me. I don't know who the hell could pull that off."

Beth tilts her head to the side and bites her lower lip.

"We could go back to Henry," I say. "He's our closest in at this point, right?"

"But what if it's not him?" Kenny spits, nodding and pouring himself another glass.

Next to him, Brian stares at the emptying bottle. We make eye contact for a second, and he shrugs, apparently okay with letting this happen.

"We need more drinks," Brian says, squeezing out of the booth. Kenny rests his elbow on the table, cradling his head in the palm of his hand, and I can't help but feel like this is a bad idea. Before Brian goes back to the bar, though, he turns around and points at me. "Time to get the creative juices flowing, brochacho. Henry's not going to cut it. What are you drinking?"

My champagne glass, I realize, is empty. "I'm cool with whatever."

"Bullshit," he says. "You've had a shit day. How about a bucket of beer?"

"Okay, then," I tell him. "Great Flood?"

"What the fuck is that?"

"Local brewery."

Brian scrunches his lips to one side, and his head bobbles up and down as he thinks over my response. Then, without saying a word, he leaves.

"So," Kenny says, "maybe you ought to move on and get back to finding out who S.A.M. really is?"

I laugh, stopping myself before rolling my eyes. It's all spiraled so far out of control that I don't know what else to do. "How the hell am I supposed to figure that out?"

"Trace the call?" Beth says. "Seems like our best chance yet. Surely this guy's slipped up at some point."

Kenny snorts a laugh.

People start cheering around the bull again, and Beth leans forward, lips parted. Before she can say anything, though, there's a knock on the table. It's Brian, setting down two buckets of beer, and behind him are two waitresses, both carrying trays of shots. Those are set on the table, too, and

Brian hands the girls cash before grabbing a shot and sliding back into the booth.

"How did you do that so quickly?" Beth asks.

"You have to see this," he says, pointing to the bull. "These dudes are hammered."

Sure enough, two guys who look like they're twenty-one at most are walking around the bull, throwing their arms in the air to cheers from the crowd. They move in half-circles, back and forth in a couple laps, high-fiving folks who reach out. The security guard, watching from the gate, rolls his eyes and crosses his arms over his chest. He's a beast of a man with arms bigger than the younger guys' legs and narrow eyes that go from one drunk to the other. For a second, I wonder if this is why Gary Shoulders struggles to smile. Looking out at this all night, every night, I can't help but feel that yeah, smiling might be tough.

Kenny stares at me from across the table, nursing a Great Flood IPA that's probably stronger than he thinks it is, and I make a mental note to not go out with him when he's drunk like this. In all fairness, though, he was one of the sober ones when we were all in college, so I guess I owe him a few.

"I bet these fuckers they wouldn't last one minute," Brian says. He cranes his neck back and looks at my hand. "Where's your drink?"

"I got it," Beth says. She reaches across the table and grabs a shot in one hand and a beer in the other. "Take your pick."

"Give him both," Brian says.

I start to say something, but Beth shrugs and hands me the drinks.

Brian grabs another shot and lifts it up. "To these fuckers falling," he says. Apparently, tonight is more about toasts than sorting out this S.A.M. business after all.

"I have five hundred dollars on this," Brian says, grinning. His eyes are wide, excited.

I stop right as the alcohol hits my lips. "Five hundred?"

Brian reaches across the table and pushes my shot back toward my face. "Don't worry about me," he says. "I wouldn't do it if I couldn't afford it."

I take the shot. Fireball. It burns like I knew it would, caking my mouth in a cinnamon that's straight out of hell, and there's a sudden haziness in my head that tells me I probably ought to slow down. I cough, and Brian laughs.

"You're such an asshole sometimes," Beth says.

Brian shrugs. "They're the ones who came up with it," he says, nodding toward the bar. "Kenny," he adds, "you all right there?"

Kenny jumps, looking like he's been woken up. "Yeah. Sorry."

Below, both guys climb onto the bull. The one on the back has taken his shirt off, which he swings in circles above his head while he holds onto his friend's waist with his free hand. When their ride starts, he tosses the T-shirt to the crowd, which a few women claw at as if it's actually worth something. The bull moves back and forth, looking like a ship making its way across some easy waves, and I start to think that Brian's going to lose his money. It jerks forward after a couple slow ones, though, and the guys both slide toward the head. Beth gasps, and Brian laughs at her. As it gets faster, the guys' bodies rock back and forth on it like they're a couple of those inflatable tube men you see in front of furniture stores, jerking one way or another with no rhyme or reason.

Brian takes a long sip of a beer, a saison from Great Flood that I can't imagine him liking. He clutches it so tightly that the can's buckling in on itself.

"You're about to blow it," Beth says, smirking. She's leaning forward again, all smiles.

A crash comes from the center of the crowd, and the onlookers erupt in *ooos* and start spreading out. Beth puts a hand to her chest, and Brian throws his arms in the air, sending beer across the booth. Kenny, despite whatever's going on with him, has his hands to his mouth too, eyes wide as they look below, where both guys are lying next to the bull, one clutching his stomach, the other wiping at vomit running down the back of his head. Before they can get up, security grabs each of them around the arm before lifting them up and parting the crowd to take them God knows where.

The security guard opens the gate into the crowd, and I lose him, because next to it is Lauren. She's wearing a black blouse that ties close to her neck, and her dark hair is pulled back. She's with a redhead, probably someone from work, and they're laughing. I imagine them laughing at me. I can almost hear her voice in my head, telling whoever this is about the stupid face I made or about how I didn't have anything to say when I saw her having sex with Jeff. I try to tell myself that of course that isn't what they're laughing at, but I can't shake the thought.

"Hey," Brian says, slapping the table. "No, no, they owe me money!" Beth reaches across the table and grabs Brian's shoulder in an attempt to keep him from running after them. She erupts in laughter, putting all her weight into her pull in a way that sends her hair falling over her shoulders, and I think of nothing but her as a lioness, like we used to joke about when we were in college. Brian gives up and grabs another beer, this time one of the IPAs, off the table before sinking into his seat. Beth relaxes back into hers too, still laughing.

The noise lowers to a hum, like I've stuffed my face in between two pillows. I used to do that when I was a kid and scared at night, when I'd have a nightmare and didn't want to wake anyone up. All I can look at is Lauren, but it isn't her with her friend that I see. It's her on top of Jeff, naked, rocking back and forth. It's her head falling back and her hair spilling over her shoulders when she moans. It's the glimmer of pleasure in her eye for a fraction of a second before she realizes I'm there.

"Next round's on me," I say, and I wiggle my way around Kenny and scoot out of the booth.

Brian's voice comes from behind me, distant, like an echo. "We have plenty, dude."

"I can't have y'all come to Kentucky without showing you some good Kentucky bourbon." Truth is, I don't know good bourbon from bad. In the back of my head, Brian makes a joke about me saying "y'all," but before he can spit it out, I'm off through the crowd, my feet moving without thinking, making my way around everyone while Lauren laughs with her friend about Jeff and how stupid I looked when I saw them fucking.

I'm pulled out of my trance when a hand wraps around my arm again.

Beth.

"I'm sorry," she says.

"What?"

"I'm sorry," she repeats, a little louder. "About everything. About S.A.M. About that," she adds, nodding back toward the bull. "It was her, wasn't it?" The noise piles up on itself around us, people talking, music blaring, but here, it somehow seems quieter, as if being with Beth dissolves the sound just enough to make it bearable. Before I can put it all together, I kiss her, and she kisses me back, her mouth over mine, her tongue on mine, and, for a second, I forget about Kenny and Lauren and the bull riders and everything else that's happened.

When it ends, Beth's eyes widen, and her jaw drops. She starts to say something but abandons it and looks down. "Let's just get you your bourbon."

"I'm sorry," I tell her. I didn't plan on saying this, but they're the first words that come to mind. "I don't know what—"

"Don't worry about it," she says, patting me on the back. Without another word, we start making our way back through the crowd, her arm around mine like it's an everyday thing. I try to find Lauren, but she's gone, having disappeared into the crowd. Beth gets us the attention of the bartender, this one not tattooed but probably still capable of kicking my ass, and who, probably because of Beth's presence, is more than patient with my lack of knowledge about bourbon. I go with his recommendation, and he pours us another round for the table. Beth offers to carry a couple of them. I think to keep them to myself so that she'll be free to grab my arm again, but, judging by her reaction to the kiss, I'm not sure what to do. Playing it safe, it seems, is probably my best bet.

When we get back, Kenny stands up. "That was cute."

In the booth, Brian looks up, but Kenny doesn't seem to notice, turning toward Beth instead. "What was that?" He stumbles a little, almost falling onto the table, then rights himself by resting his hand on it.

"Calm it down," Brian says. "What's going on?"

Beth sets the whiskey on the table. "Jack and I kissed. It was nothing. It was a stupid, drunk mistake."

"Like the stupid, drunk fuck?" Kenny spits. Beth opens her mouth to speak, but Kenny holds up a hand to hush her. "Seriously? After everything that's happened?"

"Stop it," Beth says.

"At what point does he stop getting a free pass for this shit?" Kenny snaps, pointing a finger in my face. "He fucked you," he yells, turning back toward Beth. "Literally and figuratively, and we all act like it's okay because he's finally back home and we're all hanging out again, but you know what? It's not. Because nobody's talking about how Mark started drinking after that, about how the only thing he had left was his shitty job at King's. Nobody talks about how he lost his driver's license and ended up getting hit by a fucking truck all because his best fucking friend fucked his girlfriend and ran away to Louisville so he wouldn't have to deal with it."

Brian puts a hand on Kenny's shoulder, and he shakes it away.

"And now," Kenny adds, "a little bit of karma hits him in the balls and whatever her name is starts sleeping around behind his back, so he decides to just crawl right back on top of you."

I step toward him and hold out a hand. I don't know how doing this fixes anything. He's right, after all, but that doesn't mean he has to shove it down our throats here, where Lauren is, right after I've lost my job and my girlfriend and God knows what else.

"Calm down," I tell him. "We can talk about this when—"

"No," he says. "You ruined Mark, and now he's dead, all because—"

"Dude, quit." I twitch, thinking back to when I heard the news, the hours spent trying to figure out what happened. Getting derailed by S.A.M., only to hit dead end after dead end. None of this was supposed to happen. It wasn't supposed to go this way.

Kenny picks his beer up off the table and slurps another drink. "Quit what? He's dead, Jack. He's fucking dead, and you—"

I don't mean to punch him. It's just something that happens. There's a pain in my knuckles as they meet his cheekbone, and the skin on the middle one splits, sending a sharp, tingly wave down my finger. Kenny stumbles backwards, both hands going to his face, and falls over the table, sending beer and liquor to either side in a crash the whole bar turns to see. Beth and Brian jump away, shooting backward as if they're part of the glass shattering, and I'm stuck standing in the middle of it all like some sort of pillar to everything that's been fucked up.

A few seconds of quiet follow, but they feel like an eternity. There's the rumble of the crowd, and a groan or two of Kenny's as he rolls around on the floor, but, other than that, nothing. I expect Kenny to hop back up and fight—that's what they do in the movies, after all—but he doesn't. He just lays there in his Who Gives a Crepe? shirt, holding his hand to his face until Brian goes over to him and starts looking at it. Beth's staring at me, her arms at her side, her lips parted as she takes in long, slow breaths.

"Jack?" comes a voice from the crowd

Lauren's at the edge of the onlookers, hands clasped to her chest. Her eyes are wide, and I can see her lungs fill with each of her breaths, heavy things that move her whole head up and down. She bites her lower lip for a second, and I realize that I have no idea what she's thinking. Maybe she's thinking about us, about Jeff, or about how her ex-boyfriend just punched a guy in the face. This is uncharted territory for her, a far cry from the me she once had to talk down from a panic attack when we got stuck on the top of a Ferris Wheel. What it is, I have no idea. Hell, I don't even know what we are anymore. I don't have time to figure it out, either, because before I can say anything to her, security's grabbed my arms and twisted them behind my back. They start dragging me toward the door, and Lauren takes half a step forward before pausing and staying put. I laugh, not knowing what else to do, and trudge my feet along with the guards' steps.

TWENTY

K enny and I haven't talked for two days. He tried on the way home, but I yelled at him until he stopped.

We got a talking to after getting kicked out of the bar. Security said I was lucky the cops weren't called. Brian tried to take us back to the hotel so we could calm down, and we did for a while, until 2:00 a.m. hit and I realized I'd had enough, that I was screwed no matter where I went and figured I was better off back in Lafayette. I was sober enough at that point, so I woke everyone up, made them pack their bags, and started driving north.

We got home at 5:00 a.m. and went to our respective rooms. It's 7:00 a.m. on Saturday now, and Beth and I are standing in the kitchen, sipping coffee, while Kenny and Brian sleep it off. I should have something to say to her—she didn't do anything wrong, after all—but every time I try to talk, my throat dries and tightens and I can't get any words to come out. It's like they're stuck in the memories of everything Kenny said about us fucking and Mark being dead, but they shouldn't be. She didn't do anything.

"You make good coffee," I tell her.

She takes a sip from her mug. "Thanks," she says. She forces a smile, a closed-lip thing that almost makes her look less enthusiastic than she probably is. "It's Folgers."

"Oh," I say. Then, without thinking, "I'm sorry."

She raises her eyebrows.

"About the other night. I shouldn't have kissed you. I don't know what got into me."

She doesn't say anything. Her eyes lock on mine, though, bright blue with a faint green circle around them, and I can't look away. We've never talked about us or what happened that night we slept together, and our kiss feels like the next chapter in whatever that was. Did she love me? Was she going to leave Mark for me, or was it a stupid drunk thing she did because she was pissed at her boyfriend?

"You should forgive Kenny," she says. "He's been through a lot."

I take a sip of coffee, then pause before swallowing it so I can't say anything stupid. Beth's face doesn't change. Her eyes focus on mine as tightly as ever, unblinking.

I swallow. "Not after that."

Beth sets her mug on the counter. She's wearing a massive blue sweater that swallows her torso. Her hands disappear up into the sleeves, and she crosses her arms across her chest underneath it. "Kenny would pick Mark up at the bars some-times," she says. "Mark had plenty of people he'd drink with, but nobody to drive him home. Sometimes, Mark seemed fine. Others, he'd be leaning on Kenny for support. Every time, though, Kenny said he was happy to do it."

I set my cup on the counter next to hers and stare at the floor tiles, and all I can think about are the drunk steps Mark might have taken across them. They're steps I never thought would have existed, but they were real nonetheless. I just wasn't here for them.

"I'm not trying to make you feel like an asshole," she adds.

"Just help you see that it wasn't easy on him, staying here. He saw a lot that you and your brother didn't, and I think it got the best of him the other night, so he blew up. It's not like you've never regretted something you did while you were drunk, right?"

Her eyes soften and narrow, and she cocks her head to the side.

"Was it a mistake to you?" I ask.

She closes her eyes for a second and takes in a breath. "This isn't really the time for that."

Before I can respond, Kenny pops into the kitchen doorway. He's wearing flannel pajama pants and another Who Gives A Crepe? shirt, and I'm starting to wonder if he owns anything different. His short hair is matted around his head in mismatched directions, and his cheeks are peppered with stubble. He looks like he hasn't slept for days.

He holds up an envelope. "You've got mail."

My first thought is that I shouldn't have mail because I don't live here. Then, it hits me, and my stomach ties itself into a knot.

S.A.M.

I hold my hand out, and Kenny sets the letter in it. It isn't addressed in chopped out magazine letters or anything like that. Just simple handwriting that I want to recognize but don't.

I rip open the end of the envelope. On the inside is a yellow piece of notebook paper, folded in thirds. I slowly pull the top third open, unsure of whether something's going to explode out of it. When I realize it's safe, I open the rest.

Jack Dotson,

It's become clear that you don't plan on leaving, so we'd like to discuss the terms of your presence at Mark's services over break-

*fast (our treat, don't worry). Meet us at Old Rupert's Diner at
9AM if you wish to attend.*

P.S. Bring the cat.

I reread it a couple times to make sure I'm understanding
that last bit correctly, then toss the envelope down on the table.

"They want to meet for breakfast," I say. "Today."

"You going?" Beth asks.

The yellow paper shines from the table like some sort of
shitty little star, calling me to it. "I think so," I tell her. "They
want to talk about the funeral."

Beth uncurls her arms from under her sweater and grabs
her coffee off the counter. "They can't stop you from going to
the funeral."

"They want me to bring Jack?" I don't mean for it to come
out as a question, but I haven't figured out how to swallow this
piece of information. "Can you even take a cat to a
restaurant?"

"Maybe you can say it's a service animal," Beth says.

Kenny nods. He's staring at the floor, though, like he's a
part of the conversation and not all at once. "It's not really
your problem," he says. "It's not like you wanted to bring the
cat. Whoever sent you this probably set it up so it's okay."

As if he knows we're talking about him, Jack patters into
kitchen. He stops next to Kenny and stretches his front two
paws forward, raising his ass in the air and pointing his ears
back. A couple seconds later, he's circling my ankles, so I pick
him up and scratch his neck. He purrs, a low thing, and throws
his head from side to side as he nuzzles up into my arm.

"I'm not going to take him," I say, scratching under Jack's
chin.

"Really?" Beth asks.

Kenny's staring at me now. The eye I punched is

surrounded by purple and brown. "You sure that's a good idea?"

"Fuck those guys," I say, still scratching Jack's neck. "Jack's mine."

Kenny's eye twitches. "You've barely paid attention to him since you got here."

"What?"

"Jack," he says. "He's been an afterthought. Did you even feed him before you left for Louisville?"

"I did," Beth says.

"It doesn't matter," I say, moving on to scratching behind Jack's ear. "He's my cat. We sorted this out the day I got here."

Kenny shrugs. "Your call," he says. "You want company?"

"Like backup?"

"Sure. I figure I owe you one."

I lean over to set Jack down, but he leaps out of my arms before I get him to the floor. He runs over the Beth, who shrugs as he starts circling her legs.

"Okay," I tell him.

"Cool," he says. "I'll drive." As he walks by, he slaps me on the shoulder, then leaves through the back door.

"Was that so hard?" Beth asks.

I work my way back through a handful of clips in my head. The spit trickling out of his mouth when he yelled at Beth and me. The cut on my knuckle after punching him in the face. The purple and brown ring around his eye. Then, a few more. Catching up at Stevie's Down Under when I first got to town. Huddling in the bushes, playing laser tag like a couple kids. Then, there's the wasted time with Mark. The years we could have had but didn't because I never put a foot forward and made an effort to make things right with him.

"I guess not," I say.

Beth smiles. Her eyes are wide, maybe a little teary, and I wonder if she's thinking the same thing as me. "Good luck."

TWENTY-ONE

We're parked outside of Old Rupert's Diner, staring at the front door. My brother and I used to come here after a night of drinking for the sort of greasy breakfasts that made hangovers go away. Now, all I can picture is the heartburn I'm sure to feel when I'm done eating one of those, so I tell myself that I'll take it easy and get a parfait instead.

Lauren would be proud, but I guess that doesn't matter anymore.

Old Rupert's is a two-story diner painted in thick orange-and-black stripes, making it look like some sort of pop-up Halloween store that never went away. There's a bright red Coca Cola sign on the corner and planters full of fat, orange flowers that, as far as I know, have never died. It looked like this in the '90s when my grandpa brought me here for my birthdays. And, as far as the photos tell, it looked like this in the '60s when my grandpa brought my dad here for his birthdays. It's as Lafayette as King's or Purdue or the ugly factory on the south side, the one with smokestacks pointing up like fat cigars on the skyline.

"You ever wonder what they called the place when Rupert was younger?" I ask.

"What?"

"It's called Old Rupert's Diner, but it's been open forever. What did they call it when he opened it? He wasn't old then."

Kenny blinks a couple times, and I picture his old style, the long, curly black hair he had when we were in college, fluttering in front of his eyes. "I think that's a you thing."

"Oh." I didn't anticipate being alone in this. "I guess that's fair."

He tries to smile, but it comes out slanted. "Either way, Rupert sold it off a year or so ago. You ready to go in?"

I nod.

We walk inside, and there aren't any spots available on account of the fact that the restaurant only seats thirty people at a tiny bar that snakes its way around the building. An older couple sips on their coffee toward the middle of the pack, though, and the small stack of cash tucked under the sugar tells me they're not going to order another. See, in the days of unlimited refills, Old Rupert's holds true to its roots and charges for every cup (at least, they did the last time I was here), something that's admirable when you're observing but a pain in the ass when you're drinking.

I lean over to Kenny. "You think they're here?"

"Who?"

"S.A.M."

"Oh, yeah," he says. "I don't know."

I scan the bar, looking for anyone suspicious. There's a young couple with a baby. It can't be them. S.A.M. wouldn't bring a baby. There are a few high schoolers, and I wonder if they know Henry. I make a mental note to keep an eye on them in case things go to shit.

The old couple finish off their coffee and leave, so we slide into their seats at the bar. I flip through what I can of the condiments—sugar, a stack of three of four different types of jam, a saltshaker that needs a scrubbing—while we wait for service, too nervous to look for S.A.M. and still unsure of what to say to Kenny. I'm staring at a packet of Splenda when a plastic menu slaps the side of my face. When I look up, Lisa, my ex, is staring at me from across the bar.

Lisa's short, so it isn't often that we're at eye level. She's also wearing an orange shirt and a brown apron, which makes her look more like a Thanksgiving decoration than a waitress. I want to tell her this but don't given that I've already been hit in the side of the head for, apparently, sitting down.

She smirks. "Didn't think I'd see you here."

"You," I say, and my mind goes red. "I should have fucking known."

Lisa's eyes widen, and her cheeks shine bright pink. She glances at Kenny, then back at me, but before I can say anything else, Kenny's hand claps down on my shoulder.

"Let's calm it down a minute," he says.

"Fuck that," I say, shaking his hand off me. The people on either side of us quiet down. All I can think of are the paintball welts, the glitter bomb, my meeting with Rob, Lauren fucking what's-his-name. "This bitch ruined my car, lost me my girlfriend, paintballed me—"

"It was me," he says, but I can't stop.

"She ruined everything when all I wanted was to come—"

"It was me," he repeats.

"I should have fucking known, man, the minute I saw her in Stevie's, that she'd pull something like this. You"—I say, pointing across the bar—"you goddamn piece of—"

"Jack," Kenny yells, grabbing my shoulder again and turning me toward him. "It was me. I'm S.A.M."

It's not until he says this that I notice the eyes of everyone blinking, the sudden quiet of it all. Not even silverware clattering against plates. What Kenny's said sinks in. That it's him. That he's S.A.M.

"What?"

"I'm S.A.M.," he says.

"Stop saying that. It reminds me of that fucking Sean Penn movie."

Kenny blinks, then shakes his head. "It's me." He exhales when he says this, and his shoulders slouch in on themselves. His eyes are empty for a few seconds as if he's studying a crumpled-up napkin on the floor, and he wobbles in his seat, swaying back and forth like a young tree in a rainstorm. For a second, I think he's going to pass out, but he takes in a deep breath and sits back up. "I'm behind it all," he says, suddenly sounding tired. "It was all me."

I turn to Lisa, whose arms are crossed in front of her chest. "Did you know about this?"

She glances at Kenny, then back at me.

"So that's a yes," I say. "She's in on this, isn't she?"

Kenny blinks a couple times, then nods.

"Can I at least have a cup of coffee?" I ask.

Lisa looks back, and I'm half-certain she wants to be out. With a couple full pots to greet her, though, she sighs. "Yeah."

I do my best to smile.

She turns and walks away, and I watch her as she goes, attempting to make sure she doesn't spit in my coffee or otherwise ruin my already shitty morning. A mom at the far end of the bar catches my gaze and shoots me a crooked look of disgust, and it hits me that I've caused a scene. Taking it all in, I'm fairly convinced that, despite my efforts, this city hates me and there's nothing I can do to change a damn thing about it.

"There's a lot to talk about," Kenny says. I focus on the eye I punched, still a little pink, surrounded by purple and brown splotches that look like some sort of shitty nebula. I want to punch the other one, give him a matching set and all, but there are questions I want answered. I would have expected so many people—Lisa, Henry, even the mailman—before Kenny. We used to crash at Mark's place together, hang out every weekend, sit outside of King's until Mark got off work. He was a part of everything we had, everything we'd been trying to rebuild, and none of it's true. He's just a dick.

"Like what?"

Kenny's eyes widen, and he leans back as if waiting for me to hit him again. "S.A.M.? Mark? All the shit that's been going on?"

Lisa sets my coffee on the bar.

I hike my thumb at Kenny. "It's on him, right?"

She looks at Kenny, who shrugs, then walks away.

"So, where do we start?" I ask. "Toilet paper? Glitter bomb? Mark dying?"

Kenny bites his lower lip, then tilts his head. "This goes back longer than that."

I genuinely have no idea what he's talking about.

"The end of the summer you slept with Beth," he says, "you packed up, moved to Louisville, and forgot everything. Your brother went off to do doctor things. Mark and I stayed here in Lafayette. I tried to hang out with him—you three were my friends, after all—but he wouldn't have it. I'd go over there, try to watch a movie, maybe play PS2 or something, and it was fine for a while. Then we'd have a beer or two. Eventually more. And granted, that was always a Dotson thing, but here Mark was, lonely out of his fucking mind, and he couldn't have cared less if I existed. He just wanted to get drunk and think about why you and Beth did it, why you'd betray him, why you'd run off. I tried to be a good friend and listen, but all it did was get worse."

I swallow, as if that will make me feel better. It doesn't.

"Beers turned into whiskey. Shit, one time, he bought a bottle of bourbon because he wondered if that's why you moved to Louisville. Whiskey turned into long nights, late mornings, and eventually, him getting fired. I tried to get him to cut back. Told his dad I would, that I'd help him get it under control. The only thing is, Mark didn't want to, and Beth didn't care what I had to say. It was like she didn't want to get too close to me, didn't want to risk making it seem like she was going to fuck another friend of Mark's, so it spiraled out of control until he got hit by a truck."

Kenny laughs, then grabs my cup of coffee, lifts it to his battered face, and takes a sip. I start to say something— anything to slow this down, really—but before I can, he's back at it. "You know, you've been saying he was 'pretty much crushed by a truck.' But the reality is that it hit him square on, crushed his rib cage and collapsed his lungs. That's how he died, dipshit, and you know the last thing he said to me? Two days before he died, he said he wished he could get back at you for what you did."

This is the punch to the gut, the blow that takes the air out. I open my mouth, not necessarily to speak, but Kenny holds up a finger. "I'm not done yet. Because the worst fucking thing about this is that you had the audacity to think you could waltz back into town and pick up where you left off, invalidating everything the rest of us went through while you hit the reset button on your life.

"I created S.A.M. to square things up for Mark, looped Lisa and Mark's dad into helping out, and came up with a handful of tricks to keep you busy while everything you built down in Louisville turned to—"

"You got my girlfriend to cheat on me?"

"Dude," he says, taking another sip of my coffee. "That was luck. Seems to me like she was already cheating on you."

"And my job?"

He shrugs. "Should have watched your phone instead of playing detective."

I expect him to look proud, to puff his shoulders and smirk and narrow his eyes, but there's none of that. He's hunched over in his barstool, one eye black, the other tired. He hasn't shaved in maybe a week, and his face looks like a sheet of sandpaper. There's a brightness to his eyes, though, maybe even a relief as he's spat this all out at me, and I don't know what to feel. The emotions sort of trip over each other at the finish line and all fall on top of one another, leaving me unsettled and unsure of what to do, so I take back the cup of coffee.

"I'm sorry you had to go through that, dude."

"What?"

I want to throw my coffee in his face, grab him by his stupid crepe shirt, shake him, scream at him, and beat the shit out of him. But every time I think to do it, all I can see is Mark shouting at me from across his couch, hate in his eyes, Beth holding him back. I see myself on Mark's back porch, waiting for an opportunity to step in and make it right. I see an alternate universe version of myself stopping him at Walmart and telling him with everything I have that I'm sorry, that what I did was wrong. And I can't help but feel that, in a way, I deserve this. That I'm not going to abandon a friend again.

"I'm sorry," I tell him. "I shouldn't have fucked you over like that."

Kenny grabs a sugar packet and fiddles with it, spinning it around in his fingers. His eyes are on the bar. Lisa's disappeared, serving a couple at the far end, though I know she's listening. The place has picked up again; people are back to their meals, sipping their coffee and picking at their toast and cleaning their plates. Between Kenny and me, it's silent, like nothing's gone according to plan. Because, at least as far as I can tell, it hasn't.

"Look," he says, finally looking up, "you can come to the funeral, but on one condition. You have to give Mark's dad the cat."

"Jack?"

He nods.

"No." I picture Kenny in the kitchen, the way his eye twitched when I said I wasn't bringing Jack here. "No fucking way."

He raises an eyebrow.

"That's my cat," I tell him. "He can't have it. After all you did to me—you, Lisa, him—I'm not giving him up."

"You're shitting me." Kenny wipes his hands down his face. When his fingers run down the bottom of his eyelids, they catch them, making him look like something out of a horror movie. "I get that you're having this moment, this epiphany that you're going to fix everything. But this isn't the way. It's not your cat."

"But it is," I tell him. "And it was your idea that I take him, so I couldn't care less if Mark's dad wants him."

"You weren't even sure you wanted him."

I shrug. "Things change."

"So you're going to start caring for him? Because you haven't done shit since you agreed to take him."

"Yeah," I say, shrugging, feeling like a teenager whose been caught sneaking in after curfew. "If it's that big of a deal, why did you suggest I take him in the first place?"

"I didn't know," Kenny says, slamming his fist on the bar. A few people turn toward us again. "Mark's dad didn't tell me he wanted the fucking cat. By the time I knew, I'd already told you he was yours."

The corners of my lips turn upward. I think to stop them, but I can't. "Seriously?"

"Fuck you."

"You went to all this trouble—S.A.M., the teepeeing, the glitter bomb—and you were too stupid to make sure no one wanted what you were giving away?"

I reach for the cup of coffee, but Kenny puts his hand down over the top of the mug.

"No," he says.

"It's my coffee. You offered to buy me breakfast in the letter you wrote and pretended to have delivered to the house we're sharing." Saying this aloud solidifies how dirty and fucked up this all makes me feel.

Kenny shakes his head. "I don't care," he says, but I've already wrapped my fingers around the handle. I pull, and he doesn't budge, causing a hot wave to splash up and run down the side of my hand. Whatever part of your brain tells you to shy away from burns stops working, and I pull again, but he pulls back.

"Give me the coffee," I say, tugging again.

"Give me the cat."

"You gave me the cat."

Kenny stops mid-tug, hand still on the mug. He tilts his head to the side and sticks his tongue out of the corner of his mouth, and I keep my fingers wrapped around the handle, pulling as much as he'll allow.

"Fine," he says. He lets go, and the sudden lack of tension sends me tumbling off my barstool. The coffee comes with me, spilling out of the mug and toward my face, and I try to avoid it, twisting my head to the side until my neck feels like it's about to snap. It doesn't help, though. The coffee comes at me like a drunk aunt coming in for a kiss at a family reunion, and it hits me like a hot slap to the face.

I hit the ground on my side, one arm tucked awkwardly underneath and behind me, and my right eye cracks against the tile step at the base of the wall. I groan and grit my teeth against the pain. Take in a breath. Exhale. I expect a gasp, maybe even a scream or two, but there's nothing. In my hand, though, is the handle of a now-shattered coffee mug.

I've only been on the floor for a couple seconds before two men wrap their hands around mine and drag me toward the exit. The faces of people staring come into focus the closer we get to the door—some angry, some amused—and a kid in a Spider-Man hoodie kicks me in the side for being a "bad guy" on my way, but, before it all settles, I'm through the air and onto the blacktop.

I stumble to a picnic table behind the building and collapse onto it. I want to drive home, but a headache has begun pounding against my temple, and I'm pretty sure the sun will render my eye useless as soon as I pull out of the lot. Instead, I lean back and close my eyes against the brightness, positioning my head in what shadows I can and crossing my fingers that this won't be visible for Mark's funeral, which I've decided I'm definitely attending.

I don't know how long I've been lying there when someone sits down next to me. I've either fallen asleep or passed out—is there a difference between those, really?—but someone's here, and I'm not so sure I'm in the state of mind (or body) to defend myself.

"Hey," the intruder says.

It's Lisa. Her face is fuzzy, masked by the grogginess of my nap, but the glow of her blonde hair and her pale skin shines through it all.

"You're all fucking crazy," I tell her. I want her to look down, red-faced and ashamed, but she doesn't.

"That went a little far," she says.

"There are some people who think starting a secret organization and torturing someone is more than 'a little far.'"

"Look," she says. She puts her hand on my arm. "It was an accident. I'm sorry. Kenny went overboard."

This could be, at least as far as I can remember, the first time Lisa has apologized to me since before we split. I drag my arm off from over my eyes and push myself up, squinting against the sun coming in over the top of the building.

"Oh shit," she says.

I lift my fingers to my face, only to be greeted by shots of pain and warmth radiating around my swollen eye. Tears well, and I almost want to throw up, but I don't because even though I haven't had a black eye before, I'm pretty sure crying and/or vomiting in front of your ex-girlfriend isn't the way you're supposed to respond to it.

"How bad is it?"

I never knew you could tell if someone is only staring at one of your eyes, but you can. She's wincing, too, though she's struggling for words whereas I'm struggling to see, and she tilts her head to the right like she's a doctor or dentist or someone otherwise qualified to do these things.

"It's not good."

"Like, how not good?"

"It's kind of like you have a doughnut around your eye. But not a good doughnut. More like one of those fruity ones, but after it's been run over and left out in the sun."

Something in me knows that it's only fitting that my face looks like shitty breakfast food after failing to acquire that food, but, as much as I'd like to, I'm not sure I can fully form the comparison at this point.

"I've only seen you twice since I came home," I say, "but you seem to be a lot shittier this time around than you have been in the past."

She doesn't say anything, as if something I've said resonated with her, but, through my years of experience, I know this isn't the case. As if to hammer the point home, she shrugs, feet dangling over the edge of the table like she's on a swing by a lake. "How are things going with Mark's stuff?"

"Not bad. Brian and I are staying in—"

Lisa rolls her eyes, and I see Lisas from years past doing the same thing. Senior year Lisa, rolling her eyes when I showed up to prom with a beard. College Lisa, rolling her eyes at me switching to an English major. Apartment-shopping Lisa, rolling her eyes whenever I suggested something that didn't fit her aesthetic.

"Do you remember when we were shopping for our first apartment together?" she says, as if reading my mind.

I don't like where this is going.

"Yes."

"You wasted so much time trying to find one you thought was a good 'freshman year' apartment. Nothing was just right for you, though, and it sucked because your obsession with this bullshit idea you'd come up with made nothing worthwhile. It worked out for the best, but Jesus Christ. You were awful."

I'm cornered.

"You can't do that here," she says. "Sometimes, life isn't about having everything you wish for. It isn't about a perfect life in Louisville or some promotion solving your problems. It isn't about a cat you've known for a week that you think you have a connection with. It's about making the most of what life throws at you and knowing that if you're lucky, something will stick and you'll have a semblance of what you wanted it to look like. Sometimes, that's the best you can get.

"At the end of the day, this isn't a shitty apartment. This is your friend's funeral, the last bit of anything he has in this world, so you need to stop focusing on everything you wanted this trip to be and focus on what it is. I know you knew him when we were young, but I knew him two weeks ago, when he was still alive. I'm not in on this because I don't like you. I just want what's right for those of us who stayed, and I want what's right for Mark."

Lisa and I hate each other, and in this moment, there's nothing I want to do more than hate her. Our relationship was built on this—she'd throw barbs, I'd throw worse ones, and we'd go back and forth insulting one another into oblivion until we realized there wasn't anywhere else to go. So, we calmed down and moved on. This isn't that, though. She's not mad.

"What do you want me to do?" I ask.

She smiles, as if the answer's easy. "Stop being a dick."

"Seriously."

Lisa scoffs, and she narrows her eyes, making her look like a supervillain from a '90s cartoon. "Seriously. You came here because of Marx, and you need to focus on that. This trip isn't about anything else. It isn't about fixing things with Brian or Kenny. It's about helping someone you haven't helped in years, and, frankly, it's your last chance to do it. So, despite how hard you're trying, don't fuck it up."

"How do you suggest I do that?"

She shrugs. "A week ago, I would have said stay away. Now? Just give us the fucking cat and keep your mouth shut at the funeral."

I don't know what to say, so I lean back onto the table and stare at the clouds until Lisa leaves.

TWENTY-TWO

Beth and Brian are eating lunch on the front porch when I step out of the Uber I took to get back to the house.

"Holy shit," Brian says.

Beth sets her half-eaten sandwich on the table between them and runs up to me. Her eyes are wide, and her mouth hangs open. She looks worried and shocked, which shouldn't excite me but does. When she gets close enough, she puts a hand to either side of my face and leans in, and for a second, I feel her breath on my chin.

"Brian," she says, standing on her toes and leaning in closer, "come take a look."

Brian shoves a chip into his mouth. "Fuck that," he says between crunches. "I'm on vacation."

Beth falls back on her heels. "Seriously?" she says. "His eye looks like shit."

Brian sets his plate down next to Beth's and pushes himself out of his chair. He leans back, raising his arms above his head and stretching in a way that pulls his shirt up over his gut, then falls back into place and steps off the porch.

"Just put some ice on it. There isn't much more you can do."

I force a smile. "Thanks, Doc."

Beth cups the side of my face with her hand again. Her fingers cool the heat from the bruising, and I almost want to ask her to keep them there.

"What happened?" she asks.

I don't mean to raise an eyebrow, but when I do, my eye erupts in a fresh spike of pain that makes me feel like my skull is splitting. Beth takes her hand away, and Brian snorts a laugh.

"It's like you've never had a black eye," he says.

I open my mouth to shoot back an insult, only to realize he's right.

"It's a long story," I tell them. "Can we sit down?"

Beth puts an arm around me as we walk back to the porch. Her hand on my shoulder is as comfortable as it was on my face, like the pain and drama and everything that's happened doesn't matter when she's nearby.

Brian's eyes narrow as he stares at Beth's arm. "He's just bruised," he says. "He doesn't need to be treated like he's dying."

Beth pulls her arm out from around me and steps ahead, taking her seat on the porch. I think to glare at Brian, but a dull ache in my eye reminds me not to.

When I sit down next to my brother, Beth leans forward. "So, what happened?"

"Kenny did it."

"What?" Beth asks.

"That fuck," Brian adds. "I thought those S.A.M. douchebags would have done it."

I sigh and lean back in the chair, wishing I could melt into it and make this all go away. "They did," I tell them. "Kenny is S.A.M."

I expect a look of shock, a handful of questions—anything,

really—but the two of them sit in silence, looking back and forth between one another as if they're the ones dropping a bomb on me, not the other way around.

This feels like trouble.

"What?" I ask.

The corner of Beth's tongue pokes out of the side of her mouth as she works up a response. Brian bites his lower lip.

"Not you," I say, assuming the worst. They couldn't have all been out to get me.

Brian shakes his head. "God no. You want a beer or something?"

"What?"

"A beer. You might want one for this."

"For what?" I lean forward in my seat. My back pops and groans from flying off the barstool this morning, making me feel older than I should, so I rest my elbows on my knees.

"Kenny came by," Beth says. The words almost erupt from her mouth. "He, uh, he—"

"We didn't know," Brian adds.

"Know what?"

Beth and Brian look back at one another as if I don't exist. There's a pause, and for a second, everything feels heavy. The air, the sound of the wind hitting the leaves, the swelling gathering around my eye—it all feels like it's gaining weight before crashing down.

"What the hell is it?" I ask.

"He took the cat," Brian says. He leans forward and puts a hand on my shoulder. It's a sharp contrast to the claps on the back I've been receiving since I got here. For a second, I don't even realize the hand is there. His touch is soft, like his fingers are barely on me, and he gives me a quick squeeze. "I'm sorry, man."

Suddenly, it hits me.

"That's one of your doctor moves, isn't it?"

"Fuck," he says. "Yeah," he adds, pulling his hand away. "It doesn't do much good when you call me out on it, though."

I sigh and fall back into the chair. The wood frame is hard against my back, and it crackles when I lean into it. "Jesus fucking Christ," I say. "He stole my cat."

"Did you ever find out what S.A.M. wanted with it?" Beth asks.

"Kenny," I say. "It's Kenny, not S.A.M. I'm done with this secret code name shit. And he's in on it with Mark's dad and Lisa. The cat was for Mr. King."

"Wait, what?" Brian asks. "What are they doing with him?"

I take them through Kenny's talk at breakfast. Beth and Brian react about like I thought they would, somewhere between disbelief and anger, the scales going one way or another as I make my way toward falling off the stool and getting dragged out.

When it's over, Brian sighs. "What are you going to do?"

For a few seconds, all I can feel is my head bobbling on my shoulders. I get that this isn't an answer, but truth is, I don't have one. I look out at Mark's front yard, at my car, still littered with remnants of toilet paper; at the bushes the paintballers hid in; at the porch, where the glitter bomb was delivered. I relive each of these moments, the disbelief, the questions, the fear, and it hits me that the whole time, the answer, the root of it all was in this house. That they set the whole thing up, that I tried to do the right thing, only to get shit on by a handful of assholes with nothing better to do in their stupid podunk town.

"I'm going to get my cat back," I say, "and go to that fucking funeral."

Brian bangs his fist on the table. The plates and silverware bounce off of each other in a mess of clinks and clatters, sounding for a second like a falling wind chime or someone calling for a toast. "Fuck yeah," he says. "I've been waiting for you to come to this."

Beth isn't as enthusiastic. She sits up in her seat, shoulders square, and blinks, and I can see her eyelashes touch for just a second before parting again. It's a slow blink, like the ones my dad used to give before he ripped into me, the ones he saved when he needed to buy just enough time to figure out how to tell me how much of a screw-up I was.

"How do you plan on making this work?" she asks. "You don't even know where Kenny took him." She crosses her arms, looking like a teacher questioning a kid. I try to think about when those hands were on my face, how cool they were, how much they soothed the pain in my eye and made it disappear, but now that we're here, it seems like forever ago. Now, she isn't worried. Or maybe she's too worried. I don't know.

"He's at Mark's dad's house," I tell her. "It's the only thing that makes sense. Kenny wanted Jack back to give him to Mark's dad."

Beth takes in a slow breath before speaking. "And how exactly are you going to get him?" she asks. "You can't just walk in and take the cat."

Next to me, Brian's distant. His eyes stare out over the lawn, absent, but I can almost see the thoughts forming in his head, working their way among one another like little gears in a factory. I wonder if this is what he's like when he's trying to diagnose a patient, when he's piecing together how to put someone back together or figuring out what's killing them.

He blinks, and it's gone. "You could walk in and take the cat. That's what they did to you."

"Hold on," Beth says, scooting to the edge of her seat. She leans forward, setting her elbows on her knees, and a strand of blonde hair falls loose from the messy bun on her head. "Just stop." She balls her fingers into loose fists, and for a second, I wonder if I'm going to get punched again. She keeps to herself, though, rolling them up in front of her while she stares at the ground. There are words, thoughts even, at the edge of her tongue, but she swallows them, like she knows she's outnumbered.

"That's just different," she bursts out. "You can't just break into someone's house."

"How's it different?" Brian asks.

"Kenny could walk in here any day of the week," she says. "It's not like it was out of the ordinary for him to come by and grab something. Jack," she adds. "Jack's another—"

"That doesn't make it right," I say. "He still fucked up."

"I know," she says, dragging the words out. "You're missing the point. You can't just break into Mark's parents' house. It's dangerous. Shit, it's illegal. It's not like you're in any sort of shape to be doing something like this anyway."

I pause, trying to make the moment as dramatic as she did, only I blink and my eye explodes in a fresh wave of pain, sending a tear down my cheek. Beth forces a closed-lip smile, as if I've proven her point.

"Jesus Christ." Brian rolls his eyes. "It's just a bruise. It's literally a bruise on your face."

"It doesn't have to be obvious," I say, ignoring him. "When we were kids, I'd sneak in and out through Mark's window."

"Aww," Brian says. "You guys were so cute."

"Fuck off. This is serious." I turn back toward Beth. "Anyway, I'll go in through the window when they're sleeping, steal the cat, and go back out through the window. They'll think Jack ran away or something."

"And if they do catch you," Brian says, "you can fuck 'em up."

I turn to my brother. His eyes are wide, and he's throwing a fist into his open hand, grinning, looking like some extra out of a Rocky movie.

"I'm not going to fight them," I say. "They're like, sixty years old."

"They're part of the group that did that," he says, pointing to my eye. "And that," he adds, moving to the toilet paper covering my car. "Not to mention everything else," he says. "If you get a chance to land—"

"Stop," Beth says, waving her hands in front of her like she's trying to flag down a helicopter. "Just stop. You can't fight anyone." She pauses, then adds, "Please don't fight anyone."

Jesus Christ.

"I never said I'd fight anyone. That's all Ivan Drago over there," I say, nodding toward Brian.

Beth pulls in her lips in a way that forms a thin line across her face. She stays that way for what feels like minutes, then sighs and relaxes back into her seat. "There's really no talking you out of this, is there?"

I start to open my mouth, but the "nope" I'd planned on saying falls on its ass before making it out. There should be some talking me out of this. I'm nearing thirty, and I'm about to break into someone's house to steal a cat like it's a trip to the grocery store or another thing on my list of chores at the house. For a second, I tell myself that I should be better. That it's time for me to be better. I montage through the times Amanda chewed me out at work, the times Lauren saved my ass at a dinner party or a family get-together when I did something stupid. I see Mark's face, wide-eyed at the end of the couch while he learns that I had, in fact, slept with Beth. For a second, I tell myself to pause, to assess the situation and sort out some better solution, only there's the toilet paper on my car, the paintball welts on my neck, the black eye on my face. The embarrassment, the pain, the uncertainty of everything that's been happening.

"Nah," I tell her. "They deserve this."

TWENTY-THREE

Mark's parents' house looks just like I remember it.
I'm standing across the street, half behind a
tree, watching the place glow in the soft light of
the streetlamps. It's the same chalky yellow, with brown shut-
ters and a fire-red Chevrolet S-10 in the perfect, crack-free
driveway. On the edge of the street is the custom banana split-
modeled mailbox with three scoops of frozen custard drizzled
with painted-on chocolate and raspberry sauces and a banana
for a flag. Most important, though, is the tree stretching up the
side, the one with the fat branch that leads directly to Mark's
bedroom window.

The lights have been off for an hour. They were on when
Beth and Brian drove me by, so the two of them dropped me
off about half a mile away. Before I got out of the car, Beth
cupped my face in her hands again. Her fingers were as cool as
they were when I got home from Old Rupert's, and, for a
second, I thought she was going to kiss me. Our faces were so
close that her eyes went out of focus, looking for a second like
she had four or so that were sliding back and forth, but I didn't
care. I didn't have time to care, really, because before I could

do anything, she patted the side of my face, told me not to do anything to make this any stupider, and checked for the fifth or sixth time that I'd text them when I made it back outside. That way, they'd know they could pick me up in the Tesla and we could hum away to safety.

I take in a breath, a heavy thing that puffs up my chest and makes me feel tougher than I am, like a Rambo or Rocky or someone masculine and fierce. The air is cold, sending the hair on the back of my neck on end, and I exhale and start off across the street. My instinct is to hunker down, spread out my arms, and stay low like they do in spy movies. I remind myself, though, that the goal is to look casual here, that I'm not in a spy or heist movie and I'm not trying to look like I'm sneaking around. That this is real life. Despite this, I can't shake the *Mission: Impossible* song from my head, but I guess that's okay. Nobody has to know what's going on in my head, after all.

When I get to the tree, the spy music in my head reaches full blast. I crane back my neck and stare up at the house, picturing some sort of grappling hook or gun—something cool that I'd shoot up, clip to my belt, and use to silently zip to the top. If this were a movie, I'd probably do something smooth like throw off my sunglasses or kiss a random woman before getting up there. You know, the sorts of things a Daniel Craig or Tom Cruise character might do.

There's no magic gun, though. Just a tree and a window.

Scaling the tree is like riding a bike. My feet fall into the nooks between branches like they've been waiting for this since I left town, and my fingers wrap around limbs without a thought, like they have their own little brains that remember where to go because they were made for just this moment. The moment I'm going to stick it to S.A.M.

The branch that leads up to Mark's window stretches out like an old friend ready to give me a hug. The window's cracked like it's always been. The vents in their house always left the room too warm, and Mark's dad was always too busy with the custard shop to fix it, so they always left it half an inch open. As I start out across the branch—it's just five feet or so, really—it bends and shakes in a way I don't remember. I look down at a few leaves dancing across the air, falling one way or another until they reach the ground, and realize that the branch isn't an old friend at all. Well, maybe it is, but *I'm* not the same. I'm the friend they've come across at the ten-year reunion who's twenty pounds larger and living in the past.

And like that, the music in my head is gone.

There's no going back, though, so I slide one foot, then the other, back and forth until I make it to the window, slip it open, and wiggle my way through. In my head, it's a graceful thing, my arms rippling through my sleeves, a tough-looking vein sprouting in my forehead, my smooth six-pack sliding through untouched. In reality, though, there's the huffing and puffing of a guy whose idea of a workout is walking to pick up carry out, a gut split by the window, and two clumsy, chunky legs kicking outside the house. I get in without a peep, though, and crouch down next to Mark's desk.

The room looks untouched, like a museum built in Mark's memory. There's the twin-sized bed with the navy-blue comforter, the bookshelf stuffed full of novels, comics, and DVDs, all arranged alphabetically. There's the occasional action figure pinned to the wall (near-mint in package, of course) and the Red Hot Chili Peppers poster. The memories hit me all at once, grabbing my limbs and pinning me in place, and all I can think about are the times we spent here debating comic books or playing PlayStation or talking about girls who hated us or loved us or didn't know what they thought about us.

I force myself to blink, to look away from it all for a second, and slide into the chair by Mark's desk. There's a calendar from 2004, our senior year, with our graduation date circled.

The Saturday after it is starred with a memo that the band was set to play Cody Jacobs' graduation party. I pick up Mark's pen and spin it in my fingers, trying to imagine him sitting here, scribbling it all down. In my head, he's young, sober, happy. We're best friends.

You know how this story ends, though. A few years later, Beth and I sleep together, and he tries to rip my throat out from across the couch. A few years after that, I see him at Walmart and don't say hi. And, a few years after that, he gets pretty much crushed by a truck. It's almost like the whole thing, from him saving my ass in the seventh grade to me breaking into his house and plopping down here, where he used to sit and scratch down graduation and band dates, has led to this one remarkable, daring, and stupid idea.

I lean back in Mark's chair, careful not to let it squeak, and put my fingers behind my head. Mark's special edition *Return of the Jedi* poster stares down at me. It has the whole cast of characters—Jabba and Chewbacca looking out over everyone while the Millennium Falcon zips by and Ewoks and droids wander to and fro—but in the middle of it all is Vader and Luke, deadlocked in their lightsaber fight, Luke's green lightsaber clashing in a burst of white against Vader's red. We spent hours, days probably, arguing about that lightsaber fight, about whether Luke went to the dark side in it, but what for? Now, it seems like it never even mattered.

At the base of the poster, mounted to the wall, is Mark's Luke Skywalker Force FX lightsaber. He bought it as a testament to his favorite lightsaber fight, the one in the *Jedi* poster. With a perfectly scaled metal hilt and a glass-encased blade with sound and light effects, I dreamed of one of these. I was going to get Anakin's blue blade because, well, *Revenge of the Sith*. I never saved the money to put toward it, though, so Mark got his without me. He never let me touch it, not even for a second, which is why I can't stop my fingers from reaching out toward it now. The ridges in the metal are cold with the fall air Mark's parents have been letting in, and I run my fingers across the hilt until I get to the ignition button. They've barely passed over it before the blade erupts in a bright wave of green, casting light over the desk and humming quietly on its mount. It takes me a second to register what's happened, but when I do, I wrap my fingers around it and pull it toward me, stumbling as it bobbles between my hands. Palms sweating, it slips out and clunks onto the desk so loudly I'm pretty sure the neighbors can hear, and I scramble toward it with both hands and pull it into my chest, scurrying like someone digging their fingers into the ground to pull themselves out of quicksand.

Desperate, I pat my hands over the lightsaber until I find the button again, pressing it and making the blade zip shut. The room goes black. There's no sound except my heart beating in my chest, the breaths coming in and out of my mouth, quick, short bursts that I force myself to slow. There's a squeak outside, a quiet thing like the sound of someone walking down the hall, but it disappears before squeaking again a few seconds later. I hunker down by the side of Mark's bed and stare at the door. It comes open slowly, and I wrap my fingers so tightly around the hilt that my skin squishes into the little ridges and burns.

The door opens a few inches, then stops. The breaths come faster again as I wait, looking for the tip of a rifle or maybe a baseball bat, but there's nothing. Everything stands still, like the wind has blown it open or someone has come by, started to enter, then walked away to make a snack or watch *Jeopardy* or God knows what. Then, two little orange eyes pop in, shining bright, and Jack meows and trots up to me.

"Thank God." I sigh and loosen my grip on the lightsaber, releasing the tightness in my chest. The air comes out all at once, and I suck in a quick, heavy breath to recover. "Come here," I add, giving him jazz fingers to get him to come. Jack loves jazz fingers.

The cat starts trotting across the room, but another squeak comes from the hall. Only this one's louder, heavier.

"Jack?"

It's Mark's dad.

Jack makes it to me just before a tap comes at the door. It falls all the way open now, the tip of a baseball bat pushing it into the room until it comes to a stop at the foot of the bed.

I scoop up Jack and tuck him under my arm.

"Who's there?" Mr. King says. His words slur, like his mouth's too full of spit for them to come out right. I open my mouth to say something, but before any words escape, he flips on the lights, erupting everything—the posters, the books, the comics—in a brightness that makes it look like it's all on display. I squint at the suddenness of it, making my busted eye tear up, and come to just in time for him to turn toward me.

Mr. King's wearing navy pajamas, the kind with the collared button up and all that, and they're decorated with little vanilla ice cream cones. His hair's a ruffled, gray mess, looking like a storm cloud, and his eyes are patches of red, narrow as they look down on me. In one hand is the bat, fingers wrapped tightly around it, and in the other is a bottle of Beam.

"Jack Dotson," he says, but, in his drunken slur, it comes out like Dawson. He stumbles back a half-step and points the bottle at me. "What are you doing here?"

"Getting my cat."

Mr. King's eyes widen. His fingers tighten around the bat, squeaking against the wood. The Louisville Slugger logo stares at me from the side, and I think about the time Lauren and I toured their factory. We watched bats get made that day, and I can't help but wonder if the one he's holding is one of those.

"He's not your cat, son," he says. "He belongs to Mark's mother and me. Mark would have wanted it that way."

I scratch Jack's chest with my free hand, and he purrs, humming like a little massager to calm me down. Mr. King watches us, falling from one foot to the next in small, drunk little waves, like a metronome to a song that only he can hear.

"Then why'd he name him after me?" I ask.

Mr. King snarls and shakes his head. "Come on," he says. "I've been telling you for days now. You don't really think that's after you, do you?"

I look down at Jack as if he can tell me. He stares at me for a few seconds, his orange eyes shining through his fur, then wiggles his body out from under my arm and walks toward the door. Mr. King doesn't say anything as this happens, just watches, waiting for Jack to leave as if he doesn't want to argue in front of him, like we're two parents making a cheap attempt at hiding our divorce from our kid.

When the last of Jack's fluffy, black tail disappears through the doorway, Mr. King lifts his bat and points to a poster above Mark's bed. It's the cover of *The Fantastic Four* #1. It's a cartoony thing, a stark contrast to the darker, grimier, more realistic comics we read in high school. The background is a bright white, with the Fantastic Four surrounding a big green monster that looks like a thrown-down lump of moldy mashed potatoes. My mind scans every detail, trying to figure out a part that looks like a cat or a Jack, but there's nothing. Reed Richards, Johnny Storm, Sue Storm, Ben Grimm—the heroes aren't named Jack, not a single one of them, but I am, and I was his best friend, the one who—

"Jack Kirby," Mr. King says. He plants the tip of the bat on the floor and leans on it. "He drew that."

Fuck.

Mark loved Jack Kirby. He used to say the guy revolution-ized comics. In a lot of respects, he was right—Kirby teamed

up with Stan Lee and brought all sorts of characters to print—
but Mark couldn't sing his praises enough. Even when the
comic art we grew up with was so different from this, he still
raved about how Jack Kirby was the legend, the one we needed
to thank for everything.

Mr. King takes another swig from his bottle, then sets it
down on top of the dresser. "So you can stop with that now,"
he says. "He's not named after you. He's just a cat. He's just as
much ours as he was Mark's or anyone else's, so you don't have
a right to him."

My lip starts to quiver, so I bite it to hide the fact that there
are tears welling in the corners of my eyes. Staring up at the
poster on the wall, at Mr. King with his baseball bat, I realize
that it was nothing. That maybe whatever connection I felt
with Jack wasn't real at all. That it's all bullshit. Despite this,
though, there are memories with him. There's the time he
circled my ankles in the kitchen before my breakfast with
Kenny. The time he tried to warn me before we were paintballed. The time he helped me pack up Mark's books.

My arm shakes as I start to push myself up. "Fuck you," I
say. "We don't all have this," I add, spiraling around and
staring at the comics, posters, books, and souvenirs all over the
wall. "For all the shit you and Kenny and Lisa have done, I at
least deserve the cat."

Mr. King's face shines so red I'm almost convinced I'd be
able to see it if we cut the lights. "You deserve him?" he rages.
"I have all this because he moved back in after you fucked him
over." His fingers tighten around the bat, squeaking against the
wood. "Because when things got bad with Beth or his drinking,
he needed a place that felt like home. Because everyone he
thought he could—"

"I fucked up," I shout. "Everyone in this stupid town knows
how much I fucked up, but that doesn't mean that I shouldn't
have something to remember him by or that I can't do

anything to make things right. I could have done a million things differently, we all could have, but just because we didn't doesn't mean—"

"And what would you have done differently?" he says, smirking. "Besides not break into my house?"

I open my mouth like the answer is obvious, but nothing comes out. It's all dry, like the words up and vanished and took with them any hope I had at a solution. I blink, each flap of my eyelids sending a fresh spike of pain into my head, and realize that if there were a question I couldn't answer, this might be the worst one.

I want to say I wouldn't have slept with Beth, but I keep coming back to our kiss in Louisville. The feel of her hands on my face earlier today.

"I-I don't know," I say, giving up. "I could have lied or something."

"You could have *what?*"

"I could have lied," I say, knowing from his narrow eyes and his twisted, red face that it's the wrong answer. It's a pretty shitty thing to say, and I don't know if I even believe it, but I'm going to own it because it's all I have. "About Beth. About all of that."

Mr. King's fingers glisten from the sweat as he tightens them around the baseball bat. I tighten mine around the lightsaber hilt, knowing full well that it won't do me any good but feeling better for it.

"Get out," he says, pointing his bat at the bedroom door. "Get the hell out of my house," he repeats, "and don't you dare take that cat with you."

I take in a breath through my nose, letting it sit for a few seconds before exhaling. Before I can step past him and out the door, though, he's lecturing me again.

"You could have lied?" he says. "That's really the best you've got?"

I throw my arms down at my side. "I don't know what you want," I say. "Yeah, I could have lied, and he never would have known the difference." In the anger and hurt and confusion of it all, I add, "It's not like you would have let him away from work long enough to figure it out anyway."

The first time he swings the bat, I almost don't see it happen. It's more like a blur of tans and grays that swooshes by my face as I stumble backward onto the bed. Some of the posters flutter up because Mark never pinned the bottoms to the wall. They create a little wave from one side of the room to the next, like thousands of tiny people rising and falling in their seats as they watch Mr. King try to kill me in some sort of screwed-up suburban fight club.

"He loved that job," Mr. King says. He's gritted his teeth tight, making him look menacing but sound like he's talking with his mouth full. He takes another step toward me and swings the bat down onto the bed, and I roll to the side as it puts a crater in a Spider-Man pillow.

"Look," I say, holding up the lightsaber as if it'll do anything. "Things happen, we all screw up—I screwed up, right?—but that doesn't mean that—"

Mr. King swings the bat again, and I lean back before it crunches through an X-Men poster, banging Wolverine's head straight through the drywall. Mark's dad takes in a breath, pumping his chest out, and exhales. His nostrils flare as he does so, looking like big, cavernous holes in the bottom of his nose. He takes in a few of these, and they retract, then flare up again, then fall back to normal. Even though I know I should be looking at anything other than his nose, I can't look away because it looks just like the nose Mark huffed through when I told him I slept with Beth.

I come out of this just as the bat's coming at me again, and, without much time to move, press the button on the lightsaber hilt. The green light erupting up the end of the tube is all I see for a minute, blinding me from the bat before exploding in a wave of glass shards as the Slugger erupts through it. This would have crushed Mark. He busted his ass at this prick's custard stand so he could afford it, making cones and sundaes and cleaning the lines of the shake machine, when all he wanted was to collect shit like replica lightsabers.

I charge at Mr. King. It's the only thing left to do. The second I get to him, I wrap my arms around his chest and know I'm screwed. With his free hand, he presses into my shoulder, shoves me back onto the bed, and swings again. Only this time there's no lightsaber, only a broken hilt. That won't do shit, though, so I throw my arms up over myself just before the bat hits.

There's no green light this time. Just a crunch, like someone biting into a handful of chips, but my left arm is warm like my face is warm and I know something's not right. That it's broken. Mr. King stares at me, chest huffing again, eyes wide, nostrils still flaring as he takes fat breaths in and out through them. I think I see a tear coming to one corner of his eye as he stares at my arm, which feels increasingly tingly and maybe even hot, like it might be boiling.

He drops the bat. "Jack," he says, lip trembling. "I-I don't—"

I roll out of bed and run through the bedroom door, grabbing my phone with my free hand and calling Brian as I run down the hall. It gets to half a ring before Brian picks up.

"You—"

"Now," I huff as I tear past a montage of King family photos. "Quick."

I hang up and slide my phone back into my pocket.

When I get to the top of the stairs, Jack's there, so I scoop him up with my good arm and start shuffling down. I take the steps one at a time, quick little moves that make me feel like I'm a cool Travolta or Swayze type. Only I'm not. I'm beat up and broken and not nearly as good-looking as them, and I'm stealing a cat that definitely isn't mine. It's two steps to the door when I get to the bottom, and in a couple quick moves I swing the door open and run out into the night.

The air's never felt so cool, but all I can focus on is the pain in my arm as I run across the lawn and into the street. There's nothing in sight, no sound of my rescue engine, so I do the only thing I can think of and turn off around the corner.

I hear the Tesla's tires squeal before I realize that I've stepped right in front of it. For a second, I can see through the windshield. Brian's eyes are wide, and his mouth has fallen open like he's either scared or yelling at me. Beth's face is squeezed so tight that I start to think she'll make this all disappear. Then they're gone, and there's my back crunching against the glass, the squeal of my skin rolling across the top of the car, and finally, the hot pain of my already broken arm bending in a way I know it shouldn't as I hit the concrete.

Back on the pavement, eyes on the sky, I can't hear a damn thing. Then, just as the stars start to disappear and everything in my body starts to feel like it's going lax, there's a small, high-pitched meow as Jack stretches out from under my good arm and nuzzles against my head.

TWENTY-FOUR

I wake up to a beeping. It's a steady thing that rises above the clicks and hums of the machines around me. The noises bounce off one another like a shitty robotic choir, sounding like Transformers changing from car to robot but glitching halfway through.

My left arm itches, and I throw my other one over to scratch it, only to hit not skin, but a gritty thing, like a woven little blanket that's hardened and cold. I realize that it's surrounding my arm, and everything comes back to me. The baseball bat, the Tesla, Jack. Then a groan erupts from my chest, more out of instinct than choice, and I try to push myself up in my bed only to stay still. It's like I'm some sort of fat slug, too chunky to even move.

There's a stirring from somewhere in the room, a rustling of papers and asses getting off the couch, then a hand on me. Beth's hand. Her long fingers wrap around my good arm one by one as her face comes into focus. It's a blurry thing at first, her features fading in and out of fuzzy little circles. Her hair is pulled loosely together in a dark, haphazard bun on top of her head, and I realize it isn't her at all. Not her blue eyes with the green ring around them, and not her blonde hair.

"Jack," Lauren says. Her eyes gloss over with tears, and her lower lip starts to tremble. "You're up."

I try to swallow, but my mouth is dry. Lauren leans over the bed and wraps her hands under my shoulders, sobbing into my chest and grabbing at handfuls of my hospital gown.

"I'm so sorry," she cries.

I lift my arm to hug her back, but there isn't anywhere to put it. She has my good one pinned, and, in my cast, I can't move the other one that well. I know I should say something, but I can't put a sentence together. My mind's so full of everything that happened that I'd almost forgotten that Lauren cheated on me, or that Lauren existed at all. It's like everything I ever thought or felt about her has been replaced with Jack and S.A.M. and, well, Beth.

Lauren lets go of my shoulders and pulls away, cupping my face in her hands. Her cheeks shine red now, and her makeup runs down them in little black and gray rivers that look like a map of a mountain or gorge. Her hands aren't calming like Beth's are. They're hot, her fingertips pressing into my cheekbones as she stares at me and sobs. Her touch makes me want to wrestle my head away.

The sound of footsteps draws closer from behind her, and my brother appears. He's wearing an Incubus T-shirt and glasses, and his hair's a tangled mess atop his head, showing the hints of the receding hairline he started to develop after med school.

"That's an expensive stunt you pulled," he says.

I force a smile, expecting my black eye to sting, but it doesn't. "Sorry. I never heard it coming."

He shrugs, but his eyes narrow. "You have a broken arm and a concussion to show for it, so I guess I'll let you off the hook. Plus, they let me pick the color of your cast."

I run my fingers over the cast again. It's bright pink, like something out of a glow-in-the-dark mini golf course. Across my forearm, Brian's written in big, choppy black letters:

TESLA: 1, JACKASS: 0

I cough up a laugh. "Glad you were concerned."

"I've seen worse," he says. "The real miracle is that you didn't kill the cat."

At the mention of Jack, my eyes go wide, letting me see the room for the first time. The Purdue game's on TV—they're up 14-7, though the announcers don't think they'll hold it—but, otherwise, it's all vanilla. The walls are cream, the trim white, the sheets white, the blinds white. Hell, even the machines I'm hooked up to are cream or white. The only thing that looks like anything is the paper towel dispenser, which shines metallic on the wall.

"Where is he?" I ask. I lift my head an inch or so off the pillow, turning from one side to another. My neck feels like a rusted support beam about to break, though, so I give up. "And where's Beth?"

Lauren bites her lower lip and crosses her arms. She side-eyes Brian, who forces a small, closed-lip smile.

"Beth's at the house," he says. "We've sort of been taking shifts."

Lauren puts her hand on my arm again. "What's important is that you're—"

"What about Jack?" I ask.

Brian and Lauren look at one another, reminding me of how Brian and Beth looked at each other on the porch when I told them about Kenny and S.A.M. Without either of them speaking, it hits me that Jack might have gotten away, and the memories of the bat, the car, and Mark's room all boil up, spilling onto the surface. I start to feel my face going red, my eyes tearing, my lip trembling. I picture steam erupting from my ears like it does in cartoons, so I take in a slow breath through my nose, then hold it. Exhale.

"Please say you got the cat. You have no idea what I went through to get that goddamn cat."

Brian places a hand over my chest, as if he's ready to push me down if I try to lunge at him. "He's at the house. With Beth."

A sigh falls out of me, and I sink farther into my pillow. It's a cheap thing, feeling more like a fat wad of cotton ball than anything else, but it's all I have. "So what happened?"

The way Brian looks at me reminds of when we were kids and, when even though I was the athlete, he'd stare down on me when he'd kicked my ass or made me tap out. It was a sad thing, like he knew it didn't have to be this way, and I hated it. Still do, apparently. "I mean, you darted out in front of the car. That's all there is to it."

"Where did you come from?"

"I had the headlights off," Brian says. "Thought it would be sneakier that way. You sounded pretty urgent when you called."

"And Jack's okay?"

"Yeah," he says. "You pretty much absorbed the blow."

I work back through the few memories I have. There's the sound of the ambulance, the distant shouting of the EMT running in my direction. There's Brian telling them he's a doctor, Beth sobbing as she explains what happened. I rewind a little, and there's Jack purring against my ribs in the bedroom, Mr. King's baseball crunching in Wolverine's face. Then, I'm staring at the Fantastic Four poster all over again. They're fighting the moldy mashed potato-looking monster, and Mr. King's bat is pointed right at it as he tells me that the cat's named after Jack Kirby. That he wasn't named after me, that I was an idiot to think he was.

I don't know why I wanted the cat and me to be a thing. I guess it made me feel like Mark tried to keep a piece of me with him, that even though I'd let him down, he forgave me by naming an adorable little furball after me. It sounds stupider and stupider the more I think about it, though, so I stop. Jack Kirby makes sense, after all.

The fact that I'm too sore to move and can't close one of my fists makes it all worse, like I have enough energy to run a marathon but can't do anything with it. All I want to do is lunge out of bed, run down the street, and find Kenny, but I can't. The aching in my back, the needles and stickers on my arms and chest—I'm stuck.

I prop myself up on my elbows. "We have to get him back for this."

Brian's mouth falls open. It takes my mind a second to register this, because it's not what's supposed to happen. In my head, he's the cheerleader he was on Mark's front porch, the one with the balled fists ready to kick some ass.

"I think we ought to calm it down," he says. He pauses, and for a second I think he's going to tell me I'm terminally ill. "With the cops and the accident and all, I think it's time to let it go."

Lauren sits down on a couch near the window. She's crossed her arms now, too, and she taps one foot against the linoleum while she stares at the two of us.

"Before all this," he says, pointing at me as if I'm some sort of evidence, "it was just pranks, you know? It sucked, but the paintball, the glitter bomb—it was all in good fun. But this— you could have died, dude."

I start to open my mouth, but Lauren jumps in. "What I think your brother's trying to say is that—"

"I get it," I tell her, turning my head toward the paper towel dispenser. Now that the shock's worn off, I don't want to look at either of them. Before this trip, I'd never really thought of myself as the adventurous type, but here I am, having punched someone, broken my arm, and been hit by a car, all while my girlfriend fucked another dude in my house. I want to laugh about it, but I can't. There's just a heaviness in my gut, a sinking feeling that this was all for nothing, that I fell for a trick and wasted my time, that I could be back in Louisville oblivious to my cheating girlfriend but living a quiet, peaceful, and relatively healthy life.

Honestly, I could use a Wednesday Wake-Up from Rob right now, and I don't even know what day it is.

"This is bigger than that," I say, still facing away. Half my face is mashed into the pillow, making it sound like I'm drunk. God, I'd love to be drunk right now.

Brian walks around the side of the bed, stepping directly into my frame of vision. He squats down, resting his hands on the bed's guardrail, and stares at me. He doesn't blink, looking like our dad used to look at us when we were in trouble. "Look, man," he says. "I get that this hasn't gone according to plan, and I swear we've all tried to make the most of it, but you have to slow down. The cat, S.A.M.—nobody's out to get you."

I start to open my mouth, but he interrupts me.

"Well, yeah, S.A.M. was out to get you. But that's beside the point. The funeral's tomorrow, and they're not going to be thrilled if you show up. So let's calm down the revenge talk for a while and figure out how to get you in, okay?"

This is the most serious Brian's been with me in years. He's normally full of jokes and beers, but his face—his settled eyebrows, narrow eyes, closed lips—is anything but. I imagine this is how he looks at patients when he has to give them bad news, stoic and settled and confident, and, for a second, I hate him for it. I hate how successful he is, with his stupid Tesla and medical degree, and how confident he is that he can admit that he's screwed up and not think twice about it. I have so many things I want to yell at him, but I can't, either from exhaustion or not knowing what to say or just knowing I shouldn't. So I focus instead on his eyes and do my best to keep mine steady, like his and Dac's, but I don't have those eyes. I have eyes that, in moments like these, try to look at feet or water stains on the wall or anything other than someone else. I have the unconfident, trembling eyes of an idiot who thinks he can fix things, only to get beat up and hit by a car instead.

I want to tell him to fuck off, that he should have told me to stop all along, that he owes it to me to stick this through, but I can't because he's right. I could be in much worse shape right now, and Beth and Brian are the only reason I'm not. So, I say the only thing I can.

"Fine."

TWENTY-FIVE

Lauren and I have been sitting on Mark's porch for half an hour.

We've been home from the hospital for two hours now. There was no reason for them to keep me. They'd done everything they could with the arm, and it wasn't like my concussion was going to go away, so they gave me some pain meds, told me to take it easy, and sent me on my way. When we got here, we tried to talk through a way to get me into the funeral. Beth looked up adoptable cats on craigslist that we could take in Jack's place, but we couldn't find a match. Brian suggested just showing up and seeing what happened, but the rest of us agreed that probably wouldn't end well. And Lauren, she sat there and took it all in because she's been too busy screwing around behind my back to know what's going on.

Once the conversation reached a standstill, Lauren asked if we could talk outside, so here we are. The sun has set now, and Mark's street has quieted except for the steady chirp of crickets and the hum of the occasional car driving by. Lauren has sat silently through it all, staring out at the yard and dangling a still-full bottle of Miller High Life between her fingers. In the dull porch light I can see the condensation form on the side of the bottle and roll down her hand. The way she holds it, I wait for it to slip and shatter, but it doesn't because things like that don't happen to Lauren.

I'm on my second since we got out here. The beer is warmer than I'd like, a result of the death grip I have on the bottle. I tried to grip it in my left hand—the hand I normally hold my beer in—but the cast makes it wobble in a way that's hard to hold on to. I'm slowly learning that you have hand preferences for things like drinking beer, and not being able to meet those preferences is a pain in the ass that makes moments like these all the worse.

My left leg bounces uncontrollably, looking like I'm trying to calm an invisible baby. I've stolen a few nervous glances at Lauren, and each time my throat tightens, like I'm the one who cheated and needs to talk. I've tried to say something a few times, but when I open my mouth, I'm staring at her in my bedroom again as she rides another guy and says his name like she loves him more than she's ever loved me.

I sneak another glance at Lauren, expecting her to be staring out at the lawn, but she's not. Her eyes, dark and round and open so wide that I wonder if she needs to blink, are on me. It's like she has a vise grip on my face all over again, like her hot fingers are digging into my cheeks and keeping me still. For a second, I wonder if Mark and Beth had this talk here. The cheating talk. I wonder if he felt like he couldn't look away from her, like he wanted to yell at her and cry and kiss her all at once. I wonder if he said something first, or if she did. I wonder if they talked about me, or if they talked about themselves.

Most of all, I wonder about an alternate universe where I ran up to Mark after he calmed down and apologized to him. Where it took him a while to talk to me, but he did, and we were able to rebuild. In that world, he and I would talk about this. It would be awkward, but I'd ask him how he learned to be able to look at me or Beth and overcome it, and he'd be able to tell me because we're best friends. Because we went through some terrible shit together, but we got over it.

"I'm sorry," Lauren says. The words rush everything back into focus, like a lightning strike that wakes you up in the middle of the night. "I'm so sorry."

I look down at my cast. The TESLA:1, JACKASS: 0 stares up at me, and I think of all the other scoreboards that could be there. LAUREN: 1, JACKASS: 0. BASEBALL BAT: 1, JACK-ASS: 0. KENNY: 1, JACKASS: 0. I take a swig of my luke-warm beer and let it sit in my mouth for a second, savoring the shitty carbonation bubbling off the insides of my cheeks, then swallow.

"Why are you here?"

I want Lauren to look down, to tear up or be ashamed, but she doesn't. She just stares, wide-eyed and still.

"Brian told me about your accident," she says. "I wanted to see if you were all right."

"So you're not here to say sorry."

She bites her lower lip and takes a long, slow breath that whistles in through her nose. "I am," she says, exhaling. "The circumstances just changed. I didn't realize things were like this up here."

She reaches over and runs the back of her hand across my cast. When she gets to the end of it and her fingers meet mine, I pull my arm away.

"How's Jeff?" I ask.

"We stopped seeing each other."

I think to utter a "good," but I keep it in.

"How long were you two together?"

Lauren lowers her head. "That's not going to help."

She's right, of course. There's no good answer to this ques-tion. If it was a short thing, she screwed around while I was mourning the death of my friend. If it was a long thing, she sent me off on this trip knowing she'd have a chance to shack up with him. They're both shitty, and she knows just as well as I do that I won't be happy with either one. At the same time, though, my need to know stands there in my head with an ax, taking small swings at any sort of rational, fair approach I can take to this conversation and whittling it down until all I want to do is make her say it because it will hurt her to do so.

"How long?"

She sighs. "About a year and a half."

I knew that whatever answer she gave would be the worst, but that doesn't take away the sting. All I can think about are the things we've done in that time. The dates at The Lodge, the concerts at Waterfront Park, the 5k we ran to raise money for the animal shelter. Double dates with coworkers of hers, the Christmas party at Confluence. All the while, she was thinking about someone else. Hell, there might have been things she went to with him, things I was never even invited to. Maybe her company had a Christmas party and I never knew about it because I wasn't her plus one.

"Can you say something?" she asks.

I take another drink of my beer, a long gulp that makes my throat feel like it's going to burst. "Why did you do it?"

"I don't think we should—"

"Just tell me."

"It was an accident," she says. I want to stop her now, to tell her that accidents are for people who slip on a wet floor or say "fuck" when they stub their toe at church, but I can't. "We grabbed a beer after running club one week, and he asked me to come back to his place. It just sort of happened. We had a lot in common, you know? Things to talk about. He writes. And he loves what he does. He takes his work seriously. And he tries new foods and diets and cares about his body and friends, and—"

"He sounds great," I tell her. The deepest parts of my stomach twist, and my palms start to sweat.

A tear escapes the corner of her eye, but she wipes it away before it gets past her cheekbone. "But he's not you."

My eyes water when she says this, but I don't cry because she doesn't deserve to see me cry. In some way, I always knew we were bound for something like this. Lauren, with her ambition and looks and her ability to walk into a room and make anyone feel like they're the king of the world, and me. Me, who ran away from his hometown, dropped out of college, and took a shitty office job. Me, whose biggest accomplishments are being in the mug club at Great Flood Brewing Co. and winning the cutest pet contest at Confluence. Me, with the broken arm and black eye and concussion.

Lauren scoots forward in her chair. She rests her elbows on her knees, and the tears come free now, running down her face in streams that roll off her perfect jawline and land in little splotches on her yoga pants. "We can fix this, though," she says. "After we finish with Mark and the funeral and get home, we can put everything back together."

I'm the one staring at the lawn now, and in it, I see memories of the last several days. Beth, running her fingers over my black eye. Brian, lunging over the porch and sprinting after the paintballer. Kenny, even, loading books into his truck. These versions of us move through one another, laughing and yelling and smiling and crying, and it hits me that, despite how poorly things have gone, this is where I want to be. It's where I need to be.

Lauren's lower lip starts trembling. The way she's leaned over, clasping her hands and staring at me, makes her look like she's some sort of criminal asking for a pardon.

"I don't think I can," I tell her. The words come softer than I anticipated, like there's a part of me that doesn't want to say them.

She sniffles and wipes the tears from either side of her face, nodding. She could argue with me if she wanted, and she'd probably talk me out of it. She just agrees, though, taking it in until her tears dry up.

"Is it because of Beth?" she asks.

"I don't know. I think you and I know that we're on really different paths, though."

"I could go to the funeral with you," she says. "If you need someone. Like a date or bodyguard or something."

I snort a laugh between tears. "I think I'll be okay. I don't know what else they can do to me at this point."

She sniffles again, then pushes herself up and out of her seat. I do the same, because that's what guys like me do around girls like her. We stare at one another for a moment, then she takes a step forward, wraps her fingers around my arms, and puts her head on my chest. I expect her grip to be tight, but it's not. Her fingers rest softly on my skin, and her tears soak into my T-shirt.

"At least remember why you came here, okay?" she says.

I rest my hands around her waist. I want to say "of course," but I can't. It feels like forever ago that we were sitting in our dining room, sipping coffee and talking over my decision to come home, make amends with everyone, and do right by Mark. It seemed so simple then, so well-intentioned. Then Kenny happened, and everything went to shit.

There's still time to do good, of course. All I need to do is get through this funeral before I can get back to Brian and Beth and paintball and packing and whatever else it is we're doing to help out Mark.

But first, S.A.M. They need to know that they can't keep me away from my last chance to say goodbye to my best friend.

"Of course," I tell her. There's no need to get into all that here.

"I think I'm going to go," she says. "Let me know when you want to get your stuff."

I kiss the top of her head. Her hair smells like tangerines, and I forget about S.A.M. and Kenny and everything that's gone on. It reminds me of the way her pillow smells, and I picture it next to mine, both with the teal floral pattern against the barn wood headboard she had commissioned and the light gray walls she picked out. There's the white dresser with the teal and gold handles, the photos gathered where I wanted to hang a TV, Jabba curled up on his bed. For a second, I want nothing more than to be right there, but I can't be there because I can't shake the twisting in my stomach. Because this is where we are now. And even though I could have lied and told her that everything is okay, that we could go back to our comfortable, ignorant little life in Louisville, I know where *I could have lied* has taken me, and I know I can't do that anymore.

"Travel safe," I tell her.

AFTER LAUREN LEAVES, I go to the kitchen, grab a sixer of High Life, and take it back to the porch. I sit in the chair she sat in, and, for a moment, it almost seems like she's here next to me. I can smell her hair and taste her tears, and it hits me in the deepest parts of my gut that we're done. I ended it. I think over and over again about her clasped hands, her cheeks wet with tears, how desperate and sad she looked because she knew as much as I knew that it had come to this, that it wasn't about Jeff or Beth or anyone but us.

I replay the conversation in my mind, working my way through another beer each time until I get to the kiss on her head. Then I hit rewind, watch the tears zip back into our eyes and words disappear back between our lips, and start back over from the top. Once or twice, I'm hit with the eyes that pulled me in at Fitzgerald's all those years ago, and I want to get off my ass and run down the street until I catch up with her car. You know, the way guys in movies do. Only this isn't a movie, and the last time I ran into the street, I got hit by a Tesla.

I think about Lauren offering to go to the funeral. At the time, I thought it was a last-ditch effort, a way to drag this all out until something gets better. Now that she's gone, though, I can't help but think how nice it might have been to have a date. At the least, it would surprise Kenny and Mr. King and give them a second to think before kicking me out. Now, the only person I can think to ask is Beth. Given the circumstances, that probably wouldn't go over well.

Then it hits me. The idea appears out of nowhere, jumps out from behind the bushes in my mind. I finish off my beer, set it on the porch next to me, and sit up in my chair, feeling stupid and relieved all at once that I've finally figured something out.

TWENTY-SIX

I turn on to River Road just as Old Rupert's open sign flickers to life. It flutters for a couple seconds, like it's desperate to fade back to black, but it eventually comes to, shining bright on the otherwise dark street.

The last time I was here this early was probably in college. Back then, Mark would drive me here when I was hungover (or still drunk) so I could eat. I'd order coffee and their breakfast platter—two eggs your way, a choice of bacon or sausage (bacon, duh), hash browns, and a side of toast (wheat)—and he'd order a fruit bowl, which he'd ask to have come out with my food. Sometimes, they'd bring his fruit early, but he'd wait for my food to arrive before he started eating. Over these meals, he'd ask about whatever escapade led to my current state. I'd tell him, and he'd listen, nodding between bites of cantaloupe and grapes, until I was done.

Now that I think about it, I should have asked him how he was doing, but I didn't. Not that I can remember, at least.

I had planned to get here before Old Rupert's opened, but I overslept. Last night, Brian and Beth tried to talk to me before I went to bed, but I didn't want to tell them my plan.

They'd talk me out of it or tell me it was a bad idea or that I'd end up in trouble, and, well, I didn't have a counter argument for that. I still don't, honestly. I told them I was too drunk, slumped down to the basement, and stared at the ceiling until I fell asleep.

The parking lot's empty, so I steer the Tesla into a spot near the door. For a second, I consider backing out and parking at the far corner of the lot. Mark always parked there in case someone needed one of the close spots. I told him once that they had spots reserved for those folks, but he said they might be taken when someone needed them, so we always parked at the back. He was a good guy like that.

I push through the diner's front door, and the bell above it announces my arrival. Lisa's rolling silverware into napkins, and she's just grabbed a fork and knife when she sees me. Her eyes widen, and she pauses, holding the silverware in each hand like she's ready for Thanksgiving dinner. We stay that way for a few seconds, like two animals who have stumbled across one another in the wild, each waiting for the other to strike first. Her, with an unbreakable gaze, weapons at the ready, perched in her home territory. And me, with a worthless arm, a bruised eye, and no idea what I'm doing.

Lisa inhales through her nose, puffing up her chest and raising her shoulders. She sets the fork and knife down on the bar next to her, then pulls her lips into a tight line across her face. She stays that way for a few seconds, then exhales. "What are you doing here?"

Somehow, I hadn't prepared for this question. I prepared for a lot of them—how are you doing, what's going on at Mark's house, how's the cat—but the obvious one hadn't hit me.

"Well, uh," I say, scratching the back of my neck. "I need help."

Lisa arches her eyebrow. It's a dramatic thing, looking like a bell curve and making me think that this might not be a good idea after all.

"Will you go to Mark's funeral with me?" I say, unable to keep it in. The words come out all at once, like they're rushing past one another in a race to escape. "You're the only chance I have," I add. "Kenny and Mark's dad will let me in if I'm with you."

She blinks, and it feels like her eyes are closed for minutes. It reminds me of the way she reacted when I asked her to prom. We were in between classes—she was on her way to English, and I was on my way to Algebra II—and standing in the middle of the hall, staring at one another like people do when they're dating in high school. Lisa's hair was longer then, and a brighter blonde. She was hugging her textbook to her chest—*Voices in American Literature*—and when I asked her, she inhaled so heavily that I thought she was going to drop it. She blinked, but it was a flutter, like a bird's wings or something angelic, and her lips parted and froze for a second before she gave her answer.

"Yes," she said, smiling. "Absolutely."

When present day Lisa opens her eyes, she bites her lower lip and rubs her palms on her orange apron. There's no flutter, no parting of lips as she stares me down—nothing but the clanging of pans in the kitchen and lights from the occasional car driving by.

"What the actual fuck," she says. The words come out slowly, carefully, like she's laying some sort of foundation for the rest of our conversation.

"I just need help getting into the funeral."

Lisa's eyes go to my cast, bright pink amongst Old Rupert's white-and-black tiles and faux-marble tabletops. They make their way over each letter Brian wrote, the signature from Beth. She reads these like a code-breaker, scanning the letters and the texture of my cast as if they'll unlock what's going on.

She opens her mouth to speak, her pale lips barely parting, then presses them back together and sighs. "I don't know if that's a good idea."

I sit down on a barstool across from her and rest my good arm on the table. The broken one hangs by my side like a square of toilet paper stuck to the bottom of a shoe. "Look," I tell her, "I get that it's a stupid thing to ask and that you have no reason to do it. I just don't know what else to do. Everything you said about how I shouldn't be a dick and how I need to focus on Mark and his funeral, I get it." I lug my broken arm up onto the counter, and it bounces a little, sending a dull pain radiating up to my shoulder. "I didn't get it soon enough," I add, "but I just want to say goodbye to him, and going to the funeral with you is the best chance I have."

Lisa scrunches her mouth to one side. "So just give Mark's dad the cat."

"I owe a lot of people a lot of things," I say, "but I owe Mark something I can't give him. The best I can do is say goodbye, and I don't understand why I should have to give up Jack to do it. I know S.A.M.—"

"S.A.M.'s done."

"What?"

She takes a step backward and crosses her arms. "I couldn't do it anymore. Mark's dad couldn't, either. I mean, fuck. You're a dick, but I never wanted to see you in the hospital."

"So I'm good?"

"Oh no," she says. "Kenny will lose his shit if you stroll in there."

"But you'll help me, right?"

She nods and leans against the counter. "Fine." She swallows, and her eyes lock on mine. "But you're not going to start any shit, okay?"

My eyes widen. The blackened one stings, sending a tear down my cheek that I hope Lisa reads as affection. "Absolutely," I tell her, nodding. "There won't be any shit," I add, crossing my fingers that I can make this work. Aside from giving up Jack, what other choice do I have?

TWENTY-SEVEN

I don't know who decided to paint the outside of the funeral home beige, but I can't help but think that it's unfitting. Beige is perfect for lots of things: public schools, bank lobbies, waiting rooms. It's perfect for these things because it inspires no feeling. Funerals are for every feeling, though, all at once, in a way that hits you like a punch to the face or the long cry at the end of a Nicholas Sparks movie.

Mark would have hated going out in a beige building. I'm probably a bad judge of this, given that I missed that last few years of his life, but something about it seems off. Not as off as the fact that the visitation started twenty minutes ago and I'm leaning against my toilet paper-speckled car in the parking lot, but off nonetheless. Now that I'm here, going inside is a bridge I'm not so sure I want to cross. There's a finality to it all that I don't want to deal with because dealing with it means that Mark's really gone.

Lisa's next to me, leaning against my car with her arms crossed. She's wearing a black dress, a high-necked thing with lace near the top. Her blonde hair's in a messy bun behind her head, and thin, curling strands fall down either side of her face. Her lips are red, and they haven't moved since we got here. When I picked her up, she told me she'd called the other members of S.A.M. and told them that I'd be with her. She explained to them what I said to her at Old Rupert's, and she told them that she thought Mark would appreciate my attitude. Mr. King, she told me, took this well. He said it wasn't a good idea, but that he trusted her. Kenny, on the other hand, hung up on her.

While Lisa was doing this at her house, I was back at Mark's trying to put on a suit. My cast wouldn't fit through the arm, though, and the sleeve ripped at the elbow when I tried to force it. I opted for a short-sleeved button-up instead, gray with a black tie. It's the sort of outfit that reminds me of how I dressed for middle school dances when I wanted to look like a member of Green Day, but it's all I could make work.

Lisa and I walk to the door, and before I open it, I look at myself in the glass. Face puffy, covered in purples and blues and browns, I realize that I'm more colorful than the building itself. There's no reason for this to comfort me, but it does.

When we step inside, Lisa wraps her hand around my good arm. Her fingers press into me one at a time as she squeezes the soft underside, reminding me of our senior prom. At the end of that night, she clung to my arm just like this, and we ran to my car so we could get to the after party. Back then, though, my arms weren't so squishy. I wasn't so squishy.

She pulls me in, and I tilt my head toward hers.

"Remember," she hisses. "No shit, okay?"

I nod, and one of the funeral home workers steps up to us and clears his throat. His forehead is crinkled in fat, overlapping folds, and his eyes are narrow, looking as irritated as a teacher at the front of a rowdy classroom.

"You're not supposed to be here." His words come out in a

low, mumbling drawl. "I was told to keep the kid with the pink cast out."

I freeze. All I can think to do is smile at being called a kid.

"I'm sorry," Lisa says, tugging on my arm, "but this is a misunderstanding. This is Mr. King's brother."

Hearing myself referred to as Mark's brother makes my insides twitch, and a tear gathers up in the corner of my eye. I expect the man's glare to break, but it doesn't. Instead, he narrows his eyes further, making his eyebrows almost sag over them.

"So," she adds, "we're going to go in."

For a second, he looks like he's going to stop us. My first thought is to ask him if he's really going to tell us we can't go in, but before I can, the fingers wrapped around my arm remind me that I've spent the better part of the week dueling with people who have been trying to do just that.

The man sighs and curses under his breath, looking almost cartoonish as he slumps away. Lisa squeezes my arm again, and we walk through the doorway and into the viewing. I expect everyone to turn toward us, but they don't. It's half-empty, with small islands of people separated by seas of white folding chairs.

There's less crying than I thought there'd be. A few folks make up for those who aren't, but everyone's quieter than I expected. At the front of the room, near Beth, is a blown-up copy of Mark's senior portrait. He's smiling, teeth white, black hair shaggy, and he's wearing a black suit that makes his shoulders look huge, like something out of a '90s superhero cartoon. There's no hint of the man he'll become, the alcoholic who bends and breaks because his best friend screwed him over and his dad worked him too hard. This Mark, all he cares about is doing well enough in school so he can take over his dad's custard stand one day. He's the Mark I ran away from.

I hung out with Mark the day he got his senior portraits.

He hated everything about them, from the suit to the settings and even the photographer, but his dad had insisted on them. For one of the photos, the backdrop was a collection of gears, making it look like he was in some sort of trippy steampunk movie. He had his hands stuffed in his pockets, and he stared down the camera while a fan blew his hair back. It was so campy, like something out of one of our comic books or video games, that I thought he might love it. We called it the Gear-master photo, made cracks about how he could control any watch or clock so people wouldn't know what time it was. It was our own little joke, at least until the portrait studio decided they wanted to use it for advertising. Then, Gearmaster became as much of a local legend as King's Frozen Custard or Purdue's Cradle of Quarterbacks, and Mark stopped talking about it.

A mane of flowers surrounds Mark's picture, and next to it, on a little stand that looks like a plastic Romanesque column, is a black urn. On the other side of it stands Beth, then Mark's dad, and finally, Mark's mom. People come up to them one by one, hugging them or placing a hand on their shoulder, and they smile, remaining as genuine as ever despite what I'm sure is a wave of emotion. Beth's jaw drops when she realizes who I'm with, but she recovers as quickly as she breaks, and the people she's talking to don't notice. Chin raised, shoulders square, she doesn't look half the mess I expected her to be.

I lean over to Lisa. "Are you sure I'm not going to get kicked out?"

Before she can answer, a hand claps down on my shoulder. "Never thought I'd see you two together again," Brian says.

Lisa laughs.

Brian squeezes me, then lets go. "I'm glad you were able to make it," he says. "I talked to Mark's folks before the service, and they didn't mention a thing about it. Asked how you were, even."

After everything that's happened, I hadn't considered this to be a possibility.

"You go ahead," I tell Lisa, nodding toward the front. "I'm going to let things thin out a little."

She smiles, and for a minute, she's the girl I fell for in high school. She starts to walk away, but before she can make it too far, I reach for her and tap her arm.

"Thanks, too," I say. "I appreciate this a lot."

"It wasn't for you," she says. "It was for Mark. Whatever apology or goodbye you have in store, he deserves it."

This reminds me that I have no idea what I have in store. "Well, thanks again."

When she leaves, Brian and I fall back into a couple chairs. Brian, in his suit that probably costs more than my car, and me, in a short-sleeved shirt that I think I got at a flea market. We're so different anymore, so pulled apart, but here, I've never felt closer to him. My mind flips through scenes from our past, weekends sharing the basement and meals made in Mark's kitchen, and I wonder if he's thinking about the same things.

"It's kind of funny," my brother says. "All that S.A.M. shit, and all you needed to do was talk to your ex."

"I guess." My eyes scan the room, studying the faces of everyone in attendance. "Where's Kenny, though?"

Brian shrugs. "He's been in and out. I think this was tougher than he thought it would be."

I nod, staring at the picture of Mark smiling from across the room. He's easier to look at than everyone else, and I can't help but feel that this should be more difficult. That I shouldn't be sitting here with my brother, making small talk. That I should be crying and hugging people and talking about Mark and everything he meant to me. My stomach wrenches and twists into a tight knot, and all I can think is that I've done this all wrong, the whole trip here, and that I should have done it sooner. That maybe, I should have stayed here all along.

The last of the crowd makes its way through Beth, Mark's dad, and Mark's mom. It stays quiet for a while, and the three of them eventually retreat to the refreshments in the far corner of the room.

Brian nudges my side. "You ready?"

I swallow, mostly to buy time, but nothing's there. My throat is dry, like everything has up and disappeared.

"I guess." The words come out in a whisper, like I'm parched and crawling across the desert.

"Go for it, dude," he says. I blink a couple times, expecting him to get up, but he leans farther back into his seat. "I've seen him," he adds. "Paid my respects earlier."

I wipe my hands on my pants. The cast snags on my left leg, pulling a string or two loose, and I want nothing more than to crack the plaster open and throw it away. Mark wouldn't expect me to look like this. He'd expect better.

Or, after everything that went down between us, maybe worse. Who knows?

I walk up to the photo. The flowers are more vivid up close, bright reds and whites and purples that look like something out of a parade or circus. I'm not even sure Mark would enjoy flowers, but I suppose these sorts of things are more for the attendees than anyone else. In the middle of them, his smile is huge, spreading from cheek to cheek.

"Hey," I say. I feel like an idiot, but I don't know what else to do. I picture myself at Walmart all those years ago, frozen and waving from across the discount DVD bin, and wish I'd done then what I'm doing now. My lower lip trembles, and my eyes start to sting. "I know it's late," I add, "but I'm sorry for the way things happened. For leaving and all. And for Beth."

I pause and hope for an answer. Before one comes, though, a hand slaps down on my shoulder, and I turn to face it. Kenny's staring at me through narrow, red eyes, holding onto me either because he can't stand or because he wants to apologize. He sways backward and forward, rocking as if his legs are softening underneath him. His breath smells like cheap beer, and his cheeks are red and raw from what I assume are tears he's been wiping away.

"You okay?" I ask.

Kenny closes his eyes. He stays that way for a few seconds, still rocking, then opens them. He glares at me from under half-shut lids, looking like a supervillain sizing up his enemy, and I realize that he's here because he's still pissed at me.

"You pulled it off," he says. His words slide together as they make their way off his tongue, sounding almost like Daffy Duck. "Got away with another fast one."

I look over my shoulder at the portrait of Mark, at the urn holding his ashes. I couldn't tell from across the room, but it's painted with the New York skyline, complete with a little Spider-Man swinging between the buildings. It's an older Spider-Man, with smaller eyes and a shorter body, a far cry from the scarier, bug-eyed version of the character we grew up on.

In front of me, Kenny's still glaring.

"Can we not do this here?" I say. I want to laugh and tell him that his stupid plan failed, that he was a dipshit all along, but I keep it to myself. I made a promise, after all.

He lets go and shoves me, and I stumble back a step. "Lisa called us," he says. "Told Mark's dad and me that she was bringing you. Said you deserved a chance, that you'd been through enough. Mark's dad didn't care, even after you ran off with the cat he insisted I get him. And nobody would listen to me. All this time, all this energy, all for nothing because you got what you wanted so you can give your shitty apology and disappear again."

Nobody's paying attention to us. People are immersed in conversation, sharing stories about Mark and hugging off their sorrows.

"Look," I say. I raise a hand to keep him at bay. "We can do this later, dude. We don't—"

Kenny swipes away my hand. "He didn't even like you," he says. "He used to get hammered and talk about what an idiot you were, how he carried you through high school, how you fucked him over because you knew you'd never be as good as him. He used to—"

"Jesus," I say. The tops of my cheeks burn, and the fingers of my good arm ball up in a fist. "I get it."

He takes another step toward me, and I step back into what little space I have left. The flowers brush against my back, and my cast bumps the pillar, sending the urn wobbling. Kenny's closer now, breathing between clenched teeth. He's so drunk he's practically drooling.

"I don't think Mark would want it like this," I tell him. "Not—"

"Oh," he says, eyes going wide, "you know what he'd want now, huh?"

I hold my hands up, trying to create space between us. "I didn't mean it like that."

"You suck at saying what you mean, then," he says. "Because he wouldn't have wanted you here." He pushes a finger into my chest. "He would have beat the shit out of you if he saw you here."

Behind him, across the room, Brian and Beth are talking. I lean over, trying to get their attention, but neither of them notices.

Kenny looks over his shoulder, then turns back around, grinning. It's a lopsided thing that makes him look deranged. "Looking for your crew?" he says. "Need some help before I kick your ass?"

Before I can say anything, he's winding up, bringing his fist back, and launching it forward. It comes at me in slow motion, and I stare at the wrinkles in his knuckles for a fraction of a second, feeling like a badass out of *The Matrix* before stepping to the side and shoving him away. Kenny stumbles forward, but he makes it less than a step before I realize that I've pushed him right toward the picture of Mark and the urn. I reach out to stop him from colliding with it all, but he grips onto my shirt before I can, sending me down with him.

And like that, my *Matrix* aspirations fall apart.

The two of us tear through the picture and onto the floor, and my leg catches the pillar, sending everything into a tumble. The urn hits the ground in a soft crunch and a poof, and before I can cover myself, my nose and throat go dry from the small explosion of dust. I stay still for what feels like hours, eyes closed, as the rest of my senses come to. There's a broken picture frame under my shoulder. A pillow of flowers cradling my head. Thorns pierced into my skin. There's Kenny's arm across my waist, still held tight in a sweaty ball around my shirt. My chest heaves, and I try with everything in my body to stop it because I don't want to breathe.

When I open my eyes, I wipe my hand across my face. It's covered in a gray, chalky glove of my best friend's remains. Next to me, Spider-Man's broken in half, his web attached to a shard of a building whose other half is a few inches away. My stomach rumbles, and acid rises in my throat, but I swallow down the vomit because throwing up will only make things worse.

There's the sound of heels clicking, quick and steady, and Beth steps over my torso, one leg on either side of me, staring down. Her hair dangles from either side of her face, creating a sort of wall, and I imagine the two of us locked in a room, eye to eye. Her cheeks shine red against her blonde hair, and her lips tremble. Tears grow in the corners of her eyes and make their way down her face. Her shoulders are hunched, her hands clenched in tight fists.

Next to me, Kenny groans. He pulls his arm off me and

plants it into the ground in an attempt to push himself up, only to fall back down again.

"I told you," Beth says. She shakes her head and pulls her lips in tight. "I told you days ago that this back-and-forth between you two needed to end."

"Look," I tell her, scrambling to come up with an explanation. I prop myself up on my elbow—the good one, that is—but before I can say anything else, she kicks me back down.

"No," she says. Her voice cracks, sounding like a laugh or a scream. "I don't want to hear it. You need to leave."

I turn my head toward a forest of chair legs. People's feet are in the distance, behind them all, as if Kenny and I are wild animals in need of space. One set moves closer, though, in quick steps like a doctor rushing through an emergency room.

Beth steps backward, leaving me exposed, and turns toward my brother. The tears cover her face now, making her cheeks look like a charcoal drawing. "Get rid of him," she says. "Just get him out."

Brian grabs the back of my shirt and pulls me up like a mama cat picking up a kitten. He grabs Kenny in the other one, displaying a strength I didn't know he had, and drags us toward the back of the room. I pick my feet up as soon as I can and stumble alongside my brother, letting him keep his hold on me as we make our way out. I lower my head, avoiding Lisa, Mark's dad, and even the worker who let me in. This is what they expected, who they think I am, and I don't want to see it reflected in their eyes.

When we get outside, Brian shoves us both forward. The three of us stand there, eyes darting from one to another, until Brian takes a step back. "You guys have to go," he says.

Kenny mumbles a few words, then hiccups.

"Yeah," I say, defeated. "I get it."

"You need to stay away for a while," he says. "This," he

adds, looking back into the funeral home over his shoulder, "this was a shitshow, dudes. You're both better than that."

I open my mouth to respond, but he cuts me off. "Just give everyone some space," he says. "Do us all a favor and stay away."

TWENTY-EIGHT

I push open the door to Stevie's Down Under. The place is dark, lit only by neon beer signs and a handful of TVs showing football highlights. A few folks hunker over drinks, scattered at tables by themselves, and none of them look up as I make my way across the room and settle into a seat at the far end of the bar.

It's been hours since I left the funeral home. After Brian went back inside, Kenny threw up in a flowerpot and I got into my car and left. I drove around town for a few hours afterward, letting my dirty Prius hum up and down Lafayette's empty streets while I tried to get a hold of Brian or Beth, but neither picked up. I thought about going back to Mark's place, but I couldn't convince myself that I belonged there. I couldn't convince myself that I belonged anywhere, to be honest, which is how I ended up here.

"What are we drinking?" the bartender asks. He's a big guy with muscles that force his shirt sleeves to hug them. Truth be told, he looks like he stepped right out of *Cheers* or another '80s show, with high-rise dad jeans and a bright red Stevie's T-shirt tucked into them. His hair, brown with streaks of gray, is pulled back in a tight ponytail that makes his forehead look larger than it probably is.

I rest my arms on the edge of the bar. My cast clatters against the wood, slipping a couple times before I give up and let it sit where it wants. Out of the corner of my eye I notice a small chalkboard advertising the Homewrecker, which is on special for two bucks. "I'll take one of those," I say, hiking a thumb at it.

The bartender grabs the bottle of whiskey. He fills the glass, then slides it across the bar. "Friend of Mark's?"

"I guess," I tell him, raising the shot. "I've been told this was named after me."

The bartender smirks, nodding. He stays that way for a few seconds, head bobbing up and down, then extends his hand. "Jack Dawson," he says. "I figured I'd meet you eventually. Steve Chester."

"Dotson," I say, emphasizing the "t" and grabbing his hand. His grip crushes my fingers into a wad between our palms, making me think for a second that I'll soon be out of good hands. "Jack Dawson is Leo's character from *Titanic*."

His grin widens. "Just giving you shit," he says. "Mark told me you hated that."

"You knew Mark?"

"Oh yeah," Steve says. "He came here every night. Good kid." He grabs a towel from under the bar and holds it up. "You need help cleaning up?"

I run my hand across my face, leaving my palm gray. I want to accept his offer, to wash up and get Mark's ashes off of me, but I can't bring myself to do it. As much as Mark loved this place, the thought of rinsing him down the sink makes me shiver. I feel like he should go somewhere meaningful, like over a cliff or into the ocean. You know, the places they toss ashes in movies or on Hallmark shows.

"I'm good. Thanks, though."

Behind the bar is a picture of Mark and Steve, arms around one another, grinning from ear to ear. Mark's wearing an old flannel, a red and yellow thing that's unbuttoned a few inches at the top. His hair is cut close to his head, and the undersides of his eyes are dark, heavy, like little pouches of dirt. His arms are thick, with a couple veins bulging from under the skin. He's a far cry from the fatter, softer version of my younger self that I've become.

Steve knocks on the bar a couple times, shaking me to attention. "You okay?"

"Yeah." I spin the glass of whiskey between my fingers a couple times. I hate Jack. I hate all liquor, to be honest, but ordering a Homewrecker seemed appropriate given how today's gone. "When was that picture taken?"

"A couple months ago. Business got a little too good one night, so Mark hopped behind the bar and helped me out. Didn't even keep his tips."

"So you knew him pretty well, then?"

Steve throws his towel over his shoulder and shrugs. "Guess so," he says. "We talked a lot. Like I said, he was a good kid."

I chew on my lower lip for a couple seconds, pulling on the skin with my teeth. "So, he talked about me?"

"Oh yeah," Steve says. "Every once in a while. Mostly about your falling out, but not always. He loved to talk about the band."

"Really?"

"Yeah," he says. "Guy loved making music. I think he'd convinced himself you guys were on track to be the next Zeppelin or something."

I spin the glass another couple times, then hold it to my lips and knock it back. The whiskey burns the insides of my cheeks, so I force it down. "What was he like?"

Steve raises a gray eyebrow. "I thought you guys were friends."

"We were," I say. "It just seems like he changed a little after what happened between us."

Steve nods and tucks his thumbs into his belt loops, looking like something out of a Journey or REO Speedwagon song. "Hard to say," he says. "He was a good guy, trying hard, helping out when he could, but he had an ugly side to him. He had this journal he kept here, and some nights, he'd come for hours and drink the whole time. He'd write and draw all over it, looking like some sort of crazy man. The hottest girl in the bar could walk up to him and try to talk, and he'd act like she didn't exist.

"Thing is, you couldn't predict which Mark would walk in the door. I don't think he even knew. Some days, he was laughing, cracking jokes, and watching football, and others, he was a wreck. Sucked to see him that way, you know?"

I look over Steve's shoulder at the picture of the weathered, grown-up version of my best friend. The one I know so little about. "You have that journal?"

Steve scrunches his mouth to one side, making his goatee look like it's striking a pose. "Yeah," he says, nodding. "Tucked it away as soon as I heard the news."

"You think I could read it?"

Steve's mouth falls open, and he side-eyes the photo of him and Mark on the wall. For a second, I think he's going to ask me to leave. When he opens his mouth, though, he's nodding. "Sure," he says. "No harm in that," he adds, as if he's had to talk himself into it. Without another word, he turns and walks through a doorway at the other end of the bar. I worry that a customer's going to walk in, someone from the viewing or S.A.M. or God knows what, but it doesn't happen. It stays silent except for the hum of the neon signs and the occasional crunch of the ice machine dropping fresh cubes.

Steve comes back through a couple minutes later with a

black composition notebook in one hand. He tosses it down on the counter, and it lands with a smack.

I wait for Steve to say something, but he turns and walks to the other end of the bar. The front of the notebook, speckled in white-and-black splotches like a Jackson Pollock painting, has three lines. The first and last are empty, but in the center one, in small, jagged little letters I remember from high school, is Mark's name. I run my fingers over them, hoping they'll take me back to when he wrote them, but my skin just scoots across the cheap cardboard with little more than a squeak.

I expect the notebook to scream at me when I open it, to howl across the room like a storm pounding on a window. The front side of the cover falls against the bar in a near-silent tap, though, and I tuck the corner under my cast to keep it open. On the front page is a sketch taken straight out of *The Amazing Spider-Man* #121, "The Night Gwen Stacy Died." Only it's not Spider-Man in his red-and-blue tights, and he's not holding Gwen, with her blonde hair, green coat, and purple dress. It's Mark, wearing a black T-shirt and blue jeans, and he's holding Beth, wearing one of her typical flannels and khaki shorts. To anyone else, it's just a sketch of Mark holding his girlfriend. The details, though—Mark's fist raised in the sky, his eyes wide, Beth's right arm draped over her body—are every bit the panel of a Spider-Man who realizes he's failed the love of his life.

In the comic, Spider-Man's yelling at the Green Goblin that he's going to pay for killing Gwen. I expect to find a drawing of myself across from the two of them, maybe dressed up in a Goblin costume or cackling, but it's blank. I flip through the pages, letting them fall from one side to another and hoping that something meaningful pops out, but it's nothing except sketches and notes to no one. Some of the drawings are smooth, pristine, like something out of a comic book, and some of the notes are written in Mark's jagged, blocky little letters. Others, though, are a mess of lines and shapes, curves and squiggles that trail off the edge of the page. It's these ones that fascinate me. There are pieces of him in the sentences he starts, but before I get too far down the page, they're gone. It's like seeing a familiar face on the street, but that face begins to fade away or turn into someone different once you get close.

I order another Homewrecker and start making my way through the back half of the notebook. The ink on the pages blurs together as I pass from one to the next, looking like a little cluster of storm clouds moving across the sky, until a page written in red pops out. The top, right-hand corner of it reads *December 22, 2016*. The letters are the crisp, jagged little things I remember from school, but it isn't this that sticks out. It's the date. The day I ran into Mark at Walmart.

The top line contains five words:

Things Jack should apologize for:

My heart catches in my chest, and my cheeks burn as I stare down at the letters, rereading them over and over. My hand moves to my glass of Jack, and I spin it a couple more times on the bar before picking it up and holding it to my lips. It trembles there, bouncing off of them in quick little successions as I struggle to stay still, so I take a sip and hold the whiskey in my mouth. It stings, moving backward until it hits the end of my tongue, and I swallow. The page reads:

1. *Sleeping with my girlfriend*
2. *Bailing on me and Kenny*
3. *Never apologizing to Beth*
4. *Turning his back on Lafayette*
5. *Forgetting the band*

I flip to the next page, expecting the list to continue, but it's just another Spider-Man drawing. On another one are some scribbles of Red Hot Chili Peppers lyrics, and on the one after that is another note about King's. I flip through all of them, looking for more about me, about the list and what Mark thought about it, but there's nothing.

I spent the last few years telling myself he spent all his time thinking about me and what I did to screw him over, as if he had an old T-shirt or picture of me that he hugged and cried into or threw darts at. I imagined him wondering what went wrong and when I'd come back, but he didn't. He remembered me on the one day he saw me, when I raised my hand in the air and tried to wave but couldn't, because he had a life and friends and demons he built up when he realized I wasn't coming back.

I close the notebook and suck in a heavy breath. I try to picture the version of Mark who sat here, scribbling in this notebook about music and comics, with his thick arms and his short hair. I picture him sitting with Kenny, maybe putting an arm around his shoulder and laughing about a movie they saw or a book they read. I picture his forehead hovering above the bar, eyes focused on a sketch of Spider-Man. These scenes scroll through my head, and I try to force myself into them, but I can't. I left and acted like this town was terrible, like these people were terrible, but it never was. They never were. I just wanted an excuse to stay away because I felt like shit about myself. Running away was easier than apologizing.

My chest warms, itching, and the whiskey starts to make its way back up my throat as tears gather in the corners of my eyes. I raise a finger to catch Steve's attention, and he turns my way. "Could I get the check?" I ask.

Steve raises his eyebrows. "You all right?"

"Just need some air."

"Fair enough," he says. He pushes a few buttons on the

register, then slides the receipt across the bar. Without looking,
I lay down a wad of cash, hoping it'll be enough, and leave.

The outside air is cool. I tuck Mark's composition notebook
under my left arm and stuff my good hand in my pocket as I
turn onto the sidewalk. The sweat on the back of my neck
chills against the breeze. The streetlamps shine against the dark
sky like little moons, each placed half a block or so apart, and
it hits me that I'm drunk. I focus on planting one foot in front
of the other, but despite my efforts, I stumble every couple
steps as the whiskey steeps in my blood.

After three or four blocks, I stop at the corner or 4th and
Ferry. Ahead of me, the streetlights stretch on in their careful,
measured pattern, but two blocks ahead, near Market Street
Books, are flashes of color, mounds of reds and yellows and
whites. Flowers. Pictures. Memories.

The steps come quicker now, shuffled, inconsistent things
that turn into a slow jog and eventually a run. A car drives
past, drowning out my eyes with its headlights, and I clutch the
notebook to my chest and make my way toward the spot where
Mark died. Despite it only being a couple blocks, I'm huffing
when I get there, chest warm, eyes watering. There's nothing
formal about it—just a collection of bouquets gently set on the
sidewalk next to pictures of Mark and a few cards. There's the
Gearmaster photo, Mark shaking Principal McMahon's hand
at graduation, and a few candid shots of him serving up
custard at King's. Toward the bottom of the pile, though, half-
stuffed under a white bouquet, is a picture of the two of us
playing a little set at the Java Joint, a coffee shop on 2nd Street
where you go to play if you're too young for the bars. I'm a
lanky thing, a green bean of a guy half-leaning on a stool in an
attempt to look cool. My acoustic guitar's dangling across my
waist, and Mark has two hands wrapped around his mic, his
mouth wide as he belts out what I know was our shitty cover of
Ryan Adams's cover of "Wonderwall." Mark insisted that it

wasn't a cover of Oasis's original "Wonderwall" because of the "aesthetic of our approach." I still don't know what he meant by that.

I push a couple bouquets to the side with the toe of my shoe, and a few petals fall loose. I lean down to sit, trying to balance myself with my good arm before falling on my ass next to a nearby streetlamp. On either side of me are the flowers and mementos people have left. I want to squeeze myself into the photos, push myself into another time so I can warn these kids what's going to happen, that I'm going to sleep with Beth and run away and end our band. I want to tell them to come back together, to say hi or at least bye, but I can't.

Tears run down my cheeks, rolling off my jaw and hitting the sidewalk. A couple land on Mark's notebook and sit there, flattening out like little pancakes. They lay still, and I montage through the last few hours, wondering how I could go back and make a decision that would fix things. I play through all of them—talking to Lisa at Old Rupert's, asking her for help, sitting down with Brian, dodging Kenny's punch—but I can't settle on one. It's like I've messed up at every turn, like no matter what I did, it would have led to me sitting drunk in a pile of dying flowers and old photos in the middle of the night.

It's nice out here, though. The steady yellows from the streetlamps, the faces of the little bookstores and antique shops, the light breeze rolling down the road and onto my back—it's peaceful. I take in a breath through my nose, letting it fill up my chest, and exhale as I look up, wondering if Mark looked up like this before he died, seeing the stars shine and the clouds make their way across the sky. I wonder if he thought that the town would come together in memory of him, leave flowers and photos and everything else on the ground where he was killed. He'd probably tell them not to bother, that he appreciated the gesture but they really shouldn't have spent any money on him.

I flip open the notebook to Mark's list of things I should have apologized for. That day in Walmart, he looked like the guy I went to school with. He had the same black hair, the same round, dark eyes. He was wearing the same Red Hot Chili Peppers T-shirt he wore our first day of senior year. Inside, though, he was someone else. He was someone trying to piece together how his best friend slept with his girlfriend and bailed on him without giving him a reason or trying to work it out. Someone who couldn't sort out what he did to deserve what happened because, well, he didn't.

Fresh tears well up and sting the corners of my eyes as I make my way back through the list. I shouldn't have slept with Beth, and I shouldn't have bailed on Mark and Kenny. I shouldn't have turned my back on Lafayette or skipped out on our last gig. I should have stayed and been present and been the sort of friend they all deserved. I read through it over and over, but it isn't until the ninth or tenth time that I realize that the answer I came home for has been here all along. I take in a slow breath as it hits me that I can't go back and undo things or warn past versions of myself, but there's plenty I can do.

I was stupid to tell Mark's dad that I could have lied. It would have put things off for a few weeks, maybe even a month or so, but it wouldn't have fixed anything. Even though it's late, though, I might just be able to make a difference now, so I tuck the photo of us from the Java Joint into the notebook, push myself up off the sidewalk, and start back to my car.

TWENTY-NINE

Kenny's food truck sticks out in the parking lot like a lighthouse in a storm. With its bright blues and reds and the swooping white letters of Who Gives a Crepe? painted on either side, it's a far cry from the dated sedans and beat-up trucks scattered nearby. As usual, he's set up his French and Hoosier flags next to the ordering window, and they ripple in the wind, rolling gently as if posing for a perfect snapshot. I've been meaning to ask him why he sets these up if the point of a food truck is mobility, but we haven't necessarily been on speaking terms lately.

Whatever he's doing, though, it's working. He's set up at Regent Hill, a little strip near campus with restaurants, bars, and a couple bookstores, and he's had a steady line for the better part of the last hour. Kenny's working the window, disappearing sometimes to help whomever he's hired to cook, but largely manning the register, typing in orders, taking money, making small talk—running a business, I guess. Watching him reminds me of Mark working at King's. His eyes are just as focused, his smile is just as bright, and his movements are just as intentional, as if he's practiced the most efficient way to take someone's dollars and place them in the register. It's nothing like my life at Confluence, where I'd melt into my ergonomic chair to avoid doing anything, and I can't help but wonder if I would have been better off if I'd stayed here all along.

I expected him to look worse. I figured he'd be shuffling from one side of the truck to the other, shoulders sagged, eyes bloodshot, but, at least from here, there's no hint of the drunk man who started a fistfight at a funeral and threw up in a flowerpot. He looks like he could run a marathon or climb a mountain, making me suddenly self-conscious that I'm still stuck in my middle school funeral outfit, still covered in splotches of Mark's ashes and nursing the remnants of a hangover.

I've been sitting across the parking lot since 11:00 a.m., waiting for a chance to get in line. I parked the Prius at the corner of the lot at an angle behind the truck so I could wait for my moment and minimize the risk that Kenny would see me. It's been a little more than an hour, but my legs are cramping up, and I can't sit still. Nerves, probably. I've been waiting for the line to shorten enough so that he can't spot me standing in it and run or call the cops, but business is good. I don't know what he'll do given how we left off the last time we spoke, but nothing about the way the last few weeks have gone tells me it will be good. Truth is, though, that I don't have much of an option. Given what we did at the funeral, I kind of need Kenny on my side.

Last night, after leaving the spot where Mark died, I rented a room at the Holiday Inn downtown. I hardly used it, opting instead to work on my master plan in the business center. I tried to avoid renting a room, but the hotel staff weren't crazy about a drunk, beat-up man using their computers for free in the middle of the night, so I paid for one and set up shop. I stayed up researching my plan and putting together the necessary pieces, then grabbed a bite at the continental breakfast, worked on a couple things around town, and headed here.

Kenny hands a crepe to his last customer, a girl wearing pajama pants and a Purdue sweatshirt. She smiles at him and holds it up as if to say cheers or thank him, then turns and heads toward campus. Line gone, Kenny sighs and disappears back through the window, so I grab a piece of paper from my passenger seat and get out of my car. I make my way across the parking lot slowly, taking soft steps like a spy, as if doing so will make the ash-covered old guy in a pink cast blend in near a college campus. I move to the side so I can come up on the truck from behind, minimizing the likelihood that Kenny will spot me before I want him to. He's either fiddling with the register, cleaning his equipment, or talking with his coworker, so I have the perfect chance to pull a fast one and sneak up on him.

Until the back door opens, that is. Kenny starts to step down before he notices me, and when he does, he stops, his foot lingering midair as if he's Captain Morgan posing. He grabs the inside of the door for support, then draws his leg in and takes a step back. I hold up my hand to wave, shaking my cast-covered arm back and forth, and he stares at me, wide-eyed, like Mark did in Walmart all those years ago. Only this isn't a department store, and there's nowhere for him to run. In a creepy, stalker sort of way, I've done what I can to make sure that doesn't happen.

I lower my arm and take a couple steps forward. "Hey."

Kenny's cheeks turn red, then a little blue, looking almost like he did before he threw up.

"Can we talk?" I ask. He's far enough away that I have to raise my voice, and a couple students walking nearby turn toward us.

Kenny's eyes move down to his red Who Gives a Crepe? shirt. He stays that way for a couple seconds, then looks over his shoulder, says something I can't hear to the young guy working the truck, and hops down. He shuts the back doors behind him, being careful not to slam them, and starts walking toward me. When he gets a few feet away, he stops and stuffs his hands in his pockets. The space between us is far enough that he'll have to move forward if he tries to punch me, so I relax a little and consider myself safe.

"I'm sorry," I tell him.

Kenny sighs, and his shoulders sink, making his upper half look like a pile of wet sand. "I deserved it. I shouldn't—"

"For bailing, I mean. Back then," I add, scratching the back of my neck. "When everything happened with Beth and me. I guess I thought I'd blown it all, so it was easier to say screw it and run away."

Kenny nods a couple times. "Thanks," he says. "I'm sorry too," he adds, "about S.A.M. and all of that. I was just so mad about you running off, then Mark spiraling out of control. I always felt like if you would have stayed, it never would have happened."

Despite having thought this dozens of times, hearing him say it takes the air out of my chest.

"Not that it's your fault. I get that now. I just—I don't know what got into me. When I saw everyone's faces at the funeral, saw you covered in Mark's ashes and all that, it just hit me how bad I'd screwed up, you know?"

"Yeah." I picture Beth standing over me, her blonde hair curtaining either side of her face, cheeks red, jaw clenched. "We both screwed up pretty bad, huh?"

He lowers his head and stares at the pavement.

I want to press him for information on S.A.M. because I want to know the ins and outs of starting a secret society for running someone out of town, but I decide to save it for another day.

"You talk to anyone from the funeral?" I ask.

He shakes his head.

"Me either," I say, "but I think I have a way to fix that." I hold up the piece of paper, a flyer I designed at the hotel last night, and he takes it in one hand, leaving the other in his pocket. His eyes, narrow at first, widen as they make their way across the page. His grip tightens, crinkling the paper, and as much as I want to reach out and take it from him to keep it pristine, I stand still and let him finish reading.

When he looks up, his mouth has fallen open, and his right eye is twitching. "What is this?"

"A memorial for Mark. Music, food, photos—the whole shebang."

"The 'long-anticipated reunion of The Jackals'? Sponsored by King's and Who Gives a Crepe?" A vein bulges from his forehead, and little beads of sweat start to form around his hairline. "And you're doing this tomorrow?"

I stuff my hands in my pockets and rock back on my heels. "I was kind of thinking *we* would do this tomorrow."

"You have to get permits for this sort of thing. You can't just set up a food truck and a band in a public park and put on a show."

He's right, of course. I researched this for half an hour or so on the hotel's computer last night, trying to find a loophole. The band isn't a problem—I'll take the hit for that—but Kenny could get in deep shit if his food truck randomly sets up shop, especially across the street from King's. I'd like to tell him that I figured it out, that we can get away with it without any sort of repercussion, but I can't because, well, that's not true. Knowing my luck since I got back here, it probably won't end well, either.

"Oh," I add, "I already put those flyers up around town too."

Kenny hands me back the flyer, which I try to smooth against my chest, then runs his hands over his face. "You know

I've booked a spot for tomorrow, right? Posted it on Facebook, my website, everything. And I'm supposed to bail on it because you planned something without asking?"

I force a smile. "Yeah?"

He takes in a long breath through his nose, pulling his shoulders up to his ears, then exhales. His eyes move to the flyer in my hand, and he shakes his head a couple times. "How the hell are you going to get the band back together? In case you missed it, Mark's gone, Brian isn't talking to us, and you have a broken arm."

I don't have an answer for this, either.

"Look, dude," I say, "I don't have a ton of this figured out. I do know, though, that if I can get your food truck in and say that the band will be there, and people see it, they'll come out. And if they do, they can share some memories of Mark, eat some crepes and custard, and listen to some of the songs Mark made everyone fall in love with."

Kenny starts to open his mouth, but I keep going. "I know I've pissed off a lot of people, but it kills me to think that Mark's memory is being whittled down to some flowers on the sidewalk and a fistfight at his funeral. I just want to make it all right, and the best way I can figure out to do that is to hang at Riehle Park and play music and eat food and spend time with everyone. That's really all I can come up with," I add, throwing my hands up, "and I know it'll go way better if one of my best friends is there with me."

Kenny grabs the flyer out of my hand. His eyes make their way over the letters again, scanning from left to right, top to bottom, over and over. After what feels like an hour, a smirk breaks out across his face, and he starts laughing. It's a quiet thing, a whisper almost, like he doesn't want anyone to hear that I've made him feel something good.

He sighs. "Fuck it. I'll do it."

I don't mean to hug him, but I do, throwing my arms

around his torso as tightly as I can. He winces when the plaster of the cast smashes into him, but he's laughing again, not scoffing like I expected him to. He wraps his arms around me, giving me a couple claps on the back before wedging his hand in between us and pushing me away.

"Okay, okay," he says. "Calm it down a little."

"You won't regret this."

He raises his eyebrows. "We'll see about that."

"I promise," I add. "Meet me at Riehle Park at 5:00 p.m. tomorrow. This is going to be great."

"Noted," he says, giving me a little salute.

The corners of my mouth curl up at this, and I turn back toward my car, ready to run from the sudden rush of adrenaline. I've made it five or six steps when Kenny's voice comes across the parking lot.

"Hey, Jack?"

I stop and turn. "Yeah?"

"How did you get Mark's dad in on this?"

I take in a breath and hold it there. I was hoping he wouldn't ask this.

"It's a surprise?"

"Jesus Christ," he says. He waves me away with a dismissive hand, then turns back toward his truck. "We're screwed."

I force another smile and turn back toward my car, confident for the first time since this all started that everything is going to be okay.

THIRTY

The memorial's more crowded than I expected it to be. What started as a few pockets of people has turned into a mass, like a group of cells multiplying into an unstoppable cancer. They're everywhere, huddled around collections of photos Kenny and I set out. Who Gives a Crepe? has a line running down the sidewalk, and King's is packed with people sitting at tables and leaning against railings. Their voices travel through the air in a low rumble, reminding me of the antelope running after Simba before Mufasa dies in *The Lion King*. Instead of saving someone or even facing them, though, I'm hiding behind a tree a block away.

This was a terrible idea.

A couple hours ago, Kenny and I met here to set everything up. The space isn't big by any means. There's a gazebo, which we turned into a little stage with my guitar, his drums, and a couple mics, and nearby are a handful of tables, which we decorated with the memorabilia that Kenny had available. He had boxes of photos of the four of us from college, drawings of Mark's, posters he'd made up for the band—the sorts of things you collect if you stick around, I guess.

I, on the other hand, had nothing.

For all our efforts, the display looked pathetic, like someone had left their half-assed homework sitting around. What we didn't expect was that people would bring their own artifacts, pictures and drawings and stories to tell, and before long, every table was jam-packed with memories that people circled like a museum exhibit or a science experiment.

Around 7:00, when the event was set to begin, Kenny headed to his truck and I laid low. When the crowds started to duplicate and spread and eventually turn into the overflowing congregation they are now, I tried to melt into the tree or bury my head in the ground. Anything but run away, really. I ran away once, when I was too much of a little shit to face a tough situation and do what I needed to, and I've just now dug myself out of it. Now is my moment to do better for myself, to do better for Mark and Kenny and Beth and everyone else, and I owe it to them to keep my feet planted and stick this out.

Now that I think about it, I guess I owe it to them to head to the gazebo and emcee this memorial. Not running away is hard enough, though, so I close my eyes, turn away from the crowd, and lean into the tree. The bark is harsh on my back, scratching and poking me with its jagged little fingers, but I don't care. I take in a long breath through my nose and hold it there, puffing my chest out. Lauren once made me watch a TED Talk on the power of body language and "making your-self big" to feel more confident, and for some stupid reason, it's all I can think about. After a few seconds I exhale, focusing on the wind whistling against my teeth as it makes its way out of my mouth. It takes with it some of my nerves, loosening my shoulders and the knot in my stomach.

"I don't suppose you know who's behind this, do you?"

My eyes shoot open, and my chest freezes. Mark's dad is staring at me through narrow eyes that smooth the wrinkles on his forehead, and his arms are crossed in front of teddy bears holding hands and eating frozen custard on his T-shirt. Their heads poke up over his hairy, dark, weathered skin, and I can't help but think about them staring down at me when Mark found out that I'd slept with Beth. There's no tension in Mark's dad like there was in Mark that night, though. One side of his mouth is curled up, barely containing a smirk, and his eyes, despite being narrow, are bright and lively. Happy, even. He's a far cry from the man who hit me with a baseball bat, but that doesn't mean I'm ready to trust him.

I think to take a step back, then remember I'm against a tree. "I might know a thing or two."

"Kenny told me," Mr. King says, uncrossing his arms. He hooks his thumbs into his pockets, looking like a rugged Clint Eastwood type. "Says you worked pretty hard on it."

I scratch the back of my neck. I didn't work hard, really, save for a late night at the hotel. Most of it was printing a few lies into existence and crossing my fingers they'd come together, which they did. Lucky me, I guess.

"Just thought Mark deserved something special."

Mr. King leans to the side, looking over my shoulder at the crowd. "I'd say you did all right."

I turn and look back. "I wasn't really expecting this."

"No one was really expecting you to show up and get in a fight at the funeral, either. I guess you can say it all balanced out, huh?"

The urge to run away comes back, working its way up until my fingers twitch and I'm on my heels. "About that—"

"Don't worry about it," he says. "Not that what you did is okay, but Mark's mother and I really appreciate this. You know as well as I do that Mark was troubled, but that doesn't mean he didn't work hard or love this town." A tear wells up in the corner of his eye. He obliterates it with a quick finger before it can roll onto his cheek, then tucks his thumb back into his pocket.

"I appreciate that."

"So," he says, looking over my shoulder again, "I heard there's going to be music at this thing."

I take in another breath, raising my shoulders and tensing. "Working on that."

"Mark always said you were an okay singer," he says, crossing his arms again, "but a hell of a guitarist. Granted, you didn't have a broken arm back then, but I have faith that you've figured something out."

I tilt my head to the side, unsure of how to take this. "Thanks."

"Anytime," he says. "There was something else I wanted to talk to you about, though."

"Yeah?" I look down at the cast, preparing for an apology and working through the different ways I can react. I'll accept it, sure, but that doesn't mean I can't dream about the revenge hit or making him grovel a little.

"Yeah," he says. His face is still as he looks me over. "The cat."

In between figuring out a way into the funeral, getting kicked out of said funeral, and coming up with the plan for this, I'd forgotten Jack existed. A swell of panic rises in my throat, trying to figure out if he's been given food or water or had his litter box cleaned, but it settles as quickly as it arrives. Beth and Brian are there, and, all things considered, they're more equipped to handle a cat than I am.

"You can keep him," Mr. King says.

"Really?"

He nods.

I want to ask him why we couldn't have come to this decision earlier, before he broke my arm with a baseball bat and chased me out of his home, but I don't. Everything I've felt and gone through since Mark died, Mr. King must have experienced tenfold. And while that doesn't excuse the *Throwdown at Casa del King*, as I've taken to calling it, Mark's dad is far from the only one to have made some hasty decisions.

"I'm too old for this grudge match," he adds. "When Kenny asked me to be a part of it, I'd just lost my boy and couldn't stop thinking about everything I could have done to save him. Seeing you get hit by that car scared the shit out of me, though. Thought it was Mark all over, and I couldn't stand the thought of another parent going through what Mark's mother and I have experienced." Another tear gathers in the corner of his eye, but he lets this one escape. It rolls down his tanned, leathery cheek before wobbling on his jaw and falling to the ground. "You didn't do right by my son, but I think you know that. There isn't any good in all of us drawing it out into a fight."

Somewhere between my head and my mouth, the words have frozen. I stand there, opening my lips from time to time but pausing before anything comes out.

"He was a good guy," I finally say.

"He was," Mr. King says. He takes in a heavy breath, raises his shoulders, and wipes at his eye again. "Enough of that, though," he adds, clapping me on the shoulder. "Someone decided to slam my business, so there's custard to make. Plus, you have a concert to play, no?"

I look back over my shoulder at the sea of people surrounding the gazebo. I was hoping it would have died down, but it looks larger now, the crowd spreading and folding out around the edges of our makeshift stage. "Guess so."

"You'll be fine," he says. "People are pretty forgiving at charity things, believe it or not. I think everyone's just happy you put this together." He takes another look at the crowd and nods a couple times as if assessing them, then mutters a "good luck" and heads off toward King's.

He's right, of course. Who could fault me for not playing well when most of the band is gone, my arm is broken, and we had no rehearsal time? It's the thought that counts, I tell myself. This needed to happen for Mark, and it has, albeit better than I expected it to. Plus, what other option do I have? There's no more time to run away from these sorts of decisions, to cower down when I get nervous and want to hide. This is my best chance to do right by Mark, and even though I didn't think it through and don't have much of a plan, it's my responsibility to own up to that and do the best I can with what I have.

The walk back to the memorial takes longer than I thought it would. For every step I take, it seems like the distance doubles, like one of those nightmares where you're walking toward a door and it gets farther and farther away until you break out in a sprint and realize you'll never catch it. There's no sprinting for me, though, just a focus on one step, then another.

Stay on track, Jack.

When I get to the gazebo where the equipment's set up, I hop over the back. The entrance is crowded with people turned in all sorts of directions while they talk to one another. Some are holding crepes, others custard, and a few brave souls are holding the necks of beers that definitely aren't legal to have here, but they're all smiling. They might be talking about Mark, or they might be catching up, but it doesn't matter. They're together, like people in a community should be. Like what Mark loved seeing at things like this.

I wrap the fingers of my good hand around the mic stand and clear my throat. Feedback echoes through the speakers, and my stomach ties itself back into a knot as I take in the faces. There's Mr. Arnold, who owns the pizza shop across from the fairgrounds. Kurt Klosterman, who beat me up in the seventh grade before Mark saved my ass. There's Lisa, Steve from the bar, and a bunch of other folks, and suddenly, I want to throw up and die. It's like the best and worst parts of my life have all come together for this terrible moment, and there's nothing I can do to get away from it.

"Thanks for coming," I say. "For those of you I don't know, I'm Jack Dotson. Mark and I were——" I bite my tongue, unsure of what to say. "We were best friends. I've been gone for a little while, but when we were young, we were in this band together."

"Come on, man," someone yells from the crowd. "We remember The Jackals!"

A few laughs travel across the crowd.

"Okay then," I say, smirking. "Well, I thought I'd play a few songs for you if that's all right. Mark loved playing music, so I thought it would be fitting as we take some time to remember him."

There's a weird silence between us as I wait for them to do something and they wait for me to start playing. There's a sneeze, then the hum of a car driving by, so I grab my guitar off its stand. The neck is difficult to hold onto because of my cast, so I fumble a couple times as I try to sling it over my shoulder, looking like a blown-up version of one of those string tricks kids play with their hands—cat's cradle or something. The guitar drops when I finally get it over my shoulder, and the force of the strap pinches my neck. I jump at this and bump the mic, making a few people in the audience wince.

"Sorry about that," I tell them. "Dealing with a little bit of a handicap here."

A few folks force a smile, and a few others look away. Hesitation builds up in my gut, and my palms start to sweat, but I swallow it back down and rest my fingers on the guitar strings.

"This one's called 'With Great Power.'"

The notes come back easily enough. The words, too, even though I wasn't ever the singer. My fingers, though, won't do what they're supposed to. They can't because of the cast, making what was the song that won Lafayette's 2005 Battle of the Bands sound like a middle school talent show. I push through it, focusing on belting out the words Mark wrote, ignoring the twang of the occasional missed note or the strings that sometimes get muted because of my cast stopping them. I take a step closer to the mic and close my eyes like I remember Mark doing during those shows at the Java Joint and at open mic nights, and I'm a kid again, happy with my minimum wage job and my shitty bed at Mark's place. I'm not worried about my boss ripping into me or my clients telling me what I need to do or my girlfriend cheating on me. I'm not running away. I'm just making music in a park in a small town because it's a good thing to do.

I botch the final note, making what's supposed to be drawn out disappear in a hiccup. I open my eyes, expecting to hear the crowd break out in applause like they used to, but they're staring at me, wide-eyed. There's the occasional cough and a couple attempts at a clap, but they fade out before anything can catch on. A few feet back, I catch a look at Klosterman snickering.

"Thanks," I say, not knowing what else to do. "This next one's called—"

"Hold on," someone says. "Don't put them through another one."

A few people laugh, and from the back of the crowd people start to part. I stand on my tiptoes to get a better view, but it doesn't do me any good. It isn't until Brian gets about ten feet away that I recognize him, clapping folks on the shoulder, smiling, apologizing for my shitty performance, and all other manners of greeting people. He's grinning ear to ear, a far cry from the last time I saw him staring me down and lecturing me outside of the funeral home. He's wearing an old King's shirt that he must have taken from Mark's house, looking more the part of the guy I shared a futon with in college and less the part of a doctor.

"Hey," he says when he makes his way to the front of the crowd. "Thought you could use some help."

"Was it that bad?"

Brian shrugs. "The thought was nice."

At least I got that part down.

"You guys care if I jump in on this?" comes another voice.

Brian grins, and I turn around. Kenny's sitting behind his drum set, which we set up in case he was able to make it away from the truck. He's spinning a drumstick between his fingers, and he gives the bass pedal a couple thumps, bringing out some applause from the crowd.

"Fuck yeah," Brian says. "These people won't know what hit them."

I laugh. "Thanks, dudes."

Brian and Kenny smile, and the three of us are silent for a few seconds. The two of them make eye contact, and Kenny twitches.

"What?" I ask.

Brian leans toward me, away from the mic. "You giving me that guitar?"

I look to Kenny for support, but he shakes his head and looks down at his bass pedal.

I put my hand over the mic. "I was always the guitarist."

"You're really going to do this?"

"It's my job."

"You sounded like a car wreck playing that thing," Brian says. "You literally sounded better when your limp body smashed into my windshield."

Behind Brian, the people in the crowd shuffle, eyes lit, and talk amongst themselves. Some stand up on their tiptoes, trying to get a view of us. It's a far cry from the looks they made when I performed a few minutes ago.

"Fine," I mutter, wrestling myself out of the guitar strap. Brian's hands are on it before I can get it over my shoulder, and within seconds it's over his, falling into place like it was meant to be there all along.

I clear my throat and grip the mic again with my good hand. "Looks like you guys get more of a Jackals experience than I thought you would," I say, and before the crowd can cheer, Kenny taps his drumsticks four times and Brian rips out the opening notes to "Born Again," a song Mark wrote about Kevin Smith's *Daredevil* arc from the '90s. The words come back to me like the first ones did, only this time, there's no cringing. The crowd's heads bob, and they dance and pat their thighs, listening and watching like they used to, and I can't help but picture what that show I bailed on could have been if I'd stuck around. I keep my eyes open this time, not wanting to miss the moment. Brian's leaned over the guitar, his head nodding to the beats Kenny lays out, and Kenny's as stoic as ever as he plays the drums. He flashes me an occasional grin when he catches me looking his way, and I flash one back before the song ends. Within seconds, we're starting in on the next one as if we planned the whole thing out.

By the time we get to the last song we remember, effectively bringing our set to an end, an hour has passed. The sun's disappeared, giving way to the streetlights, but the crowd hasn't died. They're as active as ever, clapping after every song and bobbing their heads to the music. Brian lets his final note draw out, and Kenny plays a short drum solo that gets the crowd cheering and clapping even louder. When it's done and the music's silent, the noise of the crowd washes over us. Brian comes up to me on one side, wrapping his arm around my sweaty shoulders, and Kenny comes up on the other, doing the same, and we stand there for a few seconds, taking it in. We bow as a unit, bringing up a few more claps, before doing it again.

I lean into the mic. "That's for you, Mark," I say, drawing up more applause. "We miss you, man." The crowd claps at this louder than anything else, making me think that somewhere, somehow, he might just be able to hear them.

THIRTY-ONE

My phone buzzes in my pocket.

I'm sitting on the patio at King's when it happens. The lights are off and the crowd is gone, but I can see everything as vividly as if it were still happening. The tables packed with people eating frozen custard, their voices rising up together in an excited buzz. The folks across the street packed shoulder to shoulder around the gazebo, bobbing their heads to the music. The memories of Mark displayed on tables, shared, and smiled about. The band, save for one important piece, picking up where it left off like nothing ever happened.

Tonight was a good night.

I reach into my pocket to check the message. The light from the screen shines out like a little star in the night, and on it, in the middle, is a green bubble with Beth's name next to it.

Where are you?

When I couldn't find Beth at the show, I assumed it was over and that she didn't want anything to do with me. It seemed fair enough; I'd shown up to Mark's viewing, and she had confidence that I'd be on my best behavior. Instead, I tumbled through a picture of him and spilled his ashes all over me. Granted, it wasn't entirely my fault, but fuckups like that don't necessarily get a shot at redemption.

I start typing out a reply before my nerves stop me from telling her.

King's.

Three dots move from one side of a little speech bubble to the other, and I can't help but feel the excitement boil up in my chest as I wait to see what she's typing. Coming to terms with Kenny, Brian, and Mr. King is one thing, but sorting things out with Beth is the cream of the crop. My Mount Everest. Whatever other monumental metaphor you want to throw at it.

Another message pops up:

I'm on my way.

The event's been over for a couple hours now. The crowd stuck around for a while afterward, but it didn't take long for people to get back to their houses or move the party to a bar. Within an hour of our set ending, it had all but emptied out. I want to think that the energy scattered, that people took their memories of Mark back home or out and about with them, spreading them all over our little Midwestern town, but I know that might not be the case. Even if it's not, taking the chance to get the band back together for a little bit, giving Mark a proper send-off—that's enough. For now, at least.

It's quiet save for the occasional shouts of high schoolers— I'm assuming they're in high school, at least—coming from Riehle Park. They're full of excitement, unrestrained by the sorts of social norms you worry about when you get older, but I can't tell what they're doing. Laser tag, maybe. I consider calling the cops on them the way someone once called the cops on Mark, Brian, Kenny, and me, but I can't bring myself to do it.

I reach into the cooler Brian left me with and pull out a PBR. It's been in there for so long that the aluminum chills through my skin and to the bone, so I crack it open and take a sip before setting it on the table next to me. I've spent the better part of an hour trying to figure out what to do now, only to come up with nothing, finish a beer, start over, and crack open a new one. With S.A.M. gone and the party over, there aren't many options for a homeless, jobless guy who's back in his hometown for the first time in years. Funny how that's worked out.

Now, though, I can walk through the possibilities with Beth. There's the chance she'll show up and hit me, but that seems unlikely. She had her chance at the viewing, after all. And if she were going to do it now, would she really text me and hunt me down? Seem all friendly about it? S.A.M. might, but that's a thing of the past. Fingers crossed it is, at least.

Maybe she'll want to talk about the viewing. My mouth dries at the thought of having to relive that, so I grab my PBR off the table and take a chilling gulp. There are words for most fuckups because you know in some part of your mind that it's possible that they'll happen. There's a chance that you'll get in a fender bender or accidentally break a glass at a friend's house. These things are so common that you're programmed to respond to them. To tumble over at a funeral and cover yourself in your friend's ashes, though, that's not supposed to happen. There aren't words for fuckups like that.

If she doesn't want to hit me and she doesn't want to talk about the viewing, there's the elephant in the room, of course: the night this all started, when she and I slept together and created the whirlwind that ended with Mark dying. The feelings associated with this—a smoothie of regret, excitement, nervousness, terror—start to work their way up, so I wipe my sweating palms on my jeans and swallow my emotions.

I'm so caught up in this that I hardly notice the sound of the cooler clicking open, the crunch of a hand plunging into the ice, or the hiss of the can opening. It's like they're in another world altogether, muffled by the noise in my mind. It isn't until Beth jumps up onto the table next to me that I fully come to. I shake my head back and forth like a cartoon character, and she smiles. She's wearing one of her flannels, this one brown and blue, and a pair of jeans that are torn at the knees. Her curly hair is pulled back in a frizzy, blonde ponytail that reminds me of the glow of streetlamps.

"Good thing I wasn't a mugger," she says. "You would have been done for."

I force a laugh, unsure of how to take her. At least I can rule out getting hit, I think.

Beth seems to understand this. She laughs a couple times, then takes a drink of her beer and sets the can down next to her. "I just wanted to let you know that I think that was a really nice thing you did."

"What?"

She nods toward the park. "That concert. The memorial. Whatever you want to call it. It was really sweet."

"You were there?"

"Over here," she says. "Helping Mark's dad."

"I didn't know you knew how to do all that."

She looks down. "You don't date Mark as long as I did and not hear enough about it to figure it out."

I think back to before I left, to Mark's enthusiasm for making a perfectly creamy batch or balancing as many scoops as he could on a cone. "That's fair."

"Listen," she says, tapping her fingers on her knee. "I wanted to talk to you about what happened. I—"

"I'm sorry," I say, thinking back to the blonde curtains of hair framing her face, the tear-smeared makeup on her cheeks, and the words she hissed through clenched teeth. She looked like she wanted to stab me in the eye with a chopstick or drop-kick my head, and now, here we are to face it. I try to come up with something else to say, something less generic than, well, "I'm sorry," but there's nothing. It's like I'm plunging toward the earth without a parachute, grasping at the air and clouds and praying that one of them turns into something I can hold on to so I don't hit the ground and go splat.

"When Kenny came at me, I just——"

"I mean what happened between us. Back then."

She might as well have grabbed me by the neck. "Oh."

"I think it's important that you know what it was. That I wasn't trying to leave Mark for you."

I swallow back the lump in my throat. Some part of me always knew this, and as much as I've tried, no part of me ever expected the two of us to talk about it.

"Of course," I say.

"I really loved him," she adds, "but we were going through a tough time, and I made a bad decision. We made a bad decision."

I make my way back through what happened that night. There's my hand on her face, then a kiss, then a mess of emotions and limbs that ends with her sitting on the other end of the couch, naked and sipping a PBR. I try to pinpoint where it was that we made a decision, but I can't. It just happened. To Beth, at least, it shouldn't have.

I don't know what I expected. If Beth wanted something more out of it, we would have made something more. We would have done it again or started dating or gotten a place of our own, but we didn't. We went our separate ways, mine in Louisville and hers here, back together with Mark.

"I'm really glad you came back, though."

"Really?""

"Yeah," she says. "I wasn't at first—I think you got that much—but there was a lot to unpack. I didn't realize how much I'd missed you, though. The creativity, the ambition—there's a lot of good in you."

I try to picture the look on Amanda's face if she were to hear someone call me creative or ambitious. "I don't know about that," I tell her. "You have to be creative when people are out to get you."

She laughs again. "Maybe," she says. "But Kenny didn't do all this," she adds, nodding toward the park. "You pulled that off."

I picture the crowd again, listen to the buzz of their voices. "I guess that's fair."

"It's nice having you back in town. Lafayette's a better place with you in it."

I don't say anything to this. I don't know what to say, really. For years now I've felt hated here, like I'd be chased out of town with pitchforks and torches if I ever came back. While it hasn't been a warm welcome, to feel at home isn't something I ever planned on experiencing again.

"So, what's next?" Beth asks.

"I don't know," I say. It's the only answer I have. "I haven't gotten that far. I could use some peace and quiet, though, you know?"

"This place can be that if you let it," she says. "It doesn't have to be affairs and revenge groups. There's a lot of good here if you're willing to give it a chance."

I look out across the street, and Beth does the same. The gazebo stares back at us like a little lighthouse or beacon, and beyond it, there are hints of the tree I hid behind, the amphitheater I crawled up onto with Brian and Kenny, and the playground where we poured out a drink in Mark's honor. Beyond them, in the distance, there's the courthouse downtown, across the street from Stevie's, and the hotel where I printed the flyers.

I slide down onto the bench next to the table and lean back, slouching into the hard plastic. The feeling reminds me of Mark's futon, worn and warm and familiar, and I cozy further into my spot and take another drink of my beer. It's lukewarm now, but that doesn't matter. The Indiana air is fresh, crisp, and it smells like dying leaves and frozen custard. It makes its way across the patio, soft like the pages of an old comic book, and I kick up my feet onto the bench across from me, close my eyes, and take in the distant sounds of the rowdy high schoolers hanging out at Riehle Park past curfew.

ACKNOWLEDGMENTS

Writing a book is a massive undertaking, and I wouldn't have come close to pulling it off if it weren't for so many amazing people.

In many ways, this is a book about friendship and the twists and turns it takes. I'm not going to say I've got it figured out, but I owe a huge thanks to my childhood best friends, The Quad: Isaac, Jayson, and Brooks. We might be spread across the world now, but the time we've spent together, the memories we've made, and the jokes we've shared inspired a lot of the good in this story. I'm glad we've got it together more than Jack and his crew.

Much of this book was written while I hung out at Great Flood Brewing Co. and Mile Wide Beer Co. here in Louisville, Kentucky. To the bartenders, friends, brewers, and trivia hosts I met, thank you for giving me a space to write, great company to enjoy, and, of course, some of the best beers in Kentucky. Louisville's lucky to have such great spots.

Thank you to everyone I met in my MFA at Concordia St. Paul—Riana, Matt, Karlajean, Maggie, Cam, Missy, Taylor, John, and tons of others I'm sure I'm forgetting—but especially to Matt Ryan, who believed in this book and pushed me to make it better, even when I pushed back. I'm so, so lucky to have spent two years in such good company.

To Brian, thanks for the feedback you offered. You have no idea how valuable it is to have such a trusted early reader. You're a good friend.

To my dad, thank you for showing me the levelheadedness

and resilience needed to do hard things. I'm not going to say that writing a book is anywhere near as difficult as working forty-something years in an aluminum factory, but the example you've set time after time has shown me that yes, even when things seem tough, we can keep going. And to my mom, thank you for the love you gave. You supported me when I wanted to study English and go on to complete my MFA, and the kindness you showed toward my writing encouraged me to keep going. I love you, and I wish I would have finished this in time for you to read it.

To my wife, Ashley, thank you for your love and strength and all-out grit. You stun me day after day, and the support you've shown, from watching our daughter so I can write to being honest with me when you read my work, has given me the awareness and confidence needed to keep going in this crazy endeavor called writing. You're the best.

Lastly, to my daughter, Cecilia, thank you for being you. Your mom and I couldn't have asked for a better kid.

ABOUT THE AUTHOR

Adam Shaw lives in Louisville, Kentucky, with his wife and daughter. *The Jackals* is his first novel.

 twitter.com/adamshaw502

instagram.com/adamshaw502

goodreads.com/adamshaw502